"Secrets and Second Chances", Book 3

Twisted Secrets

Twisted Secrets

By Donna M. Zadunajsky

Copyright

~ Dedication ~
My Forever Friend

A friend is easy to find, but a true and ever-lasting friend is something that only comes along once, maybe twice in a lifetime.

Now, when I look back over the twenty years of our friendship, I can't imagine anyone else being in your shoes.

Going back to the year of 1995, I would have to say we became instant friends. We began hanging out every weekend and telling each other our secrets, we didn't share with anyone else.

I knew then that we would be forever best friends, taking each other's secrets to our graves one day. Isn't that what true and forever friends do for each other? They share things and lean on one another through good times and bad?

Even as the year's pass, we moved around, okay, I moved around, but you were never far from my heart or my thoughts. What I miss the most after all these years is spending time with you. Living in different states isn't easy, but we try to find time to talk and to send a text in our always-busy lives.

Angie, you're an amazing person who I've looked up to all these years. You're the strongest person I know and beautiful from the inside out, but most of all, you are my best friend.

And I will always forever love you...

1

For months, Tate had done nothing but watch, plan, and learn everything about Ashley. She was beautiful, but that didn't do a woman justice, not in the world we lived in today. Beauty was just the half of it.

He watched Ashley wake in the morning. She didn't know that he could see everything she did. Like when she made her coffee, adding cream and two sugars; then stirred, and tapping the spoon twice before setting it down on the red ceramic spoon-holder next to the coffeepot.

The way she gathered her blonde hair and twisted it into a bun on the top of her head before she crawled under the covers at night to read for exactly one-half-hour before placing the book down on the nightstand and clicking off the light.

Ashley repeated this routine every day—from the moment she woke in the morning to the time she picked up her daughter Lily from her mother's place three miles down the road every evening. Although, on occasion, there were nights she didn't come home. That was when she'd sleep over at her boyfriend's house and her sweet little daughter stayed with her grandma.

Tate had on several occasions camped out and watched the grandmother who lived by herself in a two-story house surrounded by woods. Those woods made it an easy place to hide and watch the grandmother.

The grandma's house was much easier than Ashley's place to watch because Ashley lived in an apartment.

There was no place to really hide so that was when he rented the apartment across the parking lot from her. It gave him a direct view into her home.

The grandma had been a grieving widow for some time. At least that's what he'd gathered since Tate had never seen a man at her place. He watched her from time to time, but not as often as he followed Ashley around because she was who intrigued him the most.

The child, Lily, was almost a spitting image of Ashley, except for one thing; her long-wavy black hair, which Tate assumed, came from her father's side of the family. He'd never seen the little girl's father to know if she looked anything like him. The little girl's father wasn't in the picture. He hadn't been for as long as Tate had been watching them. Tate hadn't any clue where the sperm donor went or what happened to him—to them. Did they have a fight? Or did he just ditch her the moment he found out Ashley was pregnant with his baby? That would be something only God knew.

It was sad to see Ashley raise this child alone, but that would change in time. She would come to see that Tate was good for her. It would only take a little push in the right direction, and Tate knew just what to do to get her to see what love was. Show Ashley how wonderful and true it could be.

Ashley's so-called boyfriend wasn't who she thought he was. He wasn't true to her. He didn't love her the way a man should love a woman, especially someone as beautiful and smart as her—like Ashley. Her name sounded so sweet rolling off his tongue every time he said it.

As for the little girl, Lily, she would learn to love him and worship him. She would never be without a father again. A man who would give her everything she would ever need—want, but that would all come soon enough. Soon they would know all about him. Soon Ashley would be with him.

Because after today the cat would come out to play...

2

Ashley Teodora drove until she reached the state line, entering Indiana. Night was beginning to fall when she stopped at the first rest stop.

She was driving back to Illinois where she'd been just two weeks earlier to see her best friend Carla and her newborn baby Mya. Carla's friend Veronica had called yesterday telling Ashley there'd been an accident and that she needed to come back to Illinois.

Ashley had met Carla when they were six years old and had been best friends ever since. Ashley still lived in Ohio where they grew up, but Carla left after graduation and went to college in Tallahassee, Florida, where she'd met her husband Tim. After they finished college, Carla and Tim were married and moved to Tim's hometown in Homer Glen, Illinois.

Even though life at times got busy, Ashley and Carla still made time to keep in touch, even though it had been weeks since they'd talked. Carla was never far from Ashley's mind, especially since her recent visit a couple of weeks before when Carla had told her about what happened a year ago.

~ ~

Ashley went inside the rest stop, used the restroom, grabbed something small to eat, and got back in her dark blue SUV. She pulled up to the pumps, filled her gas tank, and then merged back onto Interstate 80/90.

She watched for signs showing lodging and took the next exit. On her last trip, she'd stayed at a motel that was now under an investigation because there had been some *dead bodies* found buried behind the motel. She was praying this one was different.

She drove down the road until she saw the lit-up sign MOTEL. There weren't many cars in the lot, only two if you counted hers. She pulled in and parked by the front office.

The sign on the door stated that there was Vacancy available and by the look of the place, she could see why.

She glanced out the windshield, giving the run-down motel a-once-over-look. The place definitely needed a new coat of paint. The doors and windows of each room were dirty and grimy.

She sat and wondered if she should find another motel to stay for the night. She was beyond exhausted and didn't have a lot of money to afford a room at the Hampton; this place would have to do. She'd take her chances the rooms here were clean enough to sleep in, and that there weren't any *dead bodies* buried behind the motel. She chuckled a laugh, not that it was funny. People had been killed and buried. No, it definitely wasn't funny at all, if anything she was laughing at herself for thinking that *this* motel was just like the last one. Sometimes you just have to laugh at the things that scare you the most.

She grabbed her purse from the passenger seat and got out of the car. The gravel crunched under her feet as she walked to the office door. She turned the knob, but the door wouldn't budge. She threw back her hip and bumped the door, pushing it at the same time. The door swung open, she stumbled forward, but caught herself by grabbing the counter in front of her.

After regaining her composure, she looked around the cluttered, dingy room, but saw no one. She cleared her throat loud enough for someone to hear her; still, no one came.

A bell sat to the right of her with a note stating: **ring for service**. She tapped her pointer finger down *twice* on the metal bell. The noise echoed through the room, bouncing off the walls where no pictures or decorations were hung.

A voice from the backroom called out, "I'll be right there."

"Okay, thank you," Ashley replied.

A door to the backroom opened and a short, rounded woman with shaggy white hair that could hide a bird's nest came tromping down the narrow hall; her plump butt swaying side to side.

"How can I help ya' this evening?" the woman spoke with a southern twang.

"I would like to get a room for the night."

"Well, ya' come to the right place," the woman chuckled. "I got no guests here, so ya' got your *pick-ins* of the place."

Pick-ins, Ashley thought. *What kind of place had she stopped at?* "Your best room will be fine." *Best room? Where did she think she was at, a Hilton resort or something?* Ashley almost laughed in spite of herself and the exhaustion that had brought her here.

"Well, let me see. Oh yes, I'll give you room eight. Will that do for ya'?"

"That'll be fine, thank you. Oh, do you have hot water?" She hoped she didn't sound rude.

"Hot water?" the woman snarled at Ashley. "Course there's hot water. What do ya' think this place is, an outhouse?" The woman's eyes narrowed in on Ashley's face, looking perturbed.

Well, it certainly looked like one, hoping she wasn't speaking out loud. "How much for the night?" Ashley changed the subject.

"That'll be forty-five dollars cash, and there ain't no refunds," the woman quickly added.

Ashley pulled out her wallet and counted her cash.

"Sign ya' name here for me and I'll get the key."

Ashley had seen too many horror movies and wondered if she should use a fake name. Not saying this woman was a killer or anything, but it'd probably be best if she stayed clear of her and locked the door once she was in her room. The woman made her feel uneasy; hell, the whole place reminded her of Bate's Motel. *Where was Norman,* she thought, almost chuckling? Ashley scribbled her name down before the white-haired woman returned.

The woman came back and held out a key attached to a long piece of wood. "Here ya' go. Just leave it in the box out front if ya' decide to leave before eight in the morning. I don't get up at no crack of dawn, and there ain't any room service here so you'll have to fend for yourself."

"That's fine," Ashley replied as she snatched the key and went out the door.

She hustled to her car, grabbed her bag, and hit the lock button. She looked around and spotted the room. An eerie feeling came over Ashley as if someone were watching her and she quickly bolted to her room. She stuck the key in the deadbolt, opened the door, and slammed it shut behind her. She turned, locked the door, and fastened the chain.

She leaned her forehead on the door as her heart was pulsating through her chest; she took in long shallow breaths to calm herself. She turned back around and flicked on the light switch on the wall beside her and placed her bag on the only chair in the room. As she walked further into the room, she had to pinch her nose and breathe through her mouth. There was a stench in the room, almost like a dead animal smell.

She walked to the bathroom and cracked open the window, and then decided she should probably open the window by the door as well to let the air circulate, but only a crack because the owner of this place freaked her out.

She gazed around the room, looking at the furniture and wallpaper. The place looked like it had never left the sixties or seventies with its avocado green chair, and what was that—pot leaves on the wallpaper?

She strolled back to the bed, pulled the comforter off, and shook it out. She didn't see any bed bugs, but that didn't mean they weren't there. *Were bed bugs even something you could see with the naked eye?* she asked herself. She grabbed her bag and headed into the bathroom to shower and change.

Fifteen minutes later, she stood in front of the mirror, wiping away the film that was left by the steam, and then brushed her hair and teeth. When she finished, she went back to the bed and switched on the television.

After flicking through the channels of nothing but static, she settled on the only channel that came in clear enough for her to watch. Not that she was interested in watching television; it was more for white noise if anything.

She took the comforter and folded it in half like a sleeping bag. She collected her cell phone from her purse, and then climbed between the blankets. She called and talked to her mom Catherine, hoping she could catch Lily before she went to bed.

~ ~

Lily Rose was her five-year-old daughter. Occasionally, her mind would flash back to the father of her daughter. This was one of those times. She wanted to hate him for what he'd done to her, but it was as much her fault as it was his. If she'd known that she would get pregnant after one night of hot steamy sex, she would've taken precautions. But the truth was, he didn't even know she had gotten pregnant. In fact, she hadn't seen him since that night almost six years ago.

They hadn't talked about what they wanted to do with their lives. It wasn't that kind of relationship. It wasn't even a relationship—period! They had bumped into each other at a party and the next thing she knew, they were back at her friend's place, who thankfully was still at the party, pulling off each other's clothes.

After that evening, she hadn't realized how much sex two people could have and the fact that each time he aimed to please. Oh boy, did he please her. She hadn't had an orgasm like that with another guy since. When she woke the next morning, he was gone. No name, no phone number. It was as if he'd vanished into thin air.

17

Now, Ashley had spent the last five years raising Lily Rose by herself; well, not exactly by herself, she had her mom's help when she was at work or school.

Ashley took college courses online and attended a couple classes at a college outside of town, studying to be an Architect just like her father had been—*God rest his soul.*

When she thought about Lily's father, as she so often did, and if he'd kept in contact with them; she would unquestionably consider a relationship with him. But, he didn't even know that Lily Rose existed, and Ashley didn't know anything about him. Maybe, he was married with other children?

~ ~

When Ashley finished the call with her mom, she noticed there was a voicemail and tapped the green icon. After listening to the message from Rob, her ex-fiancé, who seemed to only have called to make sure she was all right and that he wanted to talk about why she had ended it with him.

She had met Rob two years ago in college. She had gone to a frat party, but only after her friends had persuaded her to go. She didn't want to make the same mistake twice, not that Lily was a mistake. She was far from a mistake.

Once at the frat party, her friends had introduced her and Rob, and one thing led to another. But, after what she'd witnessed two weeks ago, there was by all odds not going to be a wedding; not now—not ever!

Maybe she wasn't the marrying type. It happened to some people. There was nothing wrong with staying single, but there were times when she thought too much about getting married, and the whole thing made her sick to her stomach.

She'd been dodging him ever since she'd gotten back from seeing Carla a couple of weeks ago. "Whatever," she mumbled and deleted his message. "Is he nuts or something? Does he really think I'll forgive him and things will just go back to the way they were? No chance in hell that's ever going to happen," she said into the empty room.

She flicked the switch on her phone to vibrate, set it on the nightstand, turned the volume on the TV down low, and closed her eyes.

~ ~

Ashley sprang to a sitting position, her eyes searching the room. The TV had gone black. She reached for her phone and touched the power button to give her some light. Another sound came from the direction of the bathroom, like a hammer hitting a nail.

Clank, Clank, Clank.

She tapped the flashlight icon and aimed the light towards the sound. Stepping out from under the blankets, she made her way to the bathroom. She shined the light from the floor to the ceiling and from left to right; there was nothing in the room. It wasn't like there were places to hide in a room that only had a tub, toilet, and sink.

She flicked the switch on the wall, not knowing why she didn't turn the light on in the first place, and still saw nothing. The sound stopped the moment she flipped the switch. No one had to twist her arm for her to know she needed to keep it on.

She walked back to the bed and sat down. She checked the time on her phone, 3:42 a.m. She clicked the

TV off and reached her hand inside her purse, pulling out a book. She was wide awake now; no sense in trying to go back to sleep, and it was too early to leave—still dark outside.

She tried to read, but the *crackling* of branches outside the bathroom window consumed her attention. She kept tossing around the idea whether she should stay or leave. When she heard, something pawing at the ground, she hurried off the bed, threw on her clothes, and peeked out the window towards the parking lot.

The thought of the article she read weeks ago came flooding back to her. *Could this be happening again? Could this be a coincidence or maybe even be related somehow?* She didn't want to know, but also didn't want to stay and find out; and possibly getting herself killed in the process.

When she looked out the window to the parking lot, she saw nothing but darkness lurking outside her door. She grabbed her things and threw open the door. Ashley pressed the unlock button on her key ring and ran like mad to her vehicle. Once inside she touched the door panel, waiting for the *clunk* sound to indicate the doors were locked.

"Shit," she mumbled, remembering that she had left the motel key in the room. There was no way she was going back for it and started the vehicle.

She shifted into reverse. Gravel spit from the rear tires as she slammed her foot down on the gas pedal. She whipped the SUV around, slammed the gear into drive, and raced down the road.

She made a right turn and got back on the Interstate. She'd arrive earlier than she planned, but at this moment, she really didn't give a shit.

3

Reece Garran sat on the edge of the 3-inch thick cot, pulling the T-shirt over his head; his biceps nearly ripping the fabric around his arms. He'd put on more muscle since his time in prison, filling out the shirt that was once loose. He couldn't believe how nice it felt to be in street clothes again. He looked over at the orange jumpsuit now sitting in a ball near the foot of the bed. Yeah, he wasn't going to miss that God-awful thing.

He stood when the guard unlocked the door to the cell and walked through the opening. He didn't look back over his shoulder to see if he'd forgotten anything. He had nothing to leave behind; nothing to forget. He held the only thing that meant something to him in his hand.

The single thought made him wrap his fingers around the spine of the book. The guards allowed him to take it with him. "Consider it a gift. Something to remember us by," one of the guards had said as he howled with laughter. It wouldn't be them he'd be thinking about.

He had read *The Shawshank Redemption* more times than he could count. It was one of his favorite books. In fact, his father had given Reece a copy as a birthday gift a longtime ago.

He'd thought of his father all the time since he'd died on that unforgettable fall day. The fire had started in his parents' bedroom and by the time Reece could get the door open, the room had gone up in flames. Reece could still see his father lying on the bed, his screams filling the air around him. The firemen said there was nothing he could've done to save him; it was too late.

Reece had stood outside on the street and watched like everyone else as the house burned down to the ground. Everything he had ever owned was gone. His mother had died when he was four from cancer, leaving his father to raise him on his own. His father had never remarried, saying he could never love another woman the way he loved Reece's mother.

When Reece had turned nineteen, he joined the Marines just one week later. He fought in Afghanistan during the *War on Terrorism* and left after serving eight years for his country, learning things that he could only use in the military. Things that the government didn't want anyone else to know about. After leaving the military, he traveled around and did odd jobs wherever he could find them before ending up in prison where he'd spent the last five years of his life.

It had been five years since he'd been outside these concrete walls. That didn't include the two hours each day they allowed the prisoners out for yard time, as they called it here, but anything was better than sitting inside the 6x9-foot cell, day in and day out.

He had been looking forward to this day, finally getting out of this hellhole he didn't belong in. As far back as he could remember he just always seemed to be in the wrong place at the wrong time. He'd left the last town he was in and was arrested four months later for almost killing a man. The judge gave him five years with no parole in the Lancaster Correctional Center in Lancaster, Ohio.

He didn't have a wife or a girlfriend that he had left behind. The last woman he was with was before he ended up in this place—most would call it a one-night stand, but she was more than that to him. There was just something about her that grabbed ahold of his heart and wouldn't let go. She'd been on his mind every minute of every day. This woman didn't know it, but she was the only thing that had kept him going. He was going to find her if it was the last thing he did. He had to find out if she felt the same.

~ ~

He walked down the corridor with one correctional officer in front of him and one behind him, both armed with Taser guns that would shoot a bolt of electricity through your body faster than you could tip over a cow.

Although he'd read it was against the law to use a Taser gun on inmates, it was at times used as a precaution while transporting a prisoner from their cell to the outside world. Just in case they got the idea in their head to run, but his six-foot-three-inch muscular build intimated most people more than anything.

He passed the other inmates shouting their obscenities as he walked slowly by. He hadn't flinched or cared really what they were saying. He was getting out of this place and they had years left behind bars.

A buzzer sounded, echoing around him; then, the door clicked open. They walked through the opening and the door shut behind them. He retrieved the items that had been taken from him when he came to this place—a Rolex watch and a small black velvet box. He slipped the watch on his arm and slid the box in his pants pocket.

After gathering his things, he went through three more doors before the last door slid open and sunlight pierced his eyes, blinding Reece until he shielded his eyes with his hand. He was finally outside. Finally leaving the place that had consumed his world all these years.

He ran a hand through his shoulder-length black hair, and walked straight to the vehicle that would get him out of this God-forsaken place.

A small off-green bus sat idling outside the gate entrance, waiting for him to climb aboard. Waiting to take him to the bus stop where he could catch a ride to wherever he wanted to go.

The ride into town went faster than he thought it would. Thoughts occupied his time and before he knew it, the bus pulled up to the depot and opened its doors. Three other people besides him got off the bus.

He stepped off the last step and made his way down the sidewalk. He saw a sign across the street that said, *Welcome to Craven Falls, Population 2,800.* That was more than he thought there'd be when the bus drove through town, just moments ago.

He spotted a café and his mouth began to water. It had been a long time since he had a home cooked meal. Anything was better than the prison food they'd fed him.

A bell jingled above the door as he pushed it open. Reece looked around the restaurant and saw several empty seats at the counter. He sat down, placing his book on the counter and waited for the waitress to acknowledge him.

"How can I help you today?" a dainty brown-haired woman asked.

He could tell she was a local and probably had lived here her whole life. "I'll have a cup of coffee and a menu, please," Reece replied.

The waitress reached under the counter in front of her and handed him a menu. "I'll go get your coffee while you look it over," the brown-haired woman said.

He had noticed that she was pretty, but he wasn't here for that. In fact, he hadn't thought of anyone except for the last woman he'd been with. He had no clue where she lived, only her name. The way she had looked at him was never far from his mind. He couldn't get that smile, that face, out of his head.

The server set his coffee in front of him, and he gave her his order of three eggs over easy with a side of bacon, wheat toast, and four buttermilk pancakes.

The bell rang behind him, and he looked over his shoulder. A white male, maybe a few years younger than him, walked in wearing an Army uniform. The man eyeballed the place and then headed to a seat near the back.

Reece shouldn't care what this guy was doing. He should mind his own business, but there was something odd about him that just gave Reece a red flag. He didn't need to get involved or attract any attention to himself. He was not going back to prison.

Reece turned back around just as his food arrived. He inhaled the scent and started eating. When the clacking of dishes in the kitchen stopped, he could have sworn he heard the man in the booth talking to himself. No, not talking, more like arguing with himself.

A few minutes later, the guy in the Army uniform stood, walked outside, and got into a black convertible.

Reece watched as the car drove away, but not until after he saw the two white men kiss. Not that he hadn't seen two men kiss before. Hell, he'd seen it his whole time in prison. *To each his own,* he thought, *to each his own,* and went back to eating his breakfast.

4

Catherine Teodora wiped her hands and placed the dishtowel on the counter. She and her granddaughter Lily Rose had spent the morning baking peanut butter, sugar, and snicker doodle cookies. After they finished, Catherine laid Lily down for an early afternoon nap and went back to the kitchen to clean up their mess.

She couldn't believe how exhausted she'd felt after baking cookies with her granddaughter, something she loved to do. She left the kitchen and walked into the living room. She would lie down on the sofa for a little while and then she'd feel better.

No sooner had she closed her eyes, there was a knock on the front door. She mumbled, "For the love of Jesus." She quickly sat up and threw her legs over the side of the couch; although she was nearing seventy, she would sometimes forget that she wasn't a spring chicken anymore. She'd put on some extra weight with having six children. When she got to her feet, she hurried to the door before the person knocked again and woke up Lily.

She opened the door and gasped, "Daniel."

"Hello, Mother," said her son Dan.

"Oh, Daniel, it's so good to see you again," Catherine chimed.

"Mom, you know I hate it when you call me Daniel. It was okay when I was eight or nine years old, but now that I'm twenty-nine, it just isn't manly."

"Oh, son, don't act so grown-up now." She batted her hand in the air. "Come in, come in," she said, stepping back to make room for him.

He opened the screen door and stepped inside. He stood in front of her, hesitated, then took a step closer and slowly wrapped his arms around her, giving her a hug. She was tense at first, but after he made the gesture, she relaxed and hugged him back. When it came to her youngest son Daniel, there was uncertainty. He was the only one in the family that seemed to have a bad streak of luck, as she called it. He was always getting into some kind of trouble, at least until he joined the Army.

She pulled away and held him at arms-length. He was dressed in his Army Combat Uniform with a Patrol Cap resting on his buzz-cut hair.

"I'm speechless. I can't believe you're here. How long are you staying?" she asked.

"I have a two-week leave, then I'm off to Texas for a couple of years," Dan replied.

"Oh," Catherine whispered. "Then I guess we should spend this precious time God gave us to enjoy one another," she concluded.

He nodded in return.

She let go of his arms and padded to the kitchen. "Are you hungry? Do you want some milk and cookies? Lily and I just made them this morning."

"Lily?" he questioned. "I don't remember anyone named Lily in the family. Is it someone that comes to the house and helps with the cleaning and baking?" he asked.

She stopped, turned, "No, don't be silly. I don't need help around the house. She's Ashley's daughter," she said, knowing he hadn't known. *This was actually the first time he'd been home since he signed-up for the Army, six-years ago,* she thought.

"My sister has a daughter?" he asked, his eyes wide.

"She just turned five years old last month." She could see the surprise in his eyes. *He would've known sooner if he had written letters to his only mother, but he hadn't. So now, he had to find out almost six years later. Not my fault,* she thought.

"Please, sit and I'll pour you a glass of milk. We made snicker doodles today," she smiled and turned back towards the counter to grab one of the containers full of cookies.

She placed the tin on the table and walked to the cupboard for a glass. Once she finished pouring the milk in the cup, she sat down across from him.

"Thank you," he said before grabbing a cookie from the container and taking a bite. He finished the cookie and grabbed another one.

She could tell by the look on his face that he missed her homemade cookies. It was as if she'd known he was coming to visit her today and made his favorite. He had been on her mind a lot lately, but that wasn't unusual. She always worried about her Daniel.

She could tell that he wanted to say something to her, but was hesitant. Catherine smiled, then spoke, "So, how's the Army treating you? Do you have any stories to share?" She thought she'd ask questions to get him to talk about whatever was bothering him.

"Mom, please. Please don't start with all the questions. You know I don't like a lot of questions," Dan told her, then took another bite of his cookie.

"At least tell me where you're stationed after your leave here is up."

"I told you, Texas," he replied.

She pressed her lips together and nodded.

"Grandma Cat," the little voice said from the doorway of the kitchen. Lily shoved her little thumb back in her mouth and held her pink blankie tight in her other hand.

"Hey, Lily Rose," Catherine said as she stood and went to her granddaughter. "Did we wake you?" Lily shook her head. "Come here," Catherine opened her arms and scooped Lily up. "I want you to meet your Uncle Dan. He's your mom's youngest brother."

Catherine placed Lily on her lap still gracefully sucking her thumb.

She watched as Lily's eyes traced over Dan's face, not sure what to think of him. She knew Lily hadn't met him before and was sure Ashley had never mentioned an Uncle Dan to her. If she had, Lily would've remembered something like that, maybe. Her daughter was always making sure to tell Lily how smart she was for her age when she was around.

Catherine looked up to see Dan smile at Lily, but noticed Lily didn't smile back, probably because she'd have to take her thumb out of her mouth and she didn't like to do that. She'd tried many times to get Lily to stop sucking her thumb, but nothing seemed to work.

"That's a pretty name you have," Dan said. "Is your mommy here with you?"

Lily slowly shook her head from side to side.

Catherine watched as he smiled back at Lily's response, thinking there was something more behind that mischievous grin. Leave it to Catherine, she'd find out what he was up to, she always did. That look on his face meant he was up to no good.

5

Several hours later, Ashley arrived in Illinois. She stopped at the first restaurant she saw that was open and parked. She needed a pot of coffee and something to eat. She took her time, knowing that it was only after eight in the morning. She didn't want to show up too early, but didn't know what else to do.

When she decided she'd stayed long enough, she paid her bill and got back in the car, heading towards Carla's house. She hoped her friend would be awake when she arrived, but if she wasn't she'd wait outside on the porch swing if she had to.

Instead of pulling into the driveway next to a red Prius, Ashley parked on the side of the street and dug out her phone. She gave her mom a quick call, letting her know that she'd arrived and asked how Lily was doing. She finished the call and stepped out of the car. She locked the car, crossed the street, and walked up the stone path towards the ranch style home.

She rang the doorbell and waited as she gazed around the porch and then off into the yard. She could see that the Daylilies and Irises were coming into bloom, which made her think of her mother who loved working in her flower garden. Catherine would work in her garden all year round if the weather stayed warm, but that doesn't happen in Ohio. So, that's why Ashley's father had built her mother her own greenhouse; she didn't have to worry about the weather anymore.

The door opened behind her; she turned to see a woman with blonde hair who stood about five-five, maybe five-six at the most. The woman smiled, "Can I help you?" she asked.

"Hi, I'm Ashley, Carla's friend from Ohio…" Ashley was interrupted.

"Oh, my God, yes, please come in, come in. I'm so sorry," the woman sputtered. "I'm Veronica, I work with Carla at the school. I'm so glad you could make it. Carla will be so happy to see you, well…" she paused. "Considering the circumstances, I'm sure in her heart she'll appreciate the gesture," Veronica said.

Ashley smiled, "I'm sure she will. Is she here right now?" Ashley asked.

"Yes, but I'm having a bit of trouble getting her out of bed. Though I honestly can't blame her, seeing all that she has lost," Veronica said.

They walked into the family room by the front door and sat down on the sofa. Ashley placed her purse on the floor next to her and glanced around the room. She couldn't remember ever coming into the room the last time she was here. They always seemed to sit in the kitchen and talk or on the back porch.

There was a flat screen in the corner facing her, with photos of Carla and Tim's wedding on the wall. It was the first-time Ashley had gone to Florida. She loved the beach the most, especially watching Carla get married on one. It was a beautiful sunny day, but it usually is in Florida.

This was going to hit her friend the hardest, and she didn't know what she could do or say to make it better. Nothing could make this better. Her friend's husband and child had died and she didn't know what to say to her or how to comfort her.

"Is she in her room?" Ashley asked.

Veronica nodded, "I'm sure she'll be happy to see you. Go on up and sit with her for a while. I have some calls to make anyway."

Ashley stood, "Thank you so much for calling me and letting me know about Carla and..." Ashley choked up. "Well, you know the funeral and all." Before Veronica could reply, Ashley left the room; she didn't want to start crying in front of this stranger.

She climbed the same familiar stairs she'd climbed weeks ago, but this time felt different. It was almost like walking to your own doom. She knew that going into Carla's room would be like entering a morgue, and in these circumstances, it wasn't any different than attending a funeral.

Once at the top, she walked to where Carla's room was, stopped, took in a deep breath, and tapped on the door before entering.

The room was dark from the shades being closed. She waited for her eyes to adjust to the darkness before walking to the bed where she saw a mound of blankets Carla was hibernating under. She felt for a spot on the left side of the bed and sat down.

"Carla, it's me Ashley," she whispered. The blankets moved beside her, she heard a moan. "I'm here for you, sweetie, and I'm so so sorry about everything that has happened."

Carla pushed the blankets from her face and looked up at her friend. Tears escaped from Carla's eyes and Ashley took her in her arms. "Everything will be okay,"

Ashley whispered, knowing it was probably the wrong thing to say and not something Carla would want to hear at this moment. What else could she say to help comfort her friend when there were no words for something like this? No words to take the pain away. She did the only thing she knew to do; she held her friend in her arms and let her cry.

6

After leaving his mom's house, Dan walked the three miles back into town. As he rounded a bend in the road, he spotted a young girl who looked almost like Lily and about her height and age, but as he got closer, he noticed that she had long brown curly hair, not black. The little girl slipped quickly into the woods, but he kept on walking. It wasn't his business to follow her, even if she did intrigue him. He had other things to take care of right now.

As he walked, he decided that by the end of the day he would have a car. All this walking was for the dogs. Yeah, sure, he did a lot of walking and marching in boot camp, but that was a long time ago.

When he reached the corner of Breacher and Kale, he spotted the old café he'd been in earlier this morning and the one he'd spent most of his time in growing up. That and the local bar, which was another block away. But he wasn't in the mood for a beer or to hang around the people that would probably piss him off and then he'd get into a fight and so on and so on.

Nope. He wasn't going to make that mistake twice, or three times. To be honest, he couldn't remember how many fights he'd gotten himself into over the years; maybe that was the cause of the voices in his head. Too many blows to the head rattled something loose, but part of him doubted that theory. Even as a kid, he had secret friends that he talked to.

Dan looked both ways, crossed the street, making his way towards the diner. He knew as soon as he pushed the door open the bell above would notify the people inside that someone was there. He didn't want people to look at him or to know that he was walking in, but there was nothing he could do about it. It was just one other thing that brought the voices out.

"I told you he wouldn't be here," the first voice said.

"Yeah, ya' stupid moron," the second voice replied.

Dan shook his head. Sometimes it worked and sometimes it didn't. The voices at times had their own agenda.

He had lied to his mom about the two-week leave from the Army and about going to Texas. He actually had no clue where he was going from here; he thought he'd play it by ear. He didn't want to tell his mother, but he'd arrived two weeks ago and had just went to see her.

He hadn't wanted to hurt her feelings by telling her he wasn't going to be staying with her like he had always done in the past. No, he had other plans, but even those plans seemed to be falling through the cracks. Everything seemed to be going to shit since he'd been discharged from the Army.

He walked to the back and sat down in a booth near the far corner, away from the other people. People that would hear him if he were to talk to himself, and that was something he didn't need right now. He didn't need folks looking at him. No, he just wanted to keep a low key and finish what he had planned to do, and then leave.

After ordering a cup of coffee from the petite redhead with artificial breasts, because there was no way they were real at her age, which she looked to be near her fifties, and who seemed to be flirting with him. Too bad though 'cause he wasn't interested in her. Nope not his type, instead his thoughts went to the little girl named Lily Rose.

The redhead set a cup down on the table and poured the coffee, "Anything else I can get for ya'?" she asked, snapping her gum between her teeth.

Dan shook his head, "No, thanks, ma'am." She left and went back behind the counter.

He was surprised when he walked into this diner yesterday that someone hadn't recognized him. The town wasn't overly populated; mostly everyone knew everyone, but Dan didn't know the woman who served him coffee. Nor did he remember anyone one else he'd passed by through town.

He had been gone a long time, but he would have to admit that he didn't look the same after all these years either. Or, maybe he was just losing his mind. He chuckled to himself. That was an understatement.

His mind wandered back to his sister. He couldn't believe that Ashley had a child, *"A beautiful one at that,"* the voice in his head said. *"You'd been gone so long, she'd gone out and got herself knocked-up."* Dan shook his head. The voices were getting worse since he'd left Pennsylvania. He'd been able to keep them at bay when he was around other people, but now they seemed to be getting louder. As if they were trying to escape his head and become their own person.

Dan heard the bell jingle from behind him, which meant that someone had entered the café. That someone slid in the seat in front of him. Dan didn't lift his head or make any kind of eye contact with the person; he just sat there drinking his coffee.

"I thought I told you not to stick around town," Rob said.

"Yes, you said that," Dan replied.

"Yet, you're still here?"

Dan held his cup to his lips, took a sip, and then looked over the edge of the coffee cup, right into the eyes of the man across from him. His dark blond hair was combed neatly back, away from his forehead.

"Are you going to make me ask you again, why you're still in this town?" Rob tapped his finger on the table.

"I think you already did," Dan stated matter-of-factly. "I won't stay long. I just have one more *thing* to do; then, I'll leave and you'll never see me again."

"I'll give you until Sunday to get your "*thing*", " Rob said as he made air quotes, "taken care of; after that," Rob lowered his voice almost to a whisper as he leaned forward, "then you are to leave and never come back here again. Do I make myself clear?" Rob sat back in his seat. "I helped you out and now it's time for you to leave."

Dan looked him square in the face. "What about yesterday?"

"Yesterday was a mistake," Rob replied. "So was earlier today."

Daniel set his cup down. *He should have known that this was how it was going to end. He'd been so stupid to think that anything would happen between him and Rob. Fuck him! Who needs him anyway?* Dan thought. "Sure, yeah. You'll never hear from me again. I'll leave and never come back," he replied, knowing that he wasn't leaving at all. Not while Lily Rose was still here.

After Rob left, he thought of his sister, Ashley, but only for a few seconds. He was glad that she wasn't at his mother's house because if she had been, she'd no doubt stir up a can of shit, especially after what happened two weeks ago. It didn't matter anyway; he wasn't planning to stay long. He didn't give two-shits about his sister, never had, never would. He was just here to pay a visit to his mother, then hit the road, and never come back to this run-down piece of shit town. There was no reason to stay.

Or was there?

7

Lily hopped down the last step and landed on the green grass in Grandma Cat's backyard. Lily saw her friend Sierra walking out of the woods by her swing-set and started running towards her.

When Lily reached her friend, they both fell to the ground and lay there staring up at the bright blue sky. Springtime and summer were her most favorite seasons. She loved playing outside, especially with her new friend Sierra who lived on the other side of the woods.

Lily wasn't allowed to go into the woods without an adult. Sometimes when her mom was here, she would go with Lily down to the river. Lily smiled at the thought as the sun warmed her face, making her giggle.

"What do you want to do today?" Sierra asked.

Lily turned her face towards Sierra. "Want to play on the swing? I'll push you first and then you can push me," Lily said, sitting up.

"Okay, sure," Sierra replied.

Lily gave her friend a push and then another one. As soon as Sierra came back, she pushed her again, and then again. Sierra laughed louder the higher she went, and then she jumped through the air and landed on her feet.

"That was awesome," Sierra shouted, giggling.

When it was Lily's turn to swing on the swing, her friend pushed her so high she felt like she was flying. She had to be careful because last year she broke her arm when she jumped off the swing in mid-air, and Grandma Cat had cried as she drove Lily to the hospital. Lily didn't want to make Grandma Cat cry, nor did she want to break her arm again.

She remembered being in pain all the way to the hospital, which had made her cry too. The only good thing that had come out of it was the bright pink cast the doctor had put on her arm.

Lily waited until the swing wasn't moving as fast before jumping off the seat. She jumped and landed on her feet, and then rolled on the ground laughing.

"Lily Rose, how many times do I have to tell you not to jump off that swing while it's moving?" Grandma Cat hollered as she stood outside the greenhouse door.

Lily sat up and looked at Grandma Cat. "I didn't jump that high up," Lily protested, folding her arms against her chest, almost pouting.

"That doesn't matter. Your mother and I told you not to do it. Do you remember what happened last year?"

Lily nodded and then answered back, "Yes, I remember."

"You and Sierra go find something else to do that won't get you hurt," Catherine said before turning and going back inside the greenhouse.

"Do you want to go down by the river?" Sierra asked.

"I don't know, Grandma Cat doesn't like me to go into the woods without her or Mommy. She said it can be dangerous and if something happened, she wouldn't know where I was to help me."

"It'll only be for a few minutes. She won't even know you're gone."

Lily thought for a minute, and then said, "Okay, but just for a couple of minutes." She looked over her shoulder to see where Grandma Cat was. She noticed a movement in the greenhouse and took off running with Sierra into the woods.

It only took a couple of minutes to run to the cliff and then climb down to the bottom where the water was. Once down the hill, both Lily and Sierra ran over to the huge rock and climbed up on it. They would sit there and look at the water flowing down the river. Sometimes, they would gather stones and toss them in.

Lily wasn't sure how much time had passed since they had come down here when they heard Sierra's name being called. They both walked up another path instead of climbing the hill.

Once at the top, Lily said goodbye to her friend and walked back towards Grandma Cat's house. When she saw the swing-set, she sighed a sigh of relief. She always got nervous walking back by herself even though it was still light out. That's why her and Sierra had marked an X on the trees with yellow paint.

She stepped into the yard and started running towards the house.

"Lily!"

Lily stopped in her tracks and turned around. Grandma Cat was standing by the swing-set and she didn't look happy.

"Did you just come out of the woods?"

Lily swallowed and then answered, "Yes."

"I thought your mother and I told you to stay out of the woods. You are not to go in there without one of us with you," Catherine said as she walked towards Lily. "What if something happened to you? Do you realize how hurt and lost I'd be without you? It would crush my heart to have something happen to you, my sweet child,"

Catherine said as she knelt down in front of Lily who was now crying.

"I'm sorry, Grandma Cat," Lily sniffled. "I won't do it again, promise."

"Well, okay then. Let's go inside and make something for dinner and then watch some television," Catherine said as she pulled Lily into a hug. "Your mama would never forgive me if something were to happen to you"

8

Reece sat on the bench across the street, watching the café. He had been minding his own business, walking down the sidewalk when he saw the same guy from earlier. That was enough for Reece to take a seat and see what the guy was up to. If it looked like he was just having some coffee, then he'd leave it at that, but when this other man stormed in, he could tell something was off. He could tell the guy was pissed!

The man he had seen this morning who had entered the restaurant and sat down, the one who'd been arguing with himself and then left, getting in a black car, was back in the café having coffee by himself until this other man came in the restaurant and sat down in front of the guy he'd been watching. They spoke, but of course, Reece couldn't hear them, but he'd learned how to read people's lips and knew by piecing some of the words together what was being said, *"I thought I told you not to stick around town,"* the angry guy said as the other man drank his coffee.

Reece knew the moment he saw him walk in the café yesterday that something wasn't right with him, but then he'd left and that was that.

He thought about going inside and sitting at the counter. Listen in on their conversation, but he knew better than to get involved. It was in his best interest to just walk away and pretend nothing ever happened. It was a small town, people knew people. Locals watched out for each other, and him sitting here, looked suspicious.

A few minutes later, the guy who'd just entered, left. He got in his black convertible, the same one from earlier and drove away. He didn't look happy.

Reece stood, still staring at the man in the café, and then turned and started walking down the sidewalk. He knew he should just walk away, but there was just something about the guy he didn't like or trust. He decided that he'd stay a little longer, see what the man was up to before taking a bus to somewhere else. He needed to retrace his steps back to the night he met the woman of his dreams so he could find her, but he couldn't remember where that place was.

Last night he'd slept in the woods, and it looked like he'd be doing that again tonight as long as the weather stayed nice. Maybe when he decided to leave this unpopulated town, he'd go somewhere warmer, somewhere where he could find work. Eventually he'd run out of money, and he'd have to make more in order to eat; everyone had to eat.

He stopped in front of Bailey's Pub, opened the door. Music and stale cigarette smoke spilled out as he went inside. It wasn't completely dark. There were small light fixtures by each booth along the east wall and slot machines on each table.

Near the back where the pool tables sat, there was more of a translucent lighting. To him, it looked like every other bar he'd been in. On one side of the room was a long bar with mirrors along the wall and hundreds of different liquor bottles on the other side of the room, there were booths and tables for the social drinkers or people that came to eat.

He walked over to the wood-paneled bar, swiveled the chair that was screwed into the floorboards and sat down. The bartender came to him, possibly the owner of the place. "I haven't seen you around here before," the bartender stated.

Reece wasn't much for talking; he'd keep it short and sweet. "Probably not," he replied.

The bartender gave him a cold stare. "I don't want no trouble here."

"I'm not here for trouble. I just want a whiskey on the rocks," Reece said.

The bartender didn't move his eyes from Reece as his left hand placed a glass on the bar, threw in a couple ice cubes, and then grabbed the bottle of whiskey from behind him and poured the drink.

"Thank you," Reece said before picking up the glass and knocking the drink down in one swallow. He set the glass back down and nodded for another one.

~ ~

Couple of hours later, Reece finished his third whiskey on the rocks and was about to leave for the night when a man sat down next to him and ordered a drink.

From the corner of his eye, Reece knew exactly who it was and he was about to learn the man's name.

"Hey, how's it going for you?" the bartender asked.

"Not too bad, I guess," the man replied.

Reece knew that was a crock of shit and was surprised this guy didn't start complaining about it. Reece had seen how upset the man had been when he'd seen him at the coffee shop earlier.

Everyone knew that when you walked into a bar, had a few drinks, then you usually ended up spilling your guts to the person next to you, telling that person your whole life story from beginning to end, even the embarrassing moments. Especially the embarrassing parts. Something Reece was a little curious to find out about this guy.

Either that or Reece should just stand up, walk out the door, and not look back. But Reece wasn't one to walk away, even if he should. Besides, Reece didn't have anything else to do, at least not right away until he could find the girl he'd dreamed about for so long, but he didn't even know her name. For now, he needed to know how much the world had changed while he'd been incarcerated, and he was intrigued by the drama that had been going on all day as well.

It didn't take more than an hour before Reece got the man talking, and since the man was buying the drinks, Reece wasn't going to stop him. The man was going on and on about his fiancé. Said she wasn't answering any of his calls, not that Reece could blame her.

It wasn't so much the woman that intrigued him, but the little girl named Lily the man mentioned. Said that he really loved her and that she was like his own daughter, but he would no longer be a part of the child's life, unless he stopped his fiancé from leaving him.

"I could kidnap her and no one would know," the man whispered close to Reece's ear.

"Then you'd get caught and go to jail," Reece said, looking straight into his eyes. "You don't want to go there. I've been there. They'd chew you up and spit you to high heaven. It's not a place for boys like you."

"What are you trying to imply? Do you think I'm not strong enough to be in prison? You think I'd get my ass kicked or something?" The man slurred his words, getting upset over Reece telling him he was weak and not prison-worthy.

"I think you've had too much to drink," Reece stated. "You should go home, get some rest. I think you're just upset and don't mean a word you're saying."

It was easy to get the information out of him. Reece had asked the man a couple of questions, and he fizzed like Alka-Seltzer in water.

Plop, plop, fizz, fizz.

Reece had gotten all the information he needed and left the bar, making his way down the road.

9

Ashley had stayed in the spare bedroom. The same one she'd slept in when she was here last. She tossed and turned, listening to the faint cries coming from Carla's room all night. She wanted to go to her. Comfort her friend like she did earlier, but was exhausted from the drive and what the day had brought her.

Carla wouldn't get out of bed. She wouldn't eat any of the food Ashley carried to the room. She tried to persuade her to eat, but she wouldn't budge. So, Ashley left the food that wouldn't spoil and took the rest back downstairs.

She rolled over and stared at the clock on the nightstand, 4:36 a.m. She debated on whether to lie here or just get up. Coffee did sound good to her.

She threw back the blankets, slid her legs off the bed, and stepped onto the cold wooden floor. The coolness made her hot feet feel like ice melting on a hot day. She slouched her way to the bathroom, flushed, and washed her hands. She went to the closet in the room she was staying in and slipped her feet in the slippers she'd forgotten to retrieve last night.

She paused at Carla's door, listened, and then walked down the stairs to the kitchen. She'd let Carla sleep a couple more hours, then take her some coffee and try to get her out of bed.

She knew it would be a process, but Ashley had to be back home on Sunday. She hated to leave her friend in her time of need, but she also had a daughter to care for.

Ashley discarded the old coffee grounds and searched the pantry for what she needed to make a fresh pot. Ten minutes later, she poured herself a cup and sat down at the kitchen table.

There were several newspapers still rolled up, sitting on the table. She grabbed one and scanned through it. Nothing held her interest, but once she saw the obituaries of Mya and Tim's picture, she knew she should cut it out for Carla.

Ashley glanced at the dates on the other newspapers and decided to throw them out. Carla wasn't going to read them. She couldn't even get her friend to come downstairs, let alone open the blinds in her room. It was like she was dormant like a bear in the winter.

Her stomach growled; she stood, went to the refrigerator, and opened the door. Every shelf was packed with containers of food. Food she knew friends and neighbors had probably brought over. It was the only thing people knew to do when someone died. No one feels like cooking when they're mourning.

Ashley moved a few things around, but nothing appealed to her. She went to the pantry, found a box of honey nut cheerios, and hunted through the cabinets for a bowl. She placed them on the table and went to the fridge for milk. There wasn't any. "Great," she mumbled.

She put everything back and poured another cup of coffee. *At least there was cream for her coffee,* she thought. She opened the back door and stood in the doorway looking out into the backyard. The early morning was brisk, but if it was anything like yesterday, she knew it would warm up to the mid-seventies again.

It was starting to get light outside. She went to the hall closet, grabbed a sweater of Carla's, and stepped out onto the back porch. She didn't feel like swinging on the porch swing so she sat down on the steps.

The birds were singing their morning song. She knew they were hiding in the branches of the trees; though you couldn't see them, they were there.

By the time she finished her second cup, the sky was covered in a brilliant blue. She stood and went back inside. She grabbed another coffee cup from the cabinet and poured Carla a cup. She walked upstairs, tapped on the door with the knuckle of her forefinger as she juggled the two coffee cups in one hand. She listened; there was no sound coming from inside the closed room, but she wasn't surprised.

She opened the door and went inside. After placing the cups down on the nightstand, she shuffled to the window, pulled on the cord, opening the blinds just a hair. A little light was good, and all she needed to get Carla at least sitting up. She peered around the room, clothes were scattered all around the floor and on the bed.

Ashley sighed, "I brought you some fresh coffee." No sound. "As much as I don't blame you for wanting to stay in bed, you will have to get up for the funeral later today. We have calling hours at eleven and then the funeral afterwards." Still nothing.

She saw a bottle sitting next to the bed, and for a split second, her heart stopped and then sped faster. Would her friend really try to take her own life? She remembered the conversation they had just a couple of weeks ago. Carla had said she had tried a year ago to end her life.

Ashley quickly grabbed the blankets and pulled down on them. Carla's hair was mangled around her face. Ashley brushed her hair away and placed two fingers on the side of her neck. There was a pulse. She exhaled a breath, "Thank God," she mumbled. "Carla honey, you need to wake up."

Carla moaned and rolled over onto her side.

"I know you don't want to get up, but you have to. Here, I brought you some fresh coffee."

Carla opened her eyes and quickly closed them. "It's too bright in here," she moaned.

"No, it's not," Ashley whispered. "You can do this, I know you can. You're strong enough, Carla."

"I don't think I can." She went to pull the blankets back up to cover her face, but Ashley stopped her.

"Yes, you can." Ashley picked up the bottle next to the bed and read the prescription. *Percocet,* she remembered it was what the doctor had given Carla for pain when she left the hospital after having Mya. She pushed down and turned the lid, spilling the contents in her palm. The quantity said 30, and there looked to be close to that still in the bottle.

"I only took one," Carla said, breaking the silence.

Ashley blew out a breath, feeling relieved. "Okay," was all she said. All she knew to say. She placed the lid back on the bottle and dropped it into the pocket of the sweater she was wearing.

She helped Carla sit up and handed her the cup of coffee. "Umm, this tastes good. Thank you for making me some," Carla said.

"You're welcome," Ashley replied.

They sat in silence for a while, and then Ashley suggested that Carla take a shower. She could smell the body odor coming off her, but didn't want to sound rude by telling her friend that she smelled. According to Veronica, Carla hadn't taken a shower since she'd found out four or five days ago that her husband had died. She'd kept herself in bed, mourning his loss.

"Come on, I'll help you get ready," Ashley said, and pulled the covers the rest of the way down. She positioned Carla's legs over the edge. She hadn't been aware until now, how much weight Carla had lost since the last time she'd seen her. Once she knew that Carla was up, Ashley went into the bathroom to turn on the shower.

"Okay, let's get you in the bathroom, and you can start washing yourself. Do you want me to pick out your dress and place it in the bathroom?"

Carla shook her head," I can do it, but thank you."

Ashley nodded and left the room, making her way towards the guest room.

~ ~

Once in her room, she walked to the bed, sat down, and leaned her back against the headboard. She reached for her phone that was sitting on the nightstand beside the bed. She decided to take this time and call her mom.

After hanging up, she arched her head back and closed her eyes. Her mom sounded happy and not stressed out from being with Lily these past couple of nights. Why Ashley always thought her mother couldn't handle Lily was beyond her. Her mother had given birth to six children, Ashley being the fifth child and only daughter. Before getting off the phone, her mom mentioned that

Rob had called several times and that she had told him that she would have Ashley call when she talked to her the next time.

Ashley sighed in relief that her mother didn't ask her any questions, though she could sense the concern in her voice and knew she would have to tell her everything when she got home on Sunday. The last thing her mom had said was that she was taking Lily to the zoo, just in case they weren't home when she got there on Sunday. Ashley had asked her to take some pictures of Lily for her to see when she got back home.

Ashley was surprised that her mother hadn't mentioned her brother Dan visiting. Who, she knew for a fact would stop and pay a visit to his own mother, wouldn't he? She also knew that if he did stop there, he wasn't going to tell her what had happened between the two of them. Shit, no! That would have shattered her mother's heart, knowing what he had done.

Ashley wished she could talk to Carla about the whole Rob thing and get another perspective on the matter. She already knew she wasn't going back to him, but she still needed to meet with him and give him his things back.

She was actually surprised how well she was handling the whole thing. She had cried but a couple of times after it happened; and then, it was like it didn't matter anymore. She couldn't understand why she didn't feel sad or even angry with him. She loved him, that she knew, but was she in love with him? That was something she'd have to think more about.

10

The following morning, Dan finished his coffee and asked for a refill. He thought back to yesterday when he was sitting in the same seat in the same café when Rob sat down. He wasn't intimated by the guy; the thought made him laugh. No, that was something he never got with other people.

Dan was a brute to most people. He was six-foot and weighed two-ten. In the first year of the Army, he did nothing but workout by lifting weights, just like most of them did when they weren't on duty at the Army base. Then after that, he had to find different ways to strengthen his muscles. Working out on his off-time with all the other guys on the base eventually wasn't a choice he could pursue after they found out about his voices.

Dan left the café and crossed the street. He needed to find a set of wheels. Walking wasn't an option for what he had in mind. He needed a car to complete the idea he'd gotten last night while he was sitting in the woods watching his mother's house.

With the money he'd accumulated over the years from being in the Army, the available cash he had could get him something doable, something that could get him out of town. "Four wheels and a full tank of gas," he mumbled.

Tonight, he would head back towards his mom's house and perch himself near a tree so he could see into her backyard and into the house, just like last night. He wanted to keep an eye on the little girl named Lily Rose, a pretty name at that, and make sure she didn't leave with her mama. That would ruin everything! No, he needed her to stay right where she was; at least until he came up with a good solid plan, but he knew he was on borrowed time. His sister would come back for her soon.

At the next block, he stopped and looked into the parking lot. There were several automobiles for sale, but the prices stickered on the windshield were more than he wanted to spend. If he couldn't get the owner to sell him one in his price range, then he'd just have to think of something else; maybe even have to steal one. Nah, he'd never done that before. He didn't know the first thing about stealing a car, and even less about hot-wiring an engine. He'd have to swindle a deal with the owner, scare him or something.

"Ya', man, scare the asshole!" the voice in his head said.

Dan shook his head, trying to dislodge whatever was causing him to hear these voices.

"Oh, no you're not getting rid of me that easy," the voice laughed.

"Ya', you ain't getting rid of us!" another voice shouted inside his head.

Dan turned and hid between two buildings, holding his head in his hands. Besides the voices, there was pain. Sometimes the pain would get so bad that he thought his head would explode. Sometimes he wished it would, then he wouldn't have to listen to them anymore. He wouldn't have to hide them anymore.

Normally, the voices spoke when he had one too many drinks in him, but when he was in the Army, they came when he was alone in his room, but not always. He just had to keep himself from talking back to them. Lately, he would always have pain when he heard the voices.

When the pain subsided, he leaned his back against the wall and closed his eyes. He needed a couple more minutes of peace before making an offer with or without a threat to the owner at the car dealership.

Dan weaved in between the cars, looking for something he could afford. He saw the owner step outside, looking right at him. The salesman came over and introduced himself.

"Hey, I'm Clay Blocken. If you're looking for a ride, I can help you with that," Clay said.

Dan nodded, thinking what an ass this man was making of himself. Why would he be in this parking lot if he weren't buying a fucking car?

Clay stuck his hand out. Dan hesitated and then shook it.

"What kind of deal can you give me on his one right here," Dan asked, pointing to an old Honda Civic. The price tag said $2,500.00, but he knew it wasn't worth that much.

"Well, it's got a brand-new engine in it. Can't say I can go much lower than two grand," Clay stated.

"Let me see the engine," Dan asked, knowing that Clay was bluffing.

"Yeah, okay, sure. Let me go get the keys."

Clay returned with the keys, but before popping the hood, he said, "Maybe you could give me eighteen hundred for it. I don't know that I can sell it to you any lower than that."

"Sure, you could," the voice said. Dan tightened his jaw. "Just open the hood," Dan demanded.

"Okay, okay. Fifteen hundred, no lower," Clay squealed.

"Let me ask you this, if you're lying about the new engine, does it at least run?" Dan asked.

"Sure, sure," Clay said, and ran over to the driver's side and jumped in behind the wheel. The car roared to life. Clay pushed in the gas petal a couple of times, making the engine roar loud and steady. He climbed back out of the car. "Sounds good, don't she?" he asked.

"Yes, she does, but I'm still not giving you fifteen for it," Dan replied, looking Clay straight in the eyes.

"Seriously, man, you're killing me here. Okay, I'll make you a deal—one thousand, take it or leave it?" Fifteen minutes later, Dan drove out of the lot, driving a 1992 Flint Black Metallic Honda Civic.

11

Catherine loved to look out the window of her kitchen, especially in the early morning when the dew lathered the blades of grass that sparkled in the sunlight. Just after dawn, it was cool in this part of town. In the woods you needed a jacket, but only until the sun was at high noon.

The weather was staying in the mid-sixties to seventies for the month of March. Not that it was odd because it was Ohio, and in March, there was usually still snow, but she knew better than to complain. "You take the good things and you hold on to them while they last," is what she always told her kids. It was certain that she knew about good times and bad. She'd been born and raised in the 1940s, 1948 to be exact.

Yes, she knew she wasn't a young chicken anymore, but she still had her wits about her. Although she'd given birth to six beautiful healthy babies, she could still move around and enjoyed doing yardwork.

Charley, her late husband, had been gone for five years now. She met him right after high school. He'd been on leave from the Army, and was heading back out in three weeks.

He was five years older than her, but she didn't care about the age difference. He was the most handsome man she'd ever laid her eyes on. He'd said the same about her, and also that she was the prettiest little thing like a flower—a rose to be specific.

They met in town as she was walking to the grocery store, and he had accidently bumped into her. So, he said. She had told all her kids that when she looked up and into his beautiful blue eyes, it was as if she was floating on air. He had made her heart feel as light as a feather. Of course, he had apologized multiple times for being so careless and offered her a milkshake at the ice cream parlor down the street to make up for his clumsiness.

In those three weeks, you couldn't keep them apart. Catherine, of course, didn't want to see him go, and there certainly wasn't anything to keep her here in Craven Falls. Although her parents were against them getting married, saying, *"He wouldn't amount to nothing,"* she left with him and they eloped.

It wasn't until after her first son was born that they'd moved back to Craven Falls. Catherine had gotten word that her father had become ill and wouldn't be around much longer; she'd come back to say goodbye. Her mother had asked Catherine to stay, and so they moved into the house that she grew up in. The same house she lived in now. She helped take care of her mother who was wheelchair-bound. Eighteen months later, they had buried her mother alongside her father.

Catherine's husband Charley, he didn't have much of a family himself in Craven Falls. His mother had died soon after giving birth to him, and his father after her death had drunk himself into a stupor. Charley had been physically abused when his father was drunk, but as he got older, he found himself a job so he wouldn't be at home as much. When he turned eighteen, he joined the Army. Shortly after that, he'd met Catherine when he came home for his father's funeral.

~ ~

The day had swiftly blown by and night had fallen. Catherine finished wiping off the counter, and then checked and locked the door to the backyard before turning off the light in the kitchen.

She padded down the hall, checked the front door, and went up the stairs to her bedroom, which was across the hall from where Lily was sleeping.

Since all of her kids were grown and married with their own kids and lives, she'd taken one of the boys' rooms and redecorated it for Lily. She had the room painted in three different shades of pink with a stenciled image of a castle on the wall; Lily's favorite was Bella from Beauty and the Beast.

Catherine never closed her bedroom door when her granddaughter was sleeping over. She was afraid to admit that she couldn't hear like she used to.

She walked into her bathroom, washed up, and then went to the bed where she draped her robe on the bedpost. She pulled back the covers, propped her pillow against the headboard so she could read, and slid under the blankets.

She read until her eyes grew tired, laying the book down on the nightstand. She fixed her pillow and clicked off the light. Tomorrow was going to be a busy day with Lily. Catherine was taking her granddaughter to the zoo, and she'd need as much sleep as she could get. That girl was like a kangaroo on speed.

12

Once Dan saw the light flick off, he sat back against the trunk of the tree. He'd have to wait for a least an hour before going into the house. He needed his mother to be fast asleep.

He withdrew a bag of peanuts from his coat, cracked the shell, tossing the nut in his mouth. He threw the empty shell on the ground beside him and pulled another one from the bag.

He wasn't sure how much time had passed since he didn't own a watch, and he didn't want to use the cell phone he'd purchased a few weeks ago, just in case someone in the house saw the light from the phone when he turned it on.

He stood, replaced the half-eaten bag back in his coat, and dusted himself off. He froze when he heard the snapping of twigs and underbrush, like breaking bones behind him. Had someone followed him into the woods? Had someone been watching him?

He didn't remember seeing anyone when he entered the woods. Not when it had been still light out. There were no tents or treehouses around. Not that anyone would be camping in the woods behind these houses, would they? In all reality, it certainly could be an animal. Maybe a deer, or a rabbit; both were possible.

Darkness shrouded the woods, as he peered around. The tangled branches above him, closing in. A panic attack was on the verge of kicking in; he could hear his heart pounding and the strangled feeling of shortness of breath in his throat. Quickly, he ran to the edge of the property, where he felt almost safe again. Funny, how he was a grown man, and yet scared of the dark. Scared of the noises that were all around him.

Once he was at the backdoor, he knew he'd have to be quiet inside the house. One mistake and he'd be caught. He wasn't made for prison, not that he'd ever been in one. Not if he could help it.

He lifted the only painted flowerpot that had a fake plant in it, but to his surprise, there was no key under it. His mother had actually taken his advice and removed it. Now what was he going to do? How was he going to get inside the house? He shook the pot in his hand like he was about to throw it and heard something rattle. *Could she have?* He pulled the fake plant out of the pot and there at the bottom was a key. He chuckled to himself.

"Your mom's a real piece of work," the voice said.

"Shut up," Dan mumbled through his teeth.

"Maybe you should get rid of her too while you're here," the voice said again.

He pressed his fingers against his forehead and squeezed his eyes shut. This was not a good time for him to lose it. He dropped to his knees as piercing pain shot through his head.

He rocked back and forth, cradling his head in his hands. The pain was worse than it had ever been. He pressed his hands harder against his head as though he were trying to suppress the pain, then fell to his side and all went black...

13

Reece had been sitting against an old rotted tree snoozing from all the shots he'd drunk at the Pub earlier. Shots a stranger had been buying him. He had wanted to find out his name, but after the shots kicked in, he'd forgotten all about asking the guy; and the guy had never mentioned it to him or asked Reece what his name was, either.

He didn't usually drink that much, but the guy kept ordering them. He kept going on and on about his girlfriend. Said she wouldn't take his calls. He'd done something so stupid, and she just happened to come over to his place at that moment. "Talk about dumb luck," the man at the bar had said. Then, he started talking about a little girl and how much he was going to miss her being around. That she was like a daughter to him. The guy was talking nonstop like Roadrunner on speed.

Reece was getting tired of the "poor me story," and wanted to shout, *"For the love of God, would you please shut the fuck up!"* Instead, he excused himself saying he had to use the restroom and would be right back. He did use the commode before slipping out the backdoor and walking back to where he'd slept the night before. Back to the spot, he was resting at now.

Reece was jolted awake when he heard the crackling of branches, one-hundred feet in front of him. He thought he knew the difference between animal and human. One thing was true; there were no bears in these woods, but it could be a deer.

He clawed his way up the tree trunk, until he was standing. He didn't remember seeing anyone out here when he arrived, but that didn't mean that someone could have shown up afterwards, while he was sleeping. Though the branches snapping in-half was proof that someone or something was out here with him.

He took easy steps, trying not to make any noise. When he got within twenty feet, he recognized the voice. It was the same man from the café, and he was talking to himself again. "What the shit?" Reece mumbled. *What is he doing in these woods?* The same bad vibe flowed through him. He took a few more hesitate steps forward. Branches snapped, he froze, keeping his eyes on the man.

The man turned, searching the woods around him and then took off towards the house in front of him. Reece walked as the man ran to muffle his steps. Once he hit the grass-line, Reece stopped. He had a clear view of the man and the house. *What was he up to?* Reece thought to himself.

The man walked in the shadows until he was at the backdoor of the house. He turned the doorknob, and then looked down. The man was going to break into the house. He had to stop him, but he also had to be careful not to get caught himself. That would send him straight back to prison.

Once he made it to the edge of the property, he did the same thing as the man—he hid in the shadows. The man started arguing with himself again, and then grabbed his head. Reece took his one and only shot, raising a log that he had found on the other side of the greenhouse above his head, knocking the crazy lunatic out.

14

When Dan woke, he found himself behind the wheel of his newly owed Honda Civic. He was lying across the back seat and his head hurt like a son of a bitch.

He sat up, his left hand automatically touching the huge lump on the back of his head. Dizziness took over; he squeezed his eyes shut, trying to think how he got to his car.

Nothing.

He had no recollection. Last thing he remembered was standing at the backdoor and finding the key; then, *Wham!*—he'd fallen to his knees and woke up in his car. *Strange,* he thought, surprised the voices didn't join in and state their opinions.

He removed his hand from his head, now caked with blood. Whatever had hit his head had hit him hard enough to split open his skull and cause him to bleed.

"Damn it," he swore. Did someone know what he was planning? The only other people that knew he was in town, except his mother were Ashley and Rob.

No, he knew Rob wasn't capable of bashing his head in and then carrying him to his car. Was he? Because Dan was sure it couldn't have been Ashley, she was still out of town as far as he knew. Did he know Rob well enough? It had been nearly four years now. Dan still had his doubts, but shook them off as he climbed out of the backseat and jumped behind the wheel. He had to come up with another way to get Lily.

The person that hit him could have easily killed him, but they didn't, why? He had been staying with a friend and was hoping for a future, but that had turned sour real fast. No thanks to Ashley.

He'd paid a visit to his mother after that and saw Lily for the first time. Within two weeks, his world had become a fucking mess. He didn't need this shit.

He patted the front pocket of his jeans, felt the keys, and took them out. He started the car, slammed it into gear, and drove off down the road. He'd have to contrive another way to kidnap Lily, but right now, he had to go clean up his head and make sure he didn't need stitches.

15

Saturday had come and gone. Now on this early Sunday morning, Ashley finished packing her things into her duffle bag and headed downstairs. She made a fresh pot of coffee, hoping Carla would join her before she drove back to Ohio.

While the coffee brewed, she went back upstairs and into Carla's room. A mound of blankets and clothes sat in the middle of the bed and underneath somewhere was Carla.

She sat down next to her and started peeling the covers back one by one. She combed the hair out of Carla's eyes and smoothed her cheek with her forefinger. How she wished she could make it all better and take away her friend's heartache. Carla didn't deserve this. All she wanted was Tim and a baby, but now she was left with nothing.

Ashley leaned down and kissed Carla's forehead; her friend didn't stir. She didn't want to leave without saying goodbye, but she also didn't want to wake Carla because she'd probably just gone to sleep after a long night.

Yesterday had been stressful for Carla, for everyone. The funeral seemed like a blur at times. Carla just stared at the caskets, not saying a word, not crying. She knew her friend was probably numb from all the crying she'd done already, but when they started to lower Tim's casket in the ground, she had become hysterical.

Veronica and Ashley had to hold her up and get her back in the car. They came back to the house where the gathering was to be held, but Carla went straight upstairs and crawled back under the blankets, where she stayed the rest of the day and night.

She whispered in her friend's ear that she would call or text her when she arrived home so that Carla would know that Ashley got home okay.

Nothing.

Carla just slept without saying goodbye.

~ ~

The seven-hour drive didn't take as long as Ashley thought it would. Although she was exhausted by the time she pulled into her mom's driveway, she was excited to see her Lily Bug. Although she knew there'd be no reply, she texted Carla and let her know that she'd made it back safe.

As she made her way to the porch steps, she realized that her mother's car wasn't in the driveway. *Were they still at the zoo?* she wondered. She stuck the key in the lock, pushed the door open, and went inside.

There was an eerie silence flowing throughout the house, which made Ashley feel uneasy. She'd been in the house many times before when no one was home. Why would this one time feel any different?

She went into the kitchen and grabbed a bottle of water from the refrigerator. She twisted off the cap and turned towards the window, facing the backyard. The weather outside wasn't as warm as it had been, but she decided to sit on the back porch and wait for them to return from the zoo.

A couple of hours had passed and still no sight of her mother or daughter. It was nearly 7:30 p.m., and they hadn't returned home. She knew the zoo closed at five on

Sundays so why hadn't they made it home yet? She didn't want to worry, but this was too late.

She decided to call her mom's cell phone and see if they had stopped off for something to eat. She went back inside and grabbed her cell phone from her purse.

When she went to dial her mom's number, she realized that her phone was dead. She'd forgotten to charge it on the drive home and hadn't realized the battery was low.

She grabbed the home phone, but then recalled that she didn't know what her mom's phone number was to her cell. Nowadays everyone relied on their cell phones and didn't memorize anyone's number.

She placed the phone back on the wall and went into the living room, clicked on the TV, and sat down on the sofa. She flicked through the channels and stopped on a local news channel that was broadcasting the town's local zoo. She didn't recall her mom mentioning anything special going on there this weekend.

The camera zoomed in on an area where you can feed the ducks and then said:

"A few hours ago, a young local girl was taken from this area right over here." The camera pointed to the ducks. "The local police and zoo officials have searched the area and have shut down the zoo, checking everyone as they leave," the newswoman said. "There is an Amber alert out for the missing girl named Lily Teodora, who is only five years old."

Ashley jumped to her feet when she heard her daughter's name. "Lily. My Lily. Oh, my God!" she screamed. "Oh, my God. I have to go to the station. Shit, where did I put my keys? Shit, shit, shit."

Ashley's mind was whirling, trying to figure out what she needed to do. She needed to get to the freaking police station and find out what in God's name happened and find her mother.

She stepped outside just as a car turned into the driveway. She hesitated a second or two before making her way down the stairs and to the car. The car turned off, the driver's side door opened, and her mother appeared.

"Mom, where's Lily?" Ashley questioned.

Catherine stepped back, looking down at the ground. "One minute she was there, and the next…" Catherine paused. "She was gone. I just let go of her hand for a second to get some food for the ducks, and…and when I turned to put the food in her hand, she wasn't there," Catherine sobbed. "I'm so sorry, sweetie. I…I didn't think. I…I didn't mean to lose her." Her mother cried into her hands.

Ashley stood—shocked. Had it not registered what her mother just said? That Lily was missing? That someone took her little girl?

No! No! No!

This couldn't be happening.

She reached out, placing her hands on each side of her mother's arms. Her mother's sobs became louder, echoing into the night air. Ashley started to shake her, wanting her to stop. Stop and tell her what had happened to her daughter.

Her words came out loud and before she could control herself, she was yelling.

"What happened to Lily? Who took her?" Questions she didn't have time to think about came rushing out of her. Finally, after several long minutes, Ashley stopped, exhausted. Her hands fell to her side and she dropped to her knees onto the ground.

Ashley's cries became louder with each passing moment. She began to hyperventilate. Catherine wrapped her arms around her daughter, helping her to calm down and breathe. When Ashley regained her composure, she stood up and leaned against the car.

"We need to go to the station," Catherine said. "They want to talk to you.

16

By nightfall, Tate had crossed the state-line into Pennsylvania. He wasn't planning on stopping until he got to the cabin. He knew the police would be looking for the little girl, and that's why he had left town after taking her, using a different, longer route just in case the roads were blocked off.

His head was pounding with a migraine. He'd taken at least six Tylenol, but they hadn't worked worth shit. He glanced in the mirror towards the back of the van. He could hear her breathing as she hugged her pink blanket, sucking her thumb from time to time.

After he'd followed Ashley to the motel in Indiana and tried to kidnap her, which backfired when she heard the noise through the bathroom window and ran to her car, taking off down the road. He hadn't known which way she'd gone and decided that he'd come back here and get Lily. Use her to get to Ashley.

It was easier than he'd thought it would be to take the little girl. He'd watched the house and followed them to the zoo. When the moment was right, he took his chance and grabbed her.

The grandmother had been clueless that someone could be watching them. Especially since the zoo wasn't packed. There wasn't the usual herd of people there to see the wild animals in the month of March.

He rubbed the temple on the left side of his forehead before making a right-hand turn onto the dirt road. The driveway was hidden, secluded away; only locals in the area knew the road even existed.

After the second bend, he slowed to a stop beside the black convertible that was parked in front of an old hunting cabin. He glanced over his shoulder; she was still sleeping. He got out and opened the rear door, trying not to wake her. He scooped her into his arms and walked up the dirt path to the cabin.

A couple of years ago, Rob had invited Tate to this cabin as a retreat getaway. Rob had told him that the cabin was his father's and was left to him when his dad passed away. Rob said he'd liked to come here to be alone. To think about life. That had all been a lie, of course. Tate knew the real reason Rob had brought him here.

To his left, he heard a large animal prowling around through the leaves, snuffling for food. An owl hooted as he took the last step and stood in front of the door.

Before Rob's dad went into a nursing home, Rob replaced the lock on the door with a keypad lock. He punched in the numbers and turned the knob. He didn't have to turn on a light; he knew his way in the dark. He laid the girl gently down on the bed in one of the spare rooms and placed a blanket over her, then closed the door behind him.

Tate went back to the van. He had packed a cooler with water, juice, and milk as well as a couple of boxes full of food, and some things he thought the little girl would like. He had no clue how long they'd be staying.

He made another trip to the vehicle, then drove the van behind the house out of sight. Once back in the house, he locked the doors, went to the fireplace, and lit the logs.

It wasn't chilly in the cabin, but cool enough to want a fire to keep them warm.

Once the fire was going, he went into the diminished kitchen and put away the things he'd brought. He finished and walked down a narrow hallway past another bedroom. He entered a fairly large bathroom, big enough for a family of four.

He grabbed five aspirins from the medicine cabinet on the wall, turned on the water, cupped his hand and washed them down. He stood looking into the mirror, turned his head from one side to the other, studying the hairline. His plan worked. It was foolproof and no one would know the difference.

He smiled his mischievous smile and went back into the living room where he laid down on the couch and rested his hands behind his head. He stared up at the ceiling as he listened to the wood crackling beside him.

He knew what his plans were with the little girl; he'd been thinking about it for months, years even. He wasn't going to hurt her, not unless she gave him a reason to. He just wanted to state a point. Get a reaction. He'd return her as soon as he got exactly what he wanted.

Her mother.

17

Ashley and her mother had been at the police station all night answering questions. After returning home to her mother's, she had cried most of the night and had gotten no sleep at all. How could she sleep with her daughter missing? She should be out there looking for her, but the police said that they already had people out there looking. They even had roadblocks up and were stopping every car that came through. They would notify her the minute they found something, but at this stage, there was nothing she could do, but to go home and get some rest.

~ ~

Ashley opened her eyes. They were both puffy and red from all the crying she'd done. She flung her legs over the edge of the bed and sat up. She was exhausted with worry and thoughts of what her poor little girl could be going through. She prayed whomever had taken Lily wasn't abusing her. Why would she automatically think someone would be abusing her? Maybe it was from all the shows she'd watched on TV or the books she'd read about children being abducted. She couldn't live with herself if something like that happened to Lily.

She was so angry with herself for leaving town. Although she couldn't have known that this would happen, she was still upset with herself when she should have been here. Yes, her friend Carla needed her, but what about Lily? She was the one that needed taken care of. Ashley could continue to sit here and scold herself, but that wouldn't get her Lily back to her.

She stood and shuffled to the bathroom and closed the door. She didn't feel like showering, but after looking in the mirror and seeing hair standing on edge from her restless night's sleep, she knew she couldn't leave the house looking a mess.

After showering and changing, she went downstairs where she found her mother sitting at the kitchen table. Ashley's posture stiffened. She wasn't mad at her mother. It wasn't her fault—entirely. What *if* it happened on her watch? What *if* she had taken Lily to the zoo and someone had taken her when she went to get food for the ducks? Then, she would be to blame for not watching her own daughter. She knew she needed to apologize; her mom didn't deserve to be punished. To be blamed for something she didn't have any control over.

Her mom looked up the moment she heard footsteps coming towards her. "Would you like some coffee?" she asked, always sounding polite.

"Thanks, Mom, but I can get it myself," Ashley replied, trying to keep the bitterness out of her voice. The same words kept rolling around in her head, but in different formations. It wasn't like she planned for it to happen, right? No, of course not. Her mother didn't mean for Lily to be taken. How often did kids go missing at the zoo? Not just missing, someone took her! That doesn't happen often, does it?

Ashley knew she could sit here all day and beat herself senseless about what had happened and how it could have been prevented, but it *had* happened and now she needed to sit down and figure out how to find her. To get her Lily Rose back to her.

She relied only on her movements. Lift the cup, take a sip, and put the cup back on the table. She did this several more times before realizing what she was doing. This was senseless, she needed to get in the car and go to the station and find her daughter. She needed to know what the police were doing. What evidence did they have? Did someone witness Lily being taken? Could someone identify the person? Was it a man or a woman?

So many questions entered her mind, but she didn't have the answers to any of them. They hadn't given her any of these answers last night, either. It was truly a parent's worst nightmare, having their child taken by some stranger.

Was it or could it be someone she knew? That's what it usually comes down to, right? Someone was watching them. Watching her daughter and waiting for the right moment when she was out of town; then, snatched her Lily Bug. It could be possible, but who? That's what she needed to find out. She needed to talk to her mom and find out if anyone had been hanging around more than usual.

For the first time since she'd sat down, she lifted her head and looked across the table at her mom. She hadn't realized how fragile her mother looked. Her shoulders drooped, barely holding up her head. She looked defeated and hopeless. She probably didn't get much sleep either by the looks of her.

Ashley reached out and touched her mother's hand. It was warm under her touch, just like every time she touched her mother's hand.

"Mom..." Ashley paused. "Mom, I'm sorry. I shouldn't... I mean, I don't blame you for this happening. I'm sorry," she said as the tears began to run down her face.

Ashley ended up in her mother's arms, both sobbing helplessly.

18

Catherine and Ashley left the house an hour later and headed to the station. Neither one of them was going to rest until they found Lily, her beautiful granddaughter. Why had she been so preoccupied getting the food for the ducks? Why hadn't she made Lily hold her hand? Most likely because the thought had never entered her mind that someone would take her granddaughter, that going to the zoo on a gorgeous Sunday would turn into a nightmare.

She sighed again for the hundredth time. She could sit and blame herself or do something about it. Well, in truth she was doing something about it. She and her daughter Ashley were going to talk to the police and hopefully, get some answers. Maybe even call in the FBI. She shook her head, almost laughing at the thought. As if the FBI would come out here for one missing girl. This was a small town. There was no way the FBI would even consider a case like this. The people who lived here stuck together and helped everyone else, no matter what.

She'd start calling them and get everyone together to do a search-and-rescue, but was it too late? Night had passed and her granddaughter could be anywhere. They could be long gone and in a different state, for all she knew.

She exhaled another sigh as she drove through town and parked in front of the police station. She glanced over at Ashley who had remained quiet the whole ride to the station.

Catherine squeezed her daughter's hand. Ashley looked over at her. "Are you ready to go in?" Catherine asked.

Ashley nodded.

They both opened the car doors at the same time and met in front of the car. Neither one would admit to the other, but they both needed each other for support. They held hands and walked up the cement steps and through the huge oak doors.

The police station wasn't a busy place. Not much usually happened in Craven Falls, except your normal cat in a tree or on occasion, a young kid trying to steal a candy bar from the local grocery store down the road. When something major happened, that's when you saw these officers move like roosters with their heads cut off.

As they entered through the doors, there were chairs along the wall in the hall, which she assumed was the waiting room. Catherine led them to an officer sitting behind the desk. It took a couple of seconds before they were noticed.

"Sorry, how can I help you?" the woman officer asked.

Catherine took in a deep breath than exhaled, "My granddaughter Lily was taken from me at the zoo yesterday afternoon." She explained what happened and whom she had been told to talk to. "Is Sheriff White here?"

The woman officer stood too quickly, knocking the chair to the floor. She bent over, picked up the wooden chair, and scooted it back under the desk. Her face flushed from embarrassment. She excused herself to get Sheriff White.

A few minutes later, the same lady officer returned and led them to an interrogation room. "Please have a seat until Sheriff White arrives," the woman officer said.

Catherine and her daughter pulled the chairs out at the same time and sat. The room was so quiet they could hear filing cabinets being opened and closed down the hall.

An overweight man passed the closed door of their room, his heavy boots echoing off the walls as he stomped down the hall. Catherine suddenly started to feel claustrophobic inside the small room. She took a few short breaths in and out to calm herself.

They both turned their heads when they heard a knock on the door. The door opened and in came a burly man of five ten or maybe five eleven, weighing close to two hundred and twenty pounds. "I'm Officer Richard White in charge of the missing child case," Sheriff White stated as he held out his hand in front of Ashley. "I'm sorry I wasn't here last night, but my deputy in charge filled me in on what had happened."

Ashley didn't shake his hand, instead she asked, "Do you have any leads about where and who might have taken my daughter?"

"As of right now, we don't, but we have talked to everyone that was in the vicinity where the kidnapping took place. No one heard or saw anything. They didn't hear a child scream or any signs of a struggle, which tells me that it's possible it was someone your daughter knows," Sheriff White said as he sat down across from them and continued. "As you both know being a small town and all, and the fact that I just recently moved here, I don't know people the way you do. So, I'll need for you to write down the names of all the people who have been in contact with your daughter: school, daycare, family members, and friends. Anyone and everyone is a suspect in this case. We'll do are very best to find Lily and bring her home."

Ashley stifled a cry.

"I'll also need a recent picture of Lily so we can make fliers and send it to all the News stations in the area. Any identifying marks, such as a birthmark; anything for the public to keep a look out for," Sheriff White concluded. "I'd also like to get a press conference together and have you speak to the public. The more they know about Lily the better chance we'll have of finding her."

Catherine opened her purse and pulled out several photos of Lily. When she couldn't sleep during the night, she went through the photo albums and pulled out pictures she knew they'd need to help find her granddaughter. Each photo showed Lily's vibrate eyes, her long dark curls and her radiant smile. She was the most beautiful little girl she'd ever seen besides her daughter, that is.

Catherine felt Ashley touch her arm as she began to cry harder. She must've seen the pictures in her hand, and it had become too real, the pain barreling down on Ashley once more.

Catherine slid the photos across the table into Sheriff White's view. "I gathered these last night," she said.

Sheriff White nodded before turning his gaze towards Ashley. "Ma'am, I know this is going to be upsetting, but I need for you to answer a few questions. I wasn't here last night, so some of these may be questions you have already answered."

Ashley nodded, "Sure, what do you need to know?"

"Where were you at the time of the kidnapping?"

"You can't be serious," Catherine shouted. "My daughter has nothing to do with this. Why would she have her own daughter kidnapped? This is absurd!" Catherine huffed. "We don't have to answer any of these questions." She looked at Ashley.

"Mom, it's okay. They must do their job. I've done nothing wrong," Ashley cleared her throat. "I left Illinois around eight in the morning, arriving at my mom's around four yesterday afternoon."

"When did you go to Illinois?" Sheriff White asked.

"I left Thursday evening the seventeenth and arrived at my friend's house on Friday the eighteenth."

"What's your friends name?"

"Carla Michaels."

"I'll need her phone number to verify that you were there."

"Sure, but I can't promise you that she'll answer the phone."

"And why is that?"

"Both her husband and daughter just died, and she isn't doing so well."

"Oh, well, I'm sorry to hear that, but I'll try calling her anyway, ma'am," Officer White said without making eye contact and moved on to the next question. "Why did you arrive a day later?"

"I was exhausted by the time I left on Thursday so I decided once I hit the Indiana state-line, I'd just find a place to sleep for the night and then head out the next morning."

"What's the name of the motel/hotel you stayed at? And what time did you leave in the morning?"

"Are you accusing her of something?" Catherine asked. She tried to bite her tongue, but these questions were beyond a doubt, unnecessary and ridiculous.

"No, ma'am. I'm just doing my job and getting the hard part out of the way. *If*, and I'm not accusing her of anything, but *if* your daughter didn't do anything, then there's nothing to find, but I still need to ask the questions. If I don't, someone else will," Sheriff White stated.

"Mom, it's okay. Let's just get everything out in the open now and let it be done."

Catherine snarled, "Fine."

Ashley had to think for a few minutes. "I don't remember seeing a sign for the name of the motel, just that there was a sign that said Motel; it reminded me of Bate's Motel; you know the TV show?"

Sheriff White nodded.

"Anyway, when I pulled off at the first exit after entering Indiana, that was the only place I saw. At first, I wasn't going to stay there because it looked very creepy and run down. Like I said, I was exhausted and didn't feel like driving back the way I'd come, getting back on the highway. In fact, now that I think about it, I signed my name on the registry in the office when the owner was getting my key. So, you should be able to confirm me being there."

"What time did you head out in the morning?"

"It was early, like, I think four, maybe five. I heard some noise outside my bathroom window, and was a little freaked out. You know, like the motel that was in the newspaper a couple of weeks earlier where that lady ran out into the highway screaming that her husband had been murdered. So, I got in my car and left—fast. I was in Illinois around seven, stopped off at a Denny's, had coffee and some breakfast; then drove to my friend Carla's around eight, eight-thirty the latest."

"And you stayed until what day?"

"I left Sunday morning, just like I told you, and arrived at my mom's around four yesterday afternoon."

"Anything else? Did you stop anywhere, get something to eat or drink on your way home?"

Ashley started rummaging through her purse. She pulled out a receipt. "Here," she said, handing Sheriff White the paper. "This will prove to you that I wasn't anywhere near the zoo when this happened."

He looked it over and concluded that the time stamped on the receipt was around the time of the kidnapping, but the location wasn't in the same vicinity. "Thank you, that'll be all unless there's something more you want to add?"

"No, there's nothing else. That's what happened the last four days," Ashley replied.

Catherine was the first to stand when the questioning ended. She was beyond upset that they would even think Ashley had anything to do with her granddaughter's kidnapping. Her own daughter wouldn't have any reason to have Lily taken, if that's what they're suggesting.

"Get me those names before you leave so we can start interviewing the suspects and find your daughter," Sheriff White said.

Catherine sat back down and helped Ashley write everyone they knew around town on the paper. When they finished, they handed Sheriff White the sheet, which also had Ashley's contact information on it. Catherine didn't want to spend another minute with Sheriff White, if she didn't have to.

"Before you both leave, can you tell me what you know about Sierra Miller?" he asked.

Ashley and Catherine both looked at each other. "What do you mean?"

"Do you know of her?" Officer White asked.

"Yes," Catherine replied. "She's my neighbor's daughter. Why? What's this about?" Catherine asked.

"She seems to be missing too," Sheriff White concluded.

19

Reece had slept in the woods near the house on Saturday and Sunday night. He used the restroom at the local gas station to wash up, but knew he'd eventually have to find a place to shower and get some clean clothes. Since he'd been released from prison, he had on the same shirt and jeans, and they were not looking too presentable.

His reasons for sleeping in the woods were more to ease his conscious, not anyone else's. It was more than the man talking to himself that gave Reece such an uncertainty. He would have to keep an eye out for him, just in case he returned, but he was sure after that blow to the head, it may have knocked some sense into him and he'd stay away.

Reece couldn't believe how easy it was to sneak up on the guy and hit him in the head and then carry him to the car he'd spotted while trudging back through the woods. He figured it had to belong to the man on his back because he hadn't seen the car parked there the night before and it was left unlocked, which made it easier for him to toss the man inside.

This morning he walked back into town and went to the same diner he'd been at the last couple of days. He was surprised that the waitress hadn't asked him any questions, being new to town and all, wearing the same clothes.

He took his usual seat at the counter, ordered an omelet with ham and cheese, hash browns, and a side of buttermilk pancakes. She filled his coffee cup and placed his order with a smile on her face.

He looked around the café and saw an unused newspaper sitting a few seats down from him. He asked the lady behind the counter if it belonged to anyone; when she replied no, he grabbed it.

It'd been a long time since he'd read a newspaper. He wasn't even sure if the same man was president of the United States or not. Five years in prison, a lot can happen. A lot can change.

Nothing much interested him on the front page so he moved on to the next. For a small town, there seemed to be a lot going on. In two weeks from Saturday, they were having their annual pig roast in the park with a small carnival for the kids. He hadn't been to a fair in years, and it sounded intriguing. Maybe he'd stick around a little longer and make sure that man didn't come back. Though, he should probably find work for himself and maybe even a place to stay. The woods were nice, but if someone caught him out there, they might think he was homeless or maybe even a murderer, which he wasn't... well, maybe homeless.

The bell *dinged* behind him, but he kept to his newspaper until he was sure that whomever had entered took a seat. Besides, he didn't want to seem nosy every time someone came into the diner, as long as it wasn't the man from the woods.

Reece could tell two people had entered and took a seat to his far right, which was in the opposite direction of the restroom. He pretended to read as he listened to their conversation.

"Do you really think they'll find her?"

"Of course, they will, they're the police," Catherine replied.

He was certain they were mother and daughter, and by what little he heard, someone was missing.

"She's my whole life. I can't live without my little girl," Ashley sniffled a cry.

"Sweetheart, we'll find her and bring her home. Besides, I'd know if something happened to Lily. I'd feel it in my bones," Catherine said.

His breath caught. He'd heard the name Lily before. The other night at the pub, the man buying him drinks was talking about a little girl named Lily, and that he didn't want to live without her. He even said he might kidnap her, but Reece believed he'd been too drunk and didn't mean what he was saying. That it was just two men drinking and bullshitting. The man didn't even look like he could hurt a gnat.

He definitely was going to hang around a while longer and see what he could find out about the guy at the pub and the man who was trying to break into that house the other night. There was something fishy going on in this town. He had a knack for sticking his nose where it didn't belong, but he would find out the truth.

But there was something else. Something that made him want to listen longer to their conversation. The voice of the younger woman sounded so familiar to him. Like he had heard her voice before, but where—when?

20

Light filtered through the floral printed curtains that hung on the small square window near the ceiling. If you looked close enough, you could see the dust particles glistening in the rays, before falling to the dusty wooden floor.

Lily opened her eyes, looking at the unfamiliar bedroom. She hadn't been in this room before. This wasn't her bedroom at Grandma Cat's, and she didn't recall her mommy coming to get her. In fact, the last thing she remembered was being at the zoo waiting for Grandma Cat to get some food for the ducks, and then nothing. She just went to sleep or something.

She rolled onto her back and looked up at the ceiling and then towards the door. She could hear someone moving around outside her room. Should she go out there and see who it was? She wanted to, but she was scared. She didn't like the smell of this place. It didn't smell like Grandma Cat's house—like cookies.

She slid out from under the blanket, popped her thumb in her mouth, and held the blankie tight in the other hand. She was getting hungry, but she wasn't sure if she should open the door.

Then the urge to pee came over her and once that happened, she had to get to the bathroom fast. She was getting better at holding it, but that only lasted so long. Lily also didn't want to pee in her pretty princess underwear that her Grandma Cat had bought her.

She wrapped her small hand around the faded metal knob and turned. The door squeaked open and she froze, listening to the sounds around her. When nothing jumped out at her, she stuck her head out the opening and saw what looked to be the bathroom to her left.

She could run, shut the door quickly behind her, and lock it before whomever was in the house came after her. She didn't have time to think about it as she heard footsteps moving in the other room. She flew down the hall and into the bathroom, slamming the door shut and locking it.

She pressed her trembling back against the door and squeezed her eyes shut. It felt like all the times her and her friend Sierra snuck down to the river without her Grandma Cat knowing. Grandma Cat wouldn't have allowed them to go without an adult, but Sierra always persuaded Lily into going. After the first couple of times, it was easy and they hadn't been caught.

Remembering that she had to pee, she flipped on the light switch and shuffled to the toilet. She wiped, stood, and pushed the lever down on the side. She tried to turn on the water in the sink, but she was too short to reach the faucet handles. She looked around for a stepstool, but didn't see one.

When it came to washing her hands, Lily was somewhat of a germ freak when using the bathroom. She didn't like feeling icky and dirty. She walked to the shower curtain that was hiding the tub and turned on the water. She breathed out, feeling less dirty. Now the question was how was she going to get out of the bathroom and back to the bedroom without being seen or heard? She didn't have the answer, but knew she couldn't stay in here forever.

Her stomach growled. She popped her thumb back in her mouth. Sometimes it helped when she needed food, but mostly it took her mind off the feeling of being hungry.

She jumped from the tap on the door. "Lily are you coming out?" the man asked.

The man knew her name, but she wasn't sure if she recognized his voice. It sounded muffled through the wooden door. It didn't sound like anyone she knew, but she hadn't been around that many men to tell the difference. Should she trust this man and open the door?

She pulled out her thumb, "I want my mommy," she finally said through the closed door.

"That's my whole plan, Lily. I'm going to take you to your mommy."

"You promise?" she asked

"I promise," he replied. "Why don't you come on out and have some breakfast. I made scrambled eggs with cheese."

Her stomach made a loud cry when she heard the words. She was so hungry, and besides she must know him if he knew what she liked to eat, right? She placed her hand on the knob, swallowed, and slowly opened the door.

21

Ashley could feel someone watching her, but who? Her mother was sitting in front of her, looking at her cup as she sipped her coffee. Ashley looked out the glass window beside her and searched the scenery. No one looked suspicious to her. That left the man with the jet-black hair sitting at the counter when they'd come into the café. There were a few other people, but two of them had left shortly after her and her mother had arrived.

She thought about dropping her fork on the floor to get a look behind her, but she didn't want it to seem too obvious to the man at the counter. But maybe if she got a good look at the guy, then she'd know he wasn't the one watching her.

She'd met a man once that had hair like his, but that was before Lily was born. She knew there was no way that it was Reece sitting here in this diner. He hadn't been from this town when she'd met him. She wanted to laugh at the thought of it being Lily's father. She had only known his first name when they had gotten together for that one night that had changed her whole life forever.

What would she say to him anyway, after all these years? "Hey, nice to see you again, and by the way, you have a daughter named Lily Rose." *Yeah, like that would go over well.*

"Hello," Catherine said, waving a hand in front of Ashley's face.

Ashley blinked and looked at her mother. "Sorry, what were you saying?' she asked.

"I was asking you if you've contacted Rob since you've been back? Does he know what happened to Lily? Have you talked to him?" Catherine asked. She was always known for asking a lot of questions. "I know you've been sort of distant with him lately. God knows you haven't said what the issue is with the two of you. Sweetie, you can talk to me about anything, you know that?" Catherine reassured.

"Yes, Mom, I know you're here for me, but I can handle things with Rob." She knew she still needed to talk to her mother about canceling the wedding that was supposed to happen one month from now. She needed to tell her that she wasn't going to be marrying that cheating asshole. Her plans had been to tell her mom when she'd gotten home from her first trip to Carla's two weeks before, but with finals in school and getting a resume together that didn't happen. Right now, it definitely wasn't the right time or place to bring it up. Getting and finding Lily was what she needed to do.

"Ash, maybe Rob can help. You should call him."

She nodded, "Sure I'll give him a call once we get back to your house, I promise," she replied, knowing he was the last person she wanted to talk to.

She heard the bell ding behind her, and knew that it was the man at the counter who had left because the only other people were sitting at tables in front of her and her mom.

She glanced out the window beside her. He must have walked in the opposite direction, and not in front of where she was sitting.

"Ready?" Ashley said a little too quickly to her mother. They both stood and left the café. When they stepped outside, Ashley looked up and down the street, but the man that was just here was nowhere in sight.

22

Catherine pulled her car into the driveway and shut off the engine. The sun was a muted, yolk-yellow beaming down above them as they exited the car. Rays of sunlight danced through the trees all around the two-story Victorian home, giving it a dazzling appearance. Something you'd only see in a painting. It was breathtaking.

Catherine's heart sank because she knew this was Lily's favorite time of day when the sun was beaming down on the earth at high noon.

She didn't want to confess to Ashley, but she did blame herself for Lily going missing. No matter what, it always came back to the same thing. *If* she'd just held her hand or decided not to get the food for the ducks, Lily would be here with them. How could she have been so careless and let her own granddaughter be taken by some stranger? Had this stranger been following them the entire time they were at the zoo? The thought scared her. She'd practically lived here her whole life, and nothing like this had ever happened. It wasn't as if they lived in Cleveland, Ohio, where things like this happened more often than not. This was the country for heaven's sack. Nothing happened in a small town in the middle of nowhere. Children don't just get taken!

She'd spent all of last night going over the area where they'd been, and no one looked out of the ordinary. Everyone had a child with them. There were moms and dads with their kids in strollers and some holding their children's hands. Of course, Catherine didn't keep a file in her head of the exact moment when Lily Rose had been taken. She couldn't be sure that every single man or woman there was with a child. She shook her head in disgust, wondering why someone would do this. *Who would do this?*

She watched as Ashley mounted the stairs and opened the squeaky screen door. She needed to spray some WD-40 on the hinges, but then again, it was like an alarm system. She'd hear if someone were to open it before coming into the house, just like the backdoor. Every night before bed, she'd place the string of cans around the doorknob so she'd hear if someone entered.

Catherine stood behind her daughter, waiting for her to unlock the door. The keys dropped and Ashley bent over to retrieve them. Catherine could hear her sniffle, and then saw her daughter tremble before a sob filled the air. Today wasn't going to get any better for either of them.

She took Ashley in her arms, grabbed the keys, and placed the key in the lock, pushing the door open with her hip. She guided her daughter to the sofa where they sat embracing one another. She let her daughter cry out all her tears, though she knew there'd more later. There were always more.

Once the tears subsided, Ashley released her hold around her mother and sat back against the cushions. Catherine reached for the box of Kleenex in front of her, sitting on the coffee table. Ashley took a few tissues, dried her eyes, and blew her nose, which was a running mess.

"Thank you," Ashley whispered.

"No need, my dear. I wouldn't expect you not to cry over her. So..." Catherine hung on the word. "I think we need to talk about Rob and whatever's going on between the two of you," Catherine said almost in a demanding voice.

Catherine watched as Ashley kept her head down, as if pretending to focus on the tissues in her hand. Catherine knew her daughter would answer the question, eventually.

Ashley cleared her throat. "I walked in on Rob with another..." she stopped, sucked in a breath and exhaled. "I caught him in bed with another man," Ashley said.

Catherine seemed to notice once the words were out of Ashley's mouth that this must be the first time she'd told anyone about what had happened. Catherine knew what it was like to hold something in and then release it from your hold for the first time. Catherine wasn't sure how it made Ashley feel. Maybe, it became truer, more real as the day it happened. Only a mother could feel her own daughter's grief. Her heart aching for a release that should not have been kept concealed inside herself for as long as she'd kept the secret hidden.

Ashley looked up and saw her mom's hand fly to her mouth, "Oh, sweet Jesus, Ashley, are you sure?"

"Mom, really?" Ashley questioned, rolling her eyes.

"Yeah, I guess you'd know if it had been a woman. Oh, my sweet Jesus. Rob and another man." She shook her head. "And right before the wedding. My God, what was he thinking? Oh, my poor girl, look what he's gone and done to you?" Catherine touched Ashley's cheek with her soft delicate hand.

"That's not the worst part," Ashley whispered.

Her mom's face changed from concerned to confused. "What more can there be? Isn't that enough to find your fiancé in bed with a man?"

Ashley blinked, "How about when it's your brother?"

"What?" Catherine shrieked so loud Ashley thought for sure the windows would break. "Tell me it isn't true."

"I'm sorry, Mom, but it's the truth!"

"Which brother?"

Since there were six kids, Ashley being the only daughter, that left Paul, Matthew, Kevin, Saul and Daniel, who was the youngest. "Dan."

The room fell silent. You wouldn't have heard dust hit the ground; not that you can hear dust hitting the ground, metaphorically speaking.

"Daniel," Catherine whispered. Her head sagged as her mind went back to the day he came by to visit. She could tell by the way he was acting that something wasn't right with him, but then he changed once he saw Lily. Her mind kept replaying the scene over and over again. The look on his face should have set-off an alarm. The clues were all there, right in front of her face, but she didn't want to believe he'd be capable of doing such a thing, could he?

That boy should know better than to mingle with his sister's affairs, whether he knew Rob was her fiancé or not. Although, she hadn't seen him in six years. A lot can happen to someone in that amount of time, but did she really even know her son? Did she know he was this kind of person? She wasn't thinking about him being gay, but liking children as well? She wasn't sure where this evil thought was coming from. Her own son?

No, no, no, her mind screamed. She looked up at Ashley. Was it wrong to think her son would do such a thing? Could it be true? Once the words entered her mind, she couldn't take them back. *What if Dan took Lily?*

23

Lily stood in the doorway of the bathroom. All her fears slipped away. She no longer needed to be afraid of the man she thought would hurt her because he was going to be her new daddy someday.

"Rob," she shrieked in excitement. "Why did you make me scared?"

"I'm sorry; I never meant for you to be afraid of me. I'd never hurt you. You know that right?" Tate said, playing along with the game.

Lily nodded and put her arms around him. He lifted her up and squeezed her until she squealed with laughter. "Is my mommy coming to be with us?"

"Not right now she isn't, but I need to call her later and see when she can meet with us."

"Okay," Lily said, smiling

"I made breakfast. Are you hungry?"

Lily nodded. "Starving like Marvin," she giggled.

She sat at the table eating all her eggs, and then stabbed a fork in the banana that was cut into pieces on her plate. Every once in a while, she would look up at Rob, but he wasn't looking back at her. In fact, he was staring at his phone and typing something.

She'd seen her mom type words into her phone before; she'd said it was called texting. You put in the words you wanted to say and hit send. It would then go to the person you're sending it to. Sometimes, her mommy would let her text Grandma Cat a message from her phone.

"Are you sending Mommy a text?" Lily asked.

"What?" Tate snapped.

Lily stiffened. Rob had never raised his voice at her before. She was almost afraid to say another word to him. What if he yelled at her again? She didn't like this Rob sitting here at the table. She bit her lower lip before repeating her question. "Are you texting Mommy a message to come be with us? Where are we anyway?" She turned and looked out the rectangle window beside her. Lily could see trees surrounding the house outside and past that in the distance, there was water, like a pond or lake.

She stabbed two pieces of the banana and stuck them in her mouth, chewing while waiting for a response. She looked out the window again and for a spilt second she wanted to go out there and look around. She liked looking for things to do outside, especially if the weather was warm.

"Ah, yeah, that's what I was about to do," he said, still not looking at her.

Lily tilted her head in confusion. He didn't seem like himself today and wondered if he was going to have her mommy come to the house. Daddy Rob wouldn't tell her a lie. Her mommy said lying was bad and that she was to never tell a lie. "Always tell the truth, Lily Bug," her mommy would say.

Grown-ups were hard to figure out sometimes. She didn't want to be a grown-up, ever. She ate the last bite of her banana and slid off the chair, carrying her plate to the sink like her mommy always said to do when she was done eating. When she turned, he was still staring at the phone. "Can I watch TV?" she asked.

105

"Sure, whatever you want," he said without looking at her.

He sure was acting funny, she thought as she walked into the living room and sat down on the dirty brown sofa. She grabbed the remote on the table beside her and flicked through the channels, but couldn't find any cartoons to watch. This place was going to bore her to death if she didn't find something to do.

"Can I go outside?" Lily asked.

"Sure," he replied without looking at her. He was still mesmerized by whatever was on the phone.

Lily opened the door and went outside. She stood on the creaky wooden porch, breathing in the fresh morning air. It didn't smell like Grandma Cat's place, that was for sure.

She stepped off the last step and stood on the dirt ground. She didn't see any grass around the house, just lots of trees and dirt. She glanced around and noticed there were no other houses, just woods. Grandma Cat at least had neighbors that lived near her. Even her mommy lived around other buildings.

A bird sang in the distance as Lily walked down the path in front of her. Once over the small hill, she saw the sparkling water at the bottom; it was amazing. She hadn't remembered seeing water so sparkly before. She'd never been to the ocean or gone fishing on a lake.

She looked out over the water; the sun was shining through the trees on the other side of the lake. Grandma Cat called the sun God's golden eye. She didn't know about that; she'd never seen what God's eye looked like and from what her mommy had told her, "You'll only see him when you go to heaven," but she didn't want to go there because that would mean she was dead. She didn't wanna' be dead. She had too much to learn and experience yet. At least that's what her mommy and Grandma Cat always told her.

She skipped down the trail that led to the lake. She stopped at the edge where an old rickety dock sat. It looked safe from afar, but up close, she wasn't so sure. There were missing pieces of wood and when she placed her foot down, the board creaked and moaned under her weight. She saw a fish jump in the water and quickly ran to the edge of the dock, forgetting about the wood being old and unsafe.

Another fish jumped out of the water and she giggled with excitement, jumping and clapping. She sat down on the edge of the dock, hanging her legs over. She held her blankie in her hand while she kicked her feet back and forth, like she was swinging on a swing.

"Lily," she heard Daddy Rob yell.

She didn't want to go back inside. Not when it was a beautiful day out here and besides she liked watching the fish jumping in and out of the water.

"Lily," he called again.

She turned and looked up the hill, watching him come barreling down towards her. By the time he reached the pier, he was out of breath. "Lily, what are you doing down here? I told you that you could go outside, but never said you could come to the lake by yourself," he huffed.

"I wanted to see the fishy jump," she pointed, just as a fish jumped out of the water in front of her.

"You still shouldn't come down here without me. It's too dangerous." He stepped onto the dock, the board groaning under his weight. He took his foot off the board.

"Lily, come on; it's time to go back up. I don't want you falling in the water. Now come on off of there." He waved a hand, indicating that she needed to follow him.

Lily didn't move. She placed her thumb in her mouth and turned back towards the water, watching the fish continue to jump.

"Lily, get off this dock right now!" he demanded.

Lily jumped from his abrasive voice and her blankie fell from her grasp and into the water. She let out a loud cry and bent over to grab it, but it was already sinking. "My blankie," she cried. "You have to get my blankie. I can't live without my blankie."

24

Dan hesitated before knocking on the screen door. He hadn't been at his mother's house in a couple of days, and from the extra car in the drive, he'd guessed that Ashley was here too. "Damn it," he mumbled as he rapped on the door.

"Coming," Catherine hollered from the kitchen. When she entered the foyer, she halted to a stop. "Daniel," she whispered, sucking in a breath.

He watched as she glanced past him as if looking for someone.

"Come in, come in," she said, pushing the screen door open for him to enter. "What brings you out here? I thought you had other plans," she said, looking out onto the porch after he slipped inside.

"Thought I'd come and see how you're doing before I leave town. Is everything okay? You seem to be looking for something," he said, following her eyes to the porch he'd been standing on.

She stared out the open door as if waiting for someone else to enter, except there was no one else. She turned towards him and nodded, "It's nothing, really, just tired is all." She let the screen door slam before looking back at him. "Thank you for thinking of me; shall we go into the kitchen?" she said as she walked down the hall, Dan following behind her. "Are you hungry? Do you want me to make you something to eat? Maybe you're thirsty. I have plenty of drinks, lemonade, water, coffee, soda, and juice, if you like juice. Lily likes..." she stopped rambling.

Dan sat down at the kitchen table just as Ashley came down from upstairs and entered the room. "What in the hell are you doing here?" Ashley asked. "What makes you think you're welcome in this house?"

"Watch your mouth, young lady," Catherine said. "Don't go saying something you'll regret later. Your brother is just here for a visit. He wanted to come and say goodbye. Let's all sit and talk about what happened, like adults," Catherine said, reaching for some glasses in the cupboard by the sink.

Ashley sulked as she pulled out a chair on the opposite side of the table, glaring at her brother as she sat.

"Now, Dan. Your sister told me what happened. Would you mind explaining why you were in bed with her fiancé?" Catherine said, sounding blunt.

Dan sat quiet, lifted his head, and stared at his sister before speaking, "Honestly, I didn't know he was engaged to be married to you. He never said anything, and certainly not in the four years that we've known each other," Dan stated.

Both Ashley and Catherine's mouth dropped open, shocked by the words that he'd said.

Catherine cleared her throat, "So you and Rob have been..." she paused. "Lovers for all of four years?"

Dan's mind was somewhere else when his mom had asked him a question he didn't quite hear. So, he didn't answer; instead, he asked, "Where's Lily? Is she taking a nap?"

"Why are you asking? According to our mom, you just met her two days ago and now you're asking if she's here? What's it to you? What do you want with her Dan? Did you take her?" Ashley questioned. "Did you follow Mom to the zoo and kidnap my daughter? Where is she? What have you done to her?" The questions poured out of her.

Dan didn't answer. He just sat there as if his sister hadn't asked him any questions. He was oblivious to his surroundings. He watched as she looked over at their mother sitting there with a grim look on her face. It was as if his mind shut off from the world around him, which seemed to happen from time to time. His ears would start ringing, and he would tune out everything else.

The silence in the room broke when Dan's phone received a text. They watched as he pulled the cell from his pants pocket and looked at the message. "Sorry to cut our visit short. But there's something I gotta' take care of." Dan stood and without saying another word, left the room and walked out the front door. Never answering the questions his sister had asked.

In fact, there was only one question that caught his attention. She had asked if he had taken Lily. Why would she ask him that question? Of course, he didn't have her. He hadn't had the chance to come back here and take her. Then it dawned on him that someone else must have taken her, but who?

He jumped in behind the wheel of his car and took off down the road. Maybe the person that was texting him knew the answers to these questions.

25

Tate seemed to contemplate on what to do before trudging into the water after her precious blanket. Back when he was little, he'd run down the wooden dock and jumped off the end, but after all these long winters, he didn't want to take the chance of the wood breaking and the little girl falling in the water. Then, the whole kidnapping thing would be for nothing.

His body was electrified by the coldness, making his bones ache with each step he took into the freezing water. He hadn't thought about taking off his shoes or even his jeans, not that he'd wanted to go in without them on. Did it really matter? The water was beyond cold, no matter what he wore or didn't wear. It got harder with each step he took, each leg weighing a ton. He waded towards the end of the pier where the blanket had gone under, but he couldn't see it now; it was gone.

Lily sat peering down into the water; her eyes coated with wetness. He had two choices, dive in and find it, or turn around and walk back out of the lake, making the little girl cry harder with the loss of her favorite blanket. He grumbled under his breath and dove down into the water.

It took him three tries before he found the blanket. He'd dive down and after only seconds of holding his breath, he'd freak out from the dark icy water and come back up to the surface. He'd hear her crying still and take in a breath and go back under the water.

He opened his eyes under the water, saw the pink blanket, and grasped it with his hands. He pushed off the bottom of the lake with his feet and swam to the surface; thankful it wasn't that deep. When his head was out of the water, he didn't see Lily sitting at the edge of the dock anymore.

He trudged out of the water, his boots and jeans weighing him down. He turned back towards the end of the dock, but didn't see Lily anywhere. She wasn't lying down on the dock hiding from him, playing a child's game of hide-and-go-seek.

He looked up the hill, but she wasn't there either. Maybe she'd gone back inside the cabin?

He started to move through the water, but something had ahold of his leg. He pulled his left leg towards him, but it wouldn't give. He tried to reach for the wooden post holding up the dock, but slipped and fell face-first into the water.

He tried to grab at the earth, but there was nothing for him to clamp onto. The mud and sand kept slipping through his fingers. He was running out of oxygen as he reached for the seaweed wrapped around his ankle. He tugged at the vine again; it finally loosened enough, and he rose to the surface gasping for air.

26

Reece was walking down the road when he spotted a man coming out of the house, the same man he'd seen at the diner and who'd tried breaking into the house the other night. Reece dodged behind a huge walnut tree, watching the guy. He was reading something on his phone and then got into his car and drove away. The exact same car he'd spotted two nights ago in the woods.

A couple of minutes later, a blonde-haired woman came walking out the same front door. She stood there and watched as the car drove away. She looked familiar, almost like the same woman he'd seen at the café earlier, but he wasn't sure because he'd only seen the back of her.

He wanted to know more about her and this man, who clearly was up to no good, but didn't know how to go about it. He waited until she turned towards the house before coming out from behind the tree. His boots crunched on the gravel road as he walked.

He could see from the corner of his eye that she must have heard him walking because she quickly turned back around and trotted down the stairs toward him.

"Shit," he mumbled. Should he stop and see what she was going to do or keep walking and act as if he hadn't noticed her? He kept walking, but stopped when he felt her approach him.

"Excuse me," Ashley hollered. "Do I know you?"

He swallowed and turned. The moment he saw her face, he knew she was the one from six years ago. He had prayed that he'd run into her again, but never thought in a million years it would be in this small town that he was just passing through.

"Ashley," he whispered, hoping it was really her. He imagined taking her in his arms and kissing her until they both were too weak to stand, but what if she freaked out and started screaming, then what? He wasn't going back to jail.

Her eyes widened; "Reece," she whispered.

He smiled as a tear ran down her face. He wanted to open his arms to her and embrace her while she cried. How could only one night with this beautiful woman bring him such comfort? He didn't know anything about her. Where she came from and if she had any brothers or sisters, but he did know now where she lived.

He decided it was best to just let her make the first move. Let her lead him to wherever she wanted to go. He would follow her anywhere. Love did that to people sometimes. Hell, he'd seen it in his own parents. He'd seen it in people he never met before, and in towns he'd passed through.

But he knew one thing. He knew that he loved her, had always loved her, and now that he had found her, he wasn't about to let her out of his sight. Only death could cause them not to be together.

27

*H*ow can this be? She thought. *How can he be here right now? Right when she needed him the most. When Lily needed him the most.* Ashley knew the moment she looked into his eyes that he was the same man from six years ago.

She had dreamed many times of seeing him again. She had waited and thought she'd never find him. It was a one-night stand, and she had gotten pregnant with that one-night with him. Her mind flashed back to that heated night, and her insides grew hot once again. She blushed as she stood there staring at him. She loved the look of the light stubble on his face.

Ashley wondered what he was doing here, walking down the road right in front of her mother's house? They were far from town so it wasn't like he was passing through to get there, especially if she'd just seen him an hour before at the diner.

She reached out and smoothed her hand along his cheek. Even though it had been so long, she'd never forget those deep blue eyes that stirred a longing deep within her. She'd have to tell him about Lily. He had a right to know; he was her father. "Reece," she whispered, again. "I...I have to tell you something."

The moment she touched him, she could see it in his eyes that he had missed her too. At least, she was hoping that he did. He touched her hand, watching as he searched her eyes. She wanted to know what he was thinking.

"Come to the house so we can talk. I need to tell you something," she said once more. She laced her fingers between his and turned towards the house.

Once up the steps, she took him to the swing near the end of the porch. They sat and looked at one another. Ashley had to do this now, no matter what the outcome. No matter if she lost him forever, he needed to know about their daughter, but she didn't want to lose him.

"Reece, that night we met."

He nodded and a smile surfaced.

She swallowed it was now or never, "I became pregnant and had a baby girl," she said it fast, knowing there was no easy way to tell him.

His face froze, but only for a moment before the realization of her words sunk in. "I…I have a daughter?" he asked.

Was he upset? She couldn't tell. She wouldn't blame him if he was. She'd probably be mad too, if it was the other way around.

"Her name is Lily," Ashley replied. His mouth dropped open. "I know I should've contacted you, but we never exchanged phone numbers. I didn't know how to get ahold of you when I found out." She sat, her body starting to tremble beside him. The fear of losing him right after she'd found him was unnerving.

"Can I meet her?" he asked. Tears ran down her face. "Do you know who took her?" he asked next.

She looked puzzled by his question. "How did you know she was missing?" she questioned.

"I overheard you and your mom at the diner earlier, talking about your daughter being missing. Then I remembered a guy at the bar talking about kidnapping a little girl named Lily, and there was a man trying to break into the back of your house, but they weren't the same men. They were two different guys. Something's not adding up," he said. "Do you think the two men could've been in on it together?"

"What two men? Do you know them? What are their names? My mom and I thought it was my brother Dan, but he looked shocked when I accused him of taking her, but he never said anything. He never answered my questions. Just got up and left."

"Was that the guy who just left?"

"Yes, that's my brother Dan. You said two guys?"

"Yeah. One I met at the bar in town, but I don't know his name, and your brother Dan who just left. He was the one trying to break into the back of your house."

"How do you know he was trying to break into the house? Especially, in the back of the house? Can you see that from the front? From the road?" Ashley questioned, turning to look at the road, then back at Reece.

Reece swallowed, "I was sleeping in the woods when I heard some noise. I followed the sound and it brought me to the backyard," he said "Then, I hit him over the head and threw him in a car down the road. I thought I'd seen the last of him, but then I saw him leaving here." Reece then went into telling Ashley everything he'd learned since his stay in Craven Falls and where he'd been the last five years.

"I figure I'd get everything out in the open now. There's no sense in keeping secrets. I've waited too long to be with you again and never thought I'd ever get the chance. I'll do whatever I have to do to keep you safe and find our daughter, if it's the last thing I do," Reece said.

Ashley grew warm inside. He said he would do whatever it took to find Lily and to keep her safe. That meant that he loved her, right? No matter how attractive he was, she couldn't let her hormones get the best of her. She had to tread carefully, especially after the Rob incident. She had thought she knew him well, but that turned out to be a joke. She'd need to open all the doors with Reece and hide no secrets from him.

28

After Dan stepped outside his mother's house and read the text, he got into his car and drove away. The text had come from a different number, not one that Rob had given him, but thought maybe Rob had changed his phone number. The text read: "Come meet me at the cabin." He knew Rob would change his mind about their relationship and ask him to stay.

After stopping and getting gas, it took him fifty-five minutes to get to the cabin. He pulled onto the dirt road and drove slowly up the driveway. It had been a while since he'd been out here to the place where him and Rob had met from time to time.

He passed weathered trees that rose from the earth and brushed against the sky. Most of the trees he noticed had buds on them, getting ready to produce their leaves for the summer.

The wind sent a shudder of movement through the hillside. Just for a moment, Dan thought he saw a small figure run through the woods beside him, but when he looked to his right, it had only been a fallen tree lying drunkenly against another tree. Or maybe even a deer or some other kind of animal. The woods were always filled with wild animals of all kinds, especially in the hills of Pennsylvania.

He saw the cabin ahead and accelerated until he was beside the black convertible. Dan looked at the cabin; memories flowed through him from the past. All the many days and nights him and Rob had spent here holding each other and having the best sex two people could possibly have.

He blinked, bringing himself back to the present. He looked hard at the cabin, but there was no movement. No signs of life. Maybe Rob was inside setting up a surprise for him. He smiled at the thought.

He killed the engine and got out of the car. He was about to climb the steps of the old log house when the sounds of water splashing filled his ears. He turned and walked down the dirt trail and saw the lake ahead. Someone was stomping out of the water fully clothed. He didn't think it was Rob because he hated the water. Dan had tried many times to get him to go skinny dipping with him, but Rob told him that he'd had a bad experience when he was younger and never went swimming again.

The man looked up once he noticed someone standing there; then turned towards the dock, and then up the hill. Dan could've sworn he heard him say, "Shit," but he wasn't sure. The man made his way up the trail and as he got closer, Dan realized it was Rob and made his way towards him.

"Why were you in the lake? I thought you were terrified of the water? And what is that thing in your hand?" Dan asked.

"About fucking time you got here. Did you see her run up the hill?" Tate asked.

"Her?" Dan questioned. "What… *her?*"

"Lily," Tate replied.

Dan's mouth started to drop open, but he closed it fast, not wanting Rob to see his surprise. *Why would Rob have Lily? And how did he get her? That's what Ashley meant when she asked if he'd taken Lily. She thinks he took her?* "Why do you have Lily?" Dan asked.

"None of your fucking business! Have you seen her or not?"

"Who?"

"The little girl?"

"Oh, nope, I haven't seen her at all," Dan lied.

Dan pretended to look around for her and remembered seeing something out of the corner of his eye when he was driving up the road. "I think she took off into the woods over there." Dan pointed to the back of the house, in the opposite direction.

Tate dropped the blanket and quickly took off towards the woods, leaving Dan alone. A smile surfaced; now was his chance to find Lily and take her far away from everyone that was looking for her. He'd finally get his wish and the voices. They'd get their chance to play with her too.

~ ~

Dan had searched everywhere he thought Lily would be, but still couldn't find her. He tried carefully not to step on any branches, but it seemed like the forest was covered in dried-up sticks.

He stopped and listened for any movement around him, but heard nothing. He thought back to when he was driving up the road. He'd spotted something to his right, but had thought it was an animal. Could it have been Lily? If so, then she had a head-start and was probably almost to the road by now.

He decided he'd go back, get the car, and drive down the road. She might be in plain sight since she'd be looking for someone to pick her up, and that's when he'd make his move and grab her.

"Ya', and you had better not fuck it up either," said the voice. "I want to play with little Lily."

"Me too. Me too," said the other voice.

Dan grinned before he howled in laughter. He was getting excited about the hunt and couldn't wait for his prize. He turned and headed back towards his car. He couldn't screw this up.

He needed her.

He wanted her.

This feeling inside was like a craving he just had to have. A delicious little girl he could do whatever he wanted with and no one would stop him.

29

Lily ran until she found a huge tree big enough for her to hide behind. She feared the man who was pretending to be her daddy. He had tricked her into believing he was Rob. She remembered him telling her that he couldn't swim and was afraid to go into the deep water. So, who was this man pretending to be Daddy Rob? Why did he look just like him?

She didn't know and did the only thing she knew to do. Her mommy had told her to run away if a stranger ever approached her and was trying to take her. That's just what she had done, even though she wasn't entirely sure at this time if he was a stranger or not. He *did* look like Daddy Rob, but he just didn't act like him. He acted like a stranger and that scared her.

She heard a branch snap behind her and she stiffened. She slowly peeked around the tree to see if it was the same man from the lake, but she didn't see anyone. She turned back around and scanned the scenery. She saw a huge rock in the distance and ran for it.

Crouching down, she peered around the massive rock, her heart beating fast. She heard another branch snap and then nothing. She held her breath and turned back around. She wanted to start crying, but only babies cried. No, she had to be strong. She needed to find someone and get help.

She thought she heard what sounded like a car driving by on the other side of the hill in front of her. Lily looked back over her shoulder, saw nothing, and took off running in the direction she'd heard the car. She'd get to the road and get help, and they would take her to her mommy.

Lily stopped when she got to the hill, almost falling over the edge. It looked steep. Steeper than the hill her and her friend Sierra climbed down to get to the river by Grandma Cat's house.

Lily was afraid she'd fall and hurt herself. She'd already skinned up her knee, and it hurt really bad. She tried not to think about how much it hurt her and the blood that was oozing out of it.

She looked back over the hill and wondered how she'd get down. She wrapped one hand around a skinny sapling tree and slid her foot to the mossy green rock. She grabbed another tree beside her and slowly made her way down. It wasn't easy because her arms were so short, and she couldn't reach some of the trees around her, but she had to try to get down the hill, away from this bad man who had taken her.

She placed her foot on another rock before grabbing ahold of something with her hand, but her foot slipped, and she started sliding down the hill, her arms and legs scraping against the earth before coming to a stop at the bottom.

Her body hurt all over and she wanted to cry out in pain, but she couldn't. She didn't want him to hear her and find her. Her eyes searched all around as she lay on the forest bed. Part of her was afraid to move just in case she'd broken a bone or something. She knew what that felt like from last summer.

She heard gravel crunch a little ways to her left. She didn't remember hearing that sound earlier when a car passed. Maybe she'd heard wrong, or maybe there were rocks on the road.

She stared up at the sky that was once a pale blue and now a shade of gray. She heard a rumble in the distance. Was it thunder? She hoped not. She didn't care much for storms. Last year, her mommy and Grandma Cat had to stay down in the basement because Grandma Cat said there was a tornado-warning out. She said that they'd be safe in the basement if the house were to be hit by the twister.

Tears leaked from her eyes. She wanted to go home. She wanted her blankie. She wanted to be with her mommy and Grandma Cat again. Why did the bad man have to take her away from her mommy? Lily sniffled as tears ran down the sides of her face and into her ears.

She wiggled her fingers, and then moved both of her arms. They didn't feel broken. She pushed herself up to a sitting position and looked down at her legs. The dress she had on was torn and dirty from the fall. She wiped the wetness from her face with the back of her hand, smearing dirt.

She took in a deep breath and then looked all around her. She could see something that looked like a road ahead of her, but she'd have to get a closer look to be sure.

She stood and took a step forward, wincing from the pain shooting up her leg. It didn't look broken either, but that didn't mean it wasn't. She glanced around her, looking for a stick to use to help her walk. Grandma Cat had a stick whenever she and Lily took a walk in the woods. Lily saw one several feet in front of her.

She closed her eyes and opened them. The pain shot up her leg. She took another step, more of a hop, and then another, trying not to put too much weight on her right leg. With hot salty tears on her cheeks, she bent over and grabbed the thick stick. She would have to use the trees around her to help balance each step she took. Tires crunched along the road before coming to a stop. She had quit moving when she'd heard the car slow down, but she couldn't see a car.

Lily spun around in circles as she hopped on one foot, looking everywhere for the car, but didn't see one. A twig snapped behind her. She turned just enough to see the man approach her, holding her pink blankie.

30

Ashley's body jerked awake, her eyes springing open. She wasn't sure how long she'd slept. "It was just a dream," she mumbled to herself. "Lily is here with me. I can hear her laughing."

She sat up too quick, dizziness and exhaustion hitting her all at once. The last few days had drained everything out of her. She had trouble sleeping. She barely ate.

She looked frantically around the room, but didn't see anything or anyone. Now she was hearing Lily laughing downstairs, which she knew wasn't true, was it? Was she home? Did someone find her? Ashley flew to her feet, taking the steps two at a time as she ran down the stairs. She stopped abruptly when she entered the living room where her mom and Reece sat talking and watching videos of Lily playing in the yard.

A smile crept upon her face, but then instantly disappeared because she didn't think she had the right to smile if Lily wasn't here.

Reece stood and came to her. He lifted her chin and kissed her lips. She could feel the warmth of his lips against hers and smiled.

"Are you okay? Do you want me to get you anything?" he asked.

She shook her head. "I thought I heard Lily. I mean," she said glancing at the TV. "I did hear Lily, but..." she stopped the words from leaving her mouth. She wanted to break down and cry, but she fought hard to be strong. She needed to be strong for her daughter, didn't she? She couldn't be all wishy-washy when her daughter needed her to be out there looking for her, but Ashley didn't know where to start, where to look, and who to blame.

"Come and sit down," Reece insisted. "Your mother thought I'd like to watch some of the home videos of you and Lily. You can watch them with us."

She shook her head again. "I can't watch them, knowing she's still out there alone. I can't pretend she's never coming home!" Ashley shouted into the room, anger washing over her.

"Ashley," Catherine spat. "I just thought it'd be nice for him to see her when she was little. He missed all those years with her."

"Now you want to blame me for him not seeing her. For him not being around to be her father," Ashley replied.

"Hey, no one's blaming you. It was just how things happened between us," Reece said, pulling Ashley into a hug, trying to comfort her. He could tell she was clearly agitated by him seeing the videos.

"I'm sorry," Ashley whispered. "I didn't mean to say those words. I just want my Lily Bug back. I want her home with me, with us."

Catherine paused the video, just as someone knocked at the front door. "I'll get it," Catherine said and quickly stood. She opened the door, all the blood drained from her face when she saw Rob standing on the porch. "Rob, what a surprise," she said loud enough for Ashley to hear.

Ashley stiffened in Reece's arms, then pulled away. Anger coursed through her blood again. Flashbacks from weeks ago entered her mind. *What the hell was he doing here,* she thought. *Hasn't he caused enough heartache?*

She turned and stomped over to where her mom stood. "What are you doing here? You're not welcome at this house or anywhere near me or Lily," Ashley shouted.

"Ash," Rob pleaded. "You won't answer any of my calls. I've been to your apartment, and you won't answer the door."

"Probably because I've been staying at my mother's," she hissed, feeling even more annoyed. *Didn't he get the picture that she didn't want to talk to him? Didn't want to see him?*

"I figured that out since you didn't answer your door and your car wasn't there. I knew you didn't start your new job yet. Well, not that I was aware of. The only other place I knew you'd be, was here," Rob replied, flashing a smile.

She hated it when he smiled like that, all smug like his shit didn't stink. If it weren't for the screen door blocking them, she would smack that smile right off his faggot face. "So, you think you can come over here and beg me to come back to you after I caught you in bed with another man. No! Not just another man, my *"effing"* brother," she yelled, pointing her finger at him, her body trembling all over.

Reece came up beside her and wrapped his arm around her, pulling her close to him; then looked at Rob.

"Wait, you're that guy from the Pub the other night," Reece stated.

Ashley's head that was resting on Reece's chest jolted up, looking confused by what Reece had said.

"Who's this?" Rob asked, nudging his head towards Reece. "You're already in bed with another man?"

"What you don't remember me?" Reece said. "You bought me all those drinks, and then told me you wanted to kidnap a little girl named Lily."

31

Catherine and Ashley looked at one another, confused by what was being said. Neither had known that Reece knew Rob.

"This is Lily's father, Reece," Catherine stated. Although she hadn't wanted to tell Rob who Reece was, she was just as pissed off at him as Ashley was. What right did he have to come here and beg her for forgiveness when he was the one who had cheated on her? Especially, when Rob was about to pledge his love to Ashley.

Catherine watched the scene as if seeing it in slow motion. Rob's mouth fell open, then closed; his eyes looking at Ashley wrapped in Reece's arms and red fire filling his face. She could imagine what was going through his mind at this moment. That was his fiancé in another man's arms. Not just any man, but Lily's biological father.

Then as if recollection had hit him, "Wait! Did you say you saw me in bed with your brother?" Rob questioned. "I don't know what or who you saw, but it sure as hell wasn't me."

Ashley thought for a second then spoke, "Well, it's what I saw. Why would I make something like that up just before we were to get married?"

"You're asking me? When did you supposedly see me in bed with your brother?"

"A little over two weeks ago, right when I left to visit my friend Carla in Illinois."

Rob shook his head in dismay. "Two weeks ago, I was out of town on a business trip. I told you about that," Rob stated.

"I know. I went over to your place to set up a surprise for you when you came home that night. When I walked into your apartment, I heard music playing and thought you had forgotten to shut it off. So, I opened the door to your bedroom, and that's when I saw you and my brother Dan in bed," she shook her head in disgust.

Rob stood on the porch, speechless.

Catherine opened the screen door, allowing Rob in so they could all discuss the matter inside. "Come in. Let's all go sit in the living room and figure out what Ashley saw and what happened to Lily," Catherine said as she shooed everyone into the living room.

"What do you mean? What happened to Lily?" Rob asked.

"That's a very good question?" Reece asked while staring Rob up and down.

"Why're you looking at me like that? I sure as hell didn't and wouldn't kidnap Lily," Rob said.

"Who said anything about Lily being kidnapped?" Reece said as he took several steps, blocking Rob's way to the living room. They were now standing face to face. Reece stood five inches taller, but never once took his eyes off Rob's. "I don't give a flying duck-shit if you were Ashley's fiancé. There's something about you that isn't quite right and I'm going to figure it out. You were talking shit at the bar and you're full of shit now," Reece said as spit sprayed from his mouth with each word.

"I have no idea what you're talking about," Rob said.

"Will someone please tell me what's going on here?" Rob

wiped his face with the back of his hand, removing Reece's spit.

"Everyone, please take a seat and let's discuss this like adults." Once everyone sat down, Catherine filled Rob in on what had happened at the zoo on Sunday and about Dan's visit. "Sheriff White at the police station said it's most likely someone Lily knows. She wouldn't have gone anywhere willingly," Catherine said, wiping away a tear. "I thought at first it was my son Daniel; although he seemed somewhat preoccupied, there's still a possibility that he's involved," she said and then continued, "Then, he received a text on his phone and left in a hurry. Didn't say where he was going."

Reece was watching as Rob sat staring at the floor. "You don't recall having drinks with me, do you?" Reece asked.

"I'm not sure. I was pissed off when I came to the bar. I'd already had several drinks before I came in. I don't remember saying that I was going to kidnap Lily," Rob said as his eye twitched.

"Yeah, you did say it, but I also told you that you'd never survive in prison if you were to do something as stupid as that."

"Now you're calling me stupid?" Rob said.

"If the shoe fits," Reece replied.

"Boys, knock it off," Catherine spat. "You are two grown men, but I can still bend you over my knee if I have to."

For a split second, the room was silent and then filled with laughter as Ashley visualized the sight of Catherine bending the two of them over her knee without a fight. "I can actually picture it," Ashley said as she composed herself. "So, if you didn't take her, do you mind telling me what you might know?" Ashley asked. She watched as he started to squirm in his seat from the question.

"May I have something to drink, please?" Rob asked as sweat rolled down the nape of his neck.

The temperature in the room seemed to escalate after they all sat down. The fan on the ceiling was rotating in circles, giving off a little breeze, but not fast enough to cool down the room or dry the sweat on the back of Rob's neck.

Catherine rose and went into the kitchen to get some drinks.

"Well," Ashley asked again. "Are you going to tell us or will we have to beat it out of you?" Part of her was joking about beating it out of him, but the other part of her wanted to hurt him so bad he'd cry like a momma cat giving birth.

"I don't know what you want me to tell you. I don't know anything about Dan or him taking Lily."

"Oh, come on. The longer you wait, the further this person or Dan will get away from us. What if he…" She didn't want to say it, but it was already too late. She'd already thought it. "What if someone you know has her and hurts her? Rob, please, say something. I'm begging you to tell us," she pleaded, wiping the many tears now running down her face.

"First of all, if you were around more often, then maybe this wouldn't have happened," Rob pointed out.

Ashley's mouth fell open, she was shocked by his words, and then anger surfaced. "Now you're blaming me for Lily being taken?"

"Well, if you weren't so consumed in your schooling, work, and running off to your best friend's house in Illinois every time she comes crying at your door, then maybe she'd still be here."

"What the fuck does that mean? I'm going to school to be an Architect, to better myself and to give Lily a better life. A good life," Ashley screamed at Rob.

"I'm just saying that if you'd be more of a mother to her than Catherine here is, maybe she'd be here with us," Rob replied.

Ashley flew out of her seat and smacked Rob across the face. She was so angry that she started punching him. "You piece of shit. You have no right calling me a bad mom. At least I am doing something with my life," Ashley screamed into his face.

Reece came up behind her and grabbed her arms, holding her back. "Enough," Reece said as he turned her to face him. "Although I'm sure he deserves it, this isn't going to solve anything," he whispered. "As for you," he looked right at Rob. "You have some nerve coming over to this house and throwing accusations around. How do we know that you didn't take her?" Reece stated.

Catherine returned, carrying a tray with a pitcher of homemade lemonade that she'd made earlier that morning and four empty glasses. "What was all the screaming about in here?" She placed the tray on the coffee table, poured lemonade in each glass, and then handed them out before sitting back down in the chair. "Sounded like a bunch of wolves going at it." She wasn't far from the truth.

32

Lily woke, feeling groggy. She went to move her arm, but it was tied with something to the side of the bed. She tugged the other arm, but it wouldn't move either. She frantically looked around the room; it was the same room, the same bed she'd been in this morning.

She thought back to earlier today. She woke up unsure of where she was, and then after coming out of the bathroom, she saw Daddy Rob, except he wasn't Daddy Rob, was he? She didn't know; her head was feeling all fuzzy like it did when she was sick with a bad cold.

Her right leg was hurting, but from what? Her mind flashed to her sliding down a hill and scraping her knee, and then Mommy's brother appearing out of nowhere. Then her mind went blank after that.

She wondered if she started screaming if Daddy Rob or whoever that man was would come to her and untie her. Or, would he do worse things to her? Would he hurt her, maybe kill her? She only knew about kids and people being killed by watching and hearing the news. It didn't happen where she lived, but in a place called Cleveland it seemed to happen a lot. She didn't know exactly where Cleveland was located, but she hoped it wasn't too close to where she lived.

Tears started to run down her face, thinking about bad things happening. She wanted her mommy. She wanted to go home because the man who had her wasn't a nice man. Nice men didn't strap a little girl's arms down so they couldn't move.

She could hear yelling outside her door. She sucked in a breath and heard the sound of boots coming towards her door, her room. She wanted to cry out for help, but who would help her, who would hear her? She was somewhere in the woods with no neighbors close by.

She remembered when she went outside before going down to the lake and sitting on the dock, watching the fish jump in and out of the water, that there were no other houses around.

The knob on the door turned. Should she pretend to be asleep or see who it was? She wasn't sure; the thought made her want to pee the bed.

The door squeaked open and she squeezed her eyes shut. The loud heavy boots walked towards her, and then stopped. She could hear him breathing above her, leaning over her as she lay perfectly still.

"Lilly, I know you're awake. I can see you squeezing your eyes shut," Dan said. "I'll untie you if you promise to be good and not run away."

Lily's eyes slowly opened, pretending to adjust to the light pouring in from the window to her right. She slowly looked to her left and screamed.

33

That night as Reece lay beside Ashley, he held her in his arms until she fell asleep. He wasn't sure how much time had passed as he listened to the rhythmic sound of her breathing.

He placed both arms under his head and looked up at the ceiling. He watched as shadows danced along the walls from the glimmering midnight moon outside.

Reece went over the conversations in his head from earlier. Rob seemed preoccupied and unpredictable; maybe it was because of Reece or maybe it wasn't. He retraced every part of Rob in his mind. Was he capable of kidnapping Lily? Yeah, sure, on the outside he looked weak and tactless, but that didn't mean he wasn't a cold-hearted prick that just wanted to get even with his fiancé for finding out the truth that he was gay. It didn't matter to Reece that Rob denied the accusations. It would have been easy to take Lily because she knew him. She wouldn't have suspected him to harm her, not that he would have, but that didn't mean he wouldn't either.

Catherine had said that Sheriff White thought it was someone they knew or Lily knew, which made sense to him. Although he didn't really know his daughter, he didn't think she'd just go off with some man she didn't know. A total stranger? Would she? No, his mind was already set that she was much smarter than that.

Isn't that what they teach in school? *Stranger danger?* Was she even in school yet? He didn't know. So, the Sheriff could be right, and it made perfect sense to have it be someone she knew, someone she was comfortable with, like Rob.

Still, nothing was clear. Even with all the people at the zoo, no one saw anything? Seems strange when you think about it. Had everyone been too busy watching the stupid ducks swimming around in the water like all ducks do? How was that more fascinating then seeing someone take a little girl?

Although he'd never met Lily, he wanted to believe she wasn't as naïve as most children were. As he lay next to Ashley, he thought about what he would need to do to find his daughter. *Daughter.* The word sounded so foreign to him, but in a good way.

Who would have thought after five years in prison that he had a daughter of his own? As he'd watched the videos yesterday, he had looked for some resemblance. She had—no *has*, *not* past tense—black hair like his, but with soft curls hanging down. Her face was a spitting image of her mother's. She even *has* his shade of blue eyes. She was beautiful and he was proud to be her father.

As a father, his job was to protect his child from harm, and that's exactly what he would do. He'd have to find out where this Rob character lived and follow him, hoping he would lead Reece straight to Lily.

~ ~

The following morning, Reece was up and gone before Ashley and Catherine woke up. Although it felt nice to lie in a soft comfortable bed, he hadn't slept last night. His mind was on overdrive, thinking about Lily and where this Rob guy would have taken her.

Last night he'd swindled Ashley into telling him where Rob lived without giving her the idea that he was going to go there. That he was going to follow this creep and get their daughter back.

Reece got to the middle of town where he started a couple of days ago, walked passed the diner to the opposite side of town where townhouses and apartments were built. He looked for the same make and model of car Rob drove to the house last night. Two parking lots later, he spotted the car and walked to the door of the townhouse.

To the left, there was a keypad. He looked through the names listed and saw Mahan, Rob Mahan 2B. He tried the door, but it was locked. He knew Rob wouldn't buzz him in if he pushed the button, especially after last night. Not after seeing Reece with his ex-fiancé. Nope, he was sure Rob wouldn't let him in the building, fearing that Reece would hurt him.

Although it had crossed his mind at some point last night to smash his head in, it wasn't his intention. All he wanted to do was follow Rob, but the problem was that Reece didn't have a car, and there was no way he was going to follow him by walking; he'd lose him after the first half-mile.

He remembered seeing a car dealership on his way into town and thought about buying a cheap car or maybe even ask to rent one. Reece didn't have a lot of money on him. He had two options, either ask Ashley to use her vehicle and take the chance Rob wouldn't recognize it—he'd have to stay far enough behind him so he didn't get suspicious. Or the second option, maybe he could make a tracking device.

That was the one thing he had been good at while in the Marines, making bombs and tracking devices. He'd made whatever the team had needed when they'd been out in the battlefield.

He'd need to walk back into town and check out the hardware store and see what he could find, and then all he needed was a cheap cell phone. Reece turned and walked back into town.

34

The boards creaked under Dan's feet with each step he took as he paced the living room of the cabin. When he went into the bedroom and Lily screamed when she saw him, his head began to hurt. The voices wouldn't stop. They kept getting louder and louder, and the pain at times was so unbearable it would bring him to his knees.

Sometimes he wanted to cry, but if he did then the one voice in his head would call him a *cry baby* and tell him to *man-up* and *grow some balls*.

One time at the Army base he was making his bed and started responding back to the voice, thinking it was one of the recruits in the bunker with him. A couple of the guys came over and stared at him. When they realized he'd been talking back to himself, they started calling him all kinds of names: *"You're a Looney"*, *"Faggot loser"*, *"Danny boy is talking to himself, fucking pussy."* They had teased him until their Sergeant came in asking what the hell was going on and made them all do one hundred push-ups in their underwear outside in the pouring rain.

He without question didn't miss those days. But it was those days that got him medically discharged from the Army after two years and into the psychiatric hospital where he'd spent the last four years. Although he had been released a couple of weeks ago, he still was no better at controlling the voices that wanted so badly to come out and become a part of society.

Dan froze when he heard the sound of gravel crunching outside. He ran to the window, moved the curtain aside. His stomach flipped. Dan tried to hide his feelings, but at times, it was too hard to do. Whenever Rob came around his insides melted.

He stood back when he heard the boards creaking as Rob walked across the porch, punched in the code, and opened the door.

"What the hell are you still doing here?" Tate asked.

Dan's mouth fell open. He'd just seen him hours ago, what had changed? How could he not remember? "You texted me earlier today to come up here, and now you're saying you don't know why I'm here?" Dan replied. He stood with his hands behind him, trying to keep them from shaking.

"What are you talking about?"

Dan opened his mouth, then closed it, and then reopened it. "It sounds like you don't want me anywhere near you. First at the diner, you tell me to get out of town and that you never want to see me again, and then you text me to come to the cabin. I thought maybe you changed your mind and wanted me to stay," Dan stated.

Tate's face changed as if recollection had surfaced in his mind. "Don't you realize how hard I worked to plan this kidnapping until you came into town and nearly screwed everything up?"

"And just how did I do that? How was I supposed to know what you were planning?" Dan questioned. "I came here to see you, Rob. You practically gave me your bed. I thought we could have a life together, but I see now you never cared about me in that way."

Tate smiled, "Oh, don't cry your fucking head off about it. You know how I feel about you, but I need to take care of this problem before it gets out of hand. Until I can get her mother up here, Lily will not leave this cabin. She is not to go outside without me knowing first. Do I make myself clear?" Tate demanded. "Don't, and I mean *don't* screw this up!"

Dan nodded, "But why are you doing this? Can't we just keep her for ourselves? Why do you need my sister involved?" Dan asked, not wanting Rob to know how much he liked little girls.

Tate stood in front of Dan contemplating the idea. "Maybe. I'll have to think it through first," Tate replied, knowing he wasn't going to change his mind.

Dan smiled before walking out the front door for some much needed fresh air. He had some thinking to do of his own, just in case his *so-called partner* had other plans, since he kept changing his mind about their relationship.

Dan wanted Lily all to himself, but there was only one way to do that, which meant he had to come up with a plan to get her out of here and away from Rob. His feelings for Rob didn't even come close to what he felt for the child.

No. This feeling. This urge. This longing was something unfamiliar to him. Something he'd been craving for far too long and hadn't known it. It was time for Rob to go away. Time to stand up for himself and show Rob who's boss.

35

Catherine brushed the remaining dirt into a bucket and pressed gently around the potted flower. She had been working all morning in her greenhouse, getting her plants and flowers ready for summer.

Normally, these past couple of years her granddaughter Lily would always help her. Catherine enjoyed the company since her late husband had passed. She didn't mind the quietness of the woods, but sometimes, it was very lonesome.

Her thoughts of Lily never left her mind. When Dan was here, why had she said her name? She'd been going on and on like she always did when she was flustered and out slipped Lily's name. She shouldn't be so hard on herself. She could speak her granddaughter's name whenever she wanted to. There was nothing wrong with saying her name. This had nothing to do with the kidnapping. Her son Daniel was not involved! At least that's what she wanted to believe.

She at times had to leave the room when she felt sad and was going to cry. That's how she'd ended up in the greenhouse. Keeping her mind busy was the best thing to do.

It had been two days since Lily had been taken. Two days of not hearing anything back from the Sheriff. Two days of crying and not sleeping well. Not that she slept well before her granddaughter's kidnapping, but more than she was getting these past couple of days.

Catherine had to force herself to eat, just so she wouldn't get dizzy or fall over from the lack of sugar in her system. The doctor just last week had told her that she was borderline diabetic and that she needed to eat healthier foods, and not cookies and breads all the time. Though she knew, no one died healthy. Besides, she was nearing seventy; what life she had left would be lived her way, not by some doctor's orders.

She wiped her hands on the apron tied around her waist and moved the finished pot to the shelf by the window. Once she watered the five plants, she'd clean up and head back inside to make some breakfast for her, Ashley, and Reece.

Catherine hadn't seen Ashley nor Reece this morning and figured they both were sleeping in, which would be great for her daughter, who hadn't slept more than a couple of hours since Sunday. She only knew that because she could hear Ashley crying in the room next to hers. It would get so bad, Catherine would have to leave her room and go downstairs where she couldn't hear her daughter cry out in pain. It was too much for her to bear; especially since Lily had been with her when she went missing, Catherine felt responsible.

She gave the plants some water, rinsed off her hands, replaced the hose on the hook, and then turned off the water. She untied her apron and hung it on the hook next to the door.

She hadn't realized from the heat inside the greenhouse how cool it was outside, until she stepped out the door.

She opened the door to the kitchen and stepped inside. Before making a big breakfast, she'd make sure Ashley and Reece hadn't made any plans for the morning. No sense in making a huge meal if there was no one here to eat it.

She hurried down the hall and up the stairs to where Ashley had been sleeping. She stopped abruptly when she saw the bed empty and neatly made.

Where had Ashley gone? she thought. *Had she forgotten that Ashley and Reece had left? Maybe poked her head in when she was in the greenhouse and said goodbye, that they were going out?* Catherine didn't think so.

She peered into the bathroom off the bedroom. Nope, she wasn't in there either. Catherine turned back around and went down the stairs and into the kitchen.

Catherine went to grab the phone on the wall, but reached for the counter instead. Dizziness swirled around her. She turned, sat down in the chair beside her; thankfully she was near it. She bent over as much as she could and placed her head down between her legs. Once she felt better, she sat up and slowly stood, making her way to the refrigerator to make herself something to eat.

God help her if something was to happen to her when no one was here. She needed to take better care of herself or at least try to.

She wouldn't let something happen to herself with Lily gone missing. No, she had to stay strong and eat. She'd have something small and lie down on the sofa for a short nap. Although that seemed to be all she did these days, even when her granddaughter was here.

Maybe if she slept at night she wouldn't be so tired during the day, but she doubted that was true. Her parents were good examples; they had taken naps all the time.

Catherine stood and walked over to the refrigerator and started gathering what she needed to make her some breakfast.

36

Ashley parked alongside the road and watched Reece slip inside the electronics store. Craven Falls wasn't a huge town, but they had their share of stores. If you were looking for a superstore, like Walmart or Target, then you'd have to drive out of town for about ten to fifteen miles to get to there.

Ten minutes later, Reece exited the small hardware store, carrying a plastic bag.

Earlier, she'd felt him get out of bed and heard him leave the house. She was curious to know why he was walking to town at six in the morning when he could've asked her for a ride. What was he up to? She wanted to know. No, she needed to know. Did he have anything to do with Lily's kidnapping? Why would she think he had anything to do with their daughter being missing?

Reece hadn't given her any indication that he was involved. Her mind was in overdrive and making speculations. He'd acted surprised when she told him about Lily, about getting pregnant. No, there was no way he had anything to do with her being missing, but she still knew he was up to something and she would make it her business to find out what it was.

Reece went around the corner of the building and disappeared. Her pulse raced as she opened the door of her SUV, walked across the street to the side of the building. When she looked around the corner, he was nowhere to be seen. *Where had he gone?* she questioned to herself. *Should she walk to the end and see if there was*

an open door or another place he could've slipped into?
She came this far. She wasn't going to back out now.

Ashley crept down the alleyway, looking for anything out of the ordinary. She strained to hear the sounds in front of her and around her. The smell of used cooking oil and rotten food made its way up her nose, making her stomach spasm. Part of her wanted to turn around, get back in her car, and drive to her mom's house, but she couldn't. Her curiosity outweighed any quick decision she'd thought about.

She jumped, her hair lifting on the nape of her neck and arms when a door from behind her opened and banged shut. She sucked in a quick breath then realized it was the cook from the diner, throwing boxes in the dumpster. He nodded to her and went back inside. She blew out the breath she was holding.

Ashley quickened her step and stopped when she got to the end of the building. She looked to her right and saw nothing but brick walls and more dumpsters. She looked left and there sat Reece on an over-turned wooden box with something in his hands.

He didn't see that she was there watching him; his back was to her. She walked up behind him, trying to be quiet as a mouse.

"Why are you following me, Ashley?" Reece asked.

She stopped suddenly. "How did you know it was me?" she asked.

He turned to face her. "I saw you pull up and park across the street when I was in the store. You wouldn't make a very good detective," he smiled.

She narrowed her eyes. "Well...," she paused. "Well, I wouldn't be following you if you'd just told me where you were going in the first place. I would've given you a ride," she said, crossing her arms in front of her, anger sparking.

He stood, faced her. "I don't want to involve you in this."

"What exactly are you doing that you don't want to involve me in?" she asked, tilting her head to look around him.

"Yesterday, I got a bad feeling about this Rob guy. I know he was your fiancé and everything, but..." Reece paused. "He still gives me a bad vibe. His eye kept twitching when Lily and Dan's name were mentioned. So, last night when you were sleeping, I went over everything in my head about him," he stated. "He just seems off-somehow. I just thought I'd come into town and check him out. I decided to build a tracking device and see if he leads us to Lily."

She shook her head. "And how do you know how to build one of those?" she questioned. "What were you, some secret agent or something?"

"Something like that," he replied.

Ashley was shocked beyond belief. "You're shitting me, right?" She stepped back. All of a sudden she felt claustrophobic, almost scared for her life.

He reached out and grabbed her arm, not hard, but enough to keep her from running away. "Ashley, I won't hurt you. I'd never hurt you. It took me six years to get back to you. I don't want to lose you after I've found you. You have to believe me."

She stood there, her body trembling. She had wanted nothing more at one time than to find him—to be with him, but now she was almost afraid of him. She had never really known him. So, it wasn't a surprise, no; it shouldn't be a surprise what kind of person he used to be or the person he may... still be.

Would he hurt her? Was that the kind of person he was? Was this the same man that helped conceive her Lily? He'd just said he wouldn't hurt her so why would she be afraid he would?

She sucked in a breath and took another step back. She wanted to stop the thoughts that were entering through her mind.

He let her arm slip from his grasp. "Let's sit down and talk about this. I can explain everything."

She nodded, "Okay, okay, but not here. I don't want to be where there's no one watching. I want to trust you. I mean, I do. I did trust you, but now..." she whispered. "Now, I don't know what to think."

He nodded in agreement, turned and gathered up all the stuff he'd bought and placed them back in the bag. When he finished, he turned back towards Ashley, and they walked back down the alley and to the front of the diner.

Ashley went in first, Reece following close behind. There were plenty of seats to choose from and Reece chose a booth near the back. The moment they sat, the petite redheaded waitress came over to take their order.

"Hey, Ash. What can I get you?" the waitress smiled.

"Hi, June. I'll take a coffee with cream and sugar."

"Sure thing. And what can I get you good-looking?" June smiled and winked in Reece's direction.

Reece didn't react to her words. "Same for me, thank you."

"No problem. I'll be right back with your coffees."

153

Ashley sat up straight, shoulders back, and waited until June came back with their order. A few minutes later, they both sat stirring their coffee.

"I was born and raised in Sumter, South Carolina. My mom died before I turned five years old from cancer. My father died right after I turned eighteen from a heart attack. After I graduated from high school, a couple months later, I enlisted in the Marines and served for eight years."

"What kind of things did you do when you were in the Marines? What was your job?"

"Special Forces. I was a Scout Sniper, but also learned how to make things, like bombs and trackers from just about anything. I can't go into everything with you; it's part of my commitment with the military," he said in a low voice. "I can't talk about some things. I can't discuss certain things with you, but I'll try to answer what I can," Reece replied.

Ashley nodded then asked, "So after you left the Marines, what did you do after that?"

"I became a gypsy. I didn't have a family to go home to in South Carolina, so I just floated around. I'd do side jobs for people and when I finished, I moved on to another town and did the same thing." He took a sip of coffee, and then signaled for the waitress who was wiping down the counter.

"What can I help you with?" June asked.

"Are you hungry?" he asked Ashley.

She nodded, "I could eat a little."

"We'll take a couple of menus first," Reece said.

June walked back around the counter, grabbed a couple of menus, and placed them on the table. "Just let me know when you're ready," she stated as she walked away. Both Ashley and Reece grabbed a menu at the same time and opened them. She already knew what she wanted to eat. She just needed to absorb everything he had told her. She wasn't afraid of him, but she definitely wasn't ready to jump back into a relationship so soon. Even if he was Lily's father, she still wanted to get to know him better.

Look at the whole Rob scenario. She was about to marry a man who she caught in bed with her brother. Although he denied it, she knew what she saw. There was no way her eyes were playing tricks on her. Besides, right now she needed to put all her focus on finding Lily. Nothing else mattered. She'd let Reece make this so-called tracking device and see where it led them because she didn't know any other way to get her daughter back. When she did, she'd never let her out of her sight again.

37

Lily woke the next morning finding her hands untied, but still in the same room she'd been in since he brought her here. She rolled to her side, turned to her belly, and slid off the bed until her feet touched the cold wooden floor.

It was freezing in the room so she pulled the small blanket from the foot of the bed and wrapped it around her shoulders, just the way her mommy always did.

She tiptoed towards the door, placing an ear against it. She didn't hear any noise. She turned the knob and found it locked. Now what was she going to do? She had to use the potty right now!

She turned and glanced around the semi-dark room. She needed to find something, anything to use as a potty. She crept away from the door and back around the bed. There against the wall was a potted plant. She went to the pot and touched the leaves; they were plastic. She knew how to tell if plants were real or not from Grandma Cat.

She pulled from the bottom where the stem met the bowl. Everything came out, even the Styrofoam at the bottom, which kept the plant in place.

Just as quickly, as she pulled down her pretty panties and squatted over the opening of the bowl, she started to pee. She'd have to hide the mess she made before Mommy's brother came into the room, but where? She could shove the fake plant under the bed, but would the pot fit too? She didn't think so. There wasn't a closet in the room like she had at home with Mommy or Grandma Cat's place.

For now, she'd just have to leave it in the corner where it was. She took an oversized throw pillow from the bed and placed it in front of the pot, hoping he wouldn't go looking behind it.

She couldn't wipe because there wasn't any toilet paper in the room, which she could sneak from the bathroom later when Uncle Dan let her use the normal toilet.

There was no way to wash her hands like her mommy had taught her after using the bathroom, but she didn't wipe so she hadn't gotten any pee on her hands.

She climbed back up on the bed and slipped under the covers. As much as she wanted to suck her thumb, she couldn't because it was gross. Grandma Cat always said not to suck on her thumb if it wasn't clean, and she'd have to try really hard not to.

~ ~

Lily didn't know how much time had passed or what day it was anymore. She heard the door creak open and someone walking to the bed.

"Oh, Lily Bug. It's time to get up," said the female voice, which sounded just like her mommy's voice. She hadn't heard those words in quite a while. Lily opened her eyes and saw her mommy standing beside her. A smile danced across her face. She was finally with her mommy and Grandma Cat again.

She jumped to her feet and started bouncing on the bed and cheering. "Yay! My mommy's here to be with me and Grandma Cat too."

She jumped and jumped, until she heard a man's voice beside her, shaking her. "Wake up, Lily. You're having a bad dream," he said.

When she opened her eyes and saw the same room, with the same curtains and the same man, she started to cry because she knew it was all a dream. Grandma Cat and her mommy weren't here to save her from this bad man.

Uncle Dan stared down at her, but with satisfying eyes. Those eyes scared Lily. She wished it wasn't a dream that she'd had just now about her mommy. She wished so much to be home with her.

"If you promise to be good, I'll let you out of this room today and we'll go outside, maybe even to the lake," Dan said.

Lily nodded. She'd do anything to get out of this room.

"Come on, let's go use the bathroom and get you cleaned up," he said.

Lily climbed out of bed and looked back at the big pillow by the wall. He hadn't noticed; she was safe with her secret. They left the bedroom; he followed close behind her as if she had some place to run to.

She prayed he'd let her go in alone and not want to watch her. He made her feel uncomfortable, dirty even. Dirtier than she already felt when she couldn't wash her hands after peeing in the pot.

"Go in and clean up. I'll wait right here for you."

She hurried inside and closed the door behind her, locking it. Even though she knew she'd have to come out when she finished, she felt safer with the door locked.

She flushed and went to the tub to wash her hands. She splashed some water on her face, moving her hands all around. The dirt from yesterday's fall came running off and into the tub. Should she get undressed and wash her whole body? She didn't know. She didn't want to make him angry if she took too long. She'd heard him yelling the day before and it scared her. Scared her to the point she had cried herself to sleep.

"Lily Rose, what are you doing in there? I didn't tell you to take a bath. Now, you come right out here this instant," he demanded.

Lily trembled from his yelling, quickly turned off the water, and grabbed the towel behind her to wipe off her face. At least she'd had a chance to wash her hands. They were now sparkly clean, and she plopped a thumb in her mouth before opening the door.

"What took you so long?" he huffed. "Come on, I made you something to eat." He pushed her in front of him and they went into the kitchen.

Lily sat in the same chair she'd sat in yesterday, staring at the plate in front of her. "What is it?" she asked.

"What do you mean, what is it? It's food. You know, the kind you eat?"

"Well, it looks gross," Lily replied. Even though her mommy had told her never to disrespect what others make for you, she couldn't help it. She wasn't going to eat this food that smelled like eggs but had some kind of green leaves in it and ketchup poured on the top. It looked gross so she stuck her thumb back in her mouth and sat back in her chair.

"If you don't eat, you don't go outside. In fact, you can stay locked up in your room," Dan replied. "So, which is it? Eat or sit in your room without any food for the rest of the day?"

Lily's eyes widened and her belly growled. It didn't look good or smell good, but it was either this or nothing. She took her thumb out of her mouth and picked up the fork. She wasn't sure if it was eggs or something he'd just whipped together that looked like them.

She scooped some onto her fork and took a bite. The moment she swallowed the food, she turned to the side and threw it all back up.

"Great! Now look what you've gone and done," he yelled.

Tears ran down her face. She hadn't meant to puke all over the floor, but the food was disgusting and apparently, her stomach thought so too.

"Here," Dan threw a towel at her. "Clean it up and then go to your room."

She'd thrown up many times before and her mommy and Grandma Cat never made her clean it up. Her Uncle Dan was mean and she hated him for making her do this.

She hopped off the chair and laid the towel over the vomit. The smell made her want to throw up again, but then he'd just make her clean that up too.

Once she finished, she slid a chair from the table to the sink and washed the towel and her hands.

"Okay, let's go."

She turned to see where he was standing before turning the water off and climbing down. He placed a hand on her shoulder and pushed her towards the bedroom.

"You can sit in your room and think about what you did and how ungrateful you are for not eating the food that was made for you. Didn't your mother ever tell you that you have to eat what is given to you?" Dan asked. "Food don't come free, you know."

Once in the room, Lily kept her eyes off him, waiting for him to leave. When he did and she heard him walk away, she pulled a banana from under her dress. She peeled half of it, ate it, and then placed the remaining banana in the top drawer of the night table on the other side of the bed where he wouldn't smell it and take it away.

He said she'd have to stay in here the rest of the day so she'd at least have the other half of the banana and not starve.

38

When they finished having their breakfast, Ashley drove them to her place. She hadn't been home since going to Carla's.

The moment she walked in through the door, she could smell Lily everywhere. Her toys were neatly stacked against the corner wall, and as she looked around the room, she saw Lily's favorite princess cup drying on a towel on the kitchen counter where she'd left it.

It made her heart sink further as she took in the sight and smells of her missing daughter. She'd forgotten all about Reece until he asked where he could sit.

"Right there at the table is fine," she replied. "Would you like anything to drink? Maybe some fresh coffee?"

"Sure, that'll be fine, thank you," Reece replied.

Ashley went into the kitchen and made a fresh pot of coffee. While the coffee was brewing, she noticed the light blinking on the answering machine and pressed the button.

"Ash, it's me, Rob. Come on, you can't ignore me forever. Where are you anyway? Please, call me back," Rob pleaded.

She looked over at Reece just as he looked up at her. She hit the delete button.

The next message said: "You can't stay mad at me; I didn't do anything wrong," Rob said. "I'll keep calling until you pick up the phone." The call ended and she deleted that one too. She deleted the next nine that were also from Rob. The next message was left only a few minutes ago and from someone other than Rob.

"Hi, this is Sheriff White down at the police department here in Craven Falls. I'm going to need you to come down to the station at your earliest convenience. There's been some new evidence in your case." A beep sounded, but there were no other messages.

Ashley looked over at Reece, as if they were both thinking the same thing. Reece stood and walked over to where she was standing.

"We should go to the station right away," Ashley said. "Maybe they found her or they have a lead as to who took her."

Reece nodded, "Let's go."

Ashley heard the coffee pot sputter and blow out a puff of steam as it came to a finish. She quickly shut it off before they went out the door.

Ashley's hands were shaking as she drove to the police station. She should've had Reece drive, but then she would've wanted him to drive faster.

Thoughts of Lily played in her head. She fought back the negative thoughts. She couldn't allow herself to think something bad had happened to her little girl. Wouldn't the officer have said it was an emergency or even called her cell? Shit, she'd forgotten her cell phone at her mom's house.

She was deep in thought when Reece shouted for her to stop. She stomped on the brakes, almost hitting two people walking across the street. Tears instantly streamed down her face.

"Ashley, I think I should drive," Reece said as he removed his hand from the dashboard.

"I'm sorry. I'm so sorry. I'll slow down," she replied. A few minutes later, they arrived at the police station and went inside. After telling the officer at the front desk who they were and whom they'd come to see, they took a seat.

Reece put his hand in Ashley's, caressing it with his thumb. She wondered if he could tell that she was tense and was barely hanging onto her sanity.

"Ms. Teodora," Sheriff White said.

They both looked up. "Yes," she replied.

"You can come with me." They both stood. "I'm sorry, but who's this person?"

Ashley looked over at Reece. "He's with me. He's coming with me."

Sheriff White nodded. "Follow me." They walked down the same hallway, but into a different interrogation room. "Please, have a seat."

Both Ashley and Reece sat. "What's this about?" Reece asked.

"I didn't want to say anything over the phone so it was best that you came to the station."

Ashley's body stiffened, feeling sick to her stomach. It was as if she could feel that something was wrong. Very wrong. Her voice cracked a little when she spoke, "Please, just tell us what this is about."

"A child's body was found down near the river, just outside of town. There's a chance the body may have drifted down the river," Sheriff White said, then continued. "I have my men searching up and down the bank for any evidence of foul play. It's also possible that the incident happened somewhere else, and they just wanted to get rid of the body, but we're checking into all scenarios," Sheriff White said as he cleared his throat.

"There's some resemblance to the child from the picture you have provided to us of your daughter."

Ashley's body trembled. "No!" she gasped. "Not my Lily!" Reece wrapped his arm around her back and held her close to him. There was no way she could hold it together much longer.

"I called you down here to identify the body. Do you think you can do that for us?"

She felt as if she'd left her body and was looking at herself from a distance. She didn't want to believe that her daughter was dead. There was no way she could be, right? She stared down at the table as if waiting for it to speak to her. To tell her what she needed to do. Wouldn't she feel her absence inside her? As a mother, wouldn't she know that something was wrong? She slowly nodded. "Can Reece come with me? I..." she paused. "I don't think I can stand. I need him with me," she said as the tears poured from her eyes.

Reece whispered in her ear, "It's not her. It's not our Lily. I'll be right here beside you." He squeezed her into him again.

"If you'll follow me, I'll take you down to our forensic lab in the basement where the medical examiner will go over any questions you may have, but only if you can identify her as your daughter," Sheriff White stated. "There will be tests run to help identify the child as well, but it doesn't help if we don't have anything to compare the samples to." Ashley seemed confused by what Sheriff White had said. Compare samples to?

When they arrived at the end of the hallway where the stairs were located, Ashley stopped. "I don't know if I can do this, Reece. What if it's my baby girl? I can't..."

Ashley shook her head side to side. "I don't know if I want to see her this way. My poor Lily Bug," Ashley sniffled.

"I'll be right here with you. We'll do this together," Reece said.

"I'm sorry," Sheriff White interrupted, "You can't go in with her. Parents of the child only."

"I'm Lily's father," Reece replied.

"Oh, well, then of course you can go in. I'm sorry, I didn't know."

"How could you, I just found out yesterday that I had a daughter," Reece informed him.

Sheriff White fell silent, turned, pushed the door to the stairwell open, and trudged down the steps, while holding onto the railing. They both followed him down two sets of stairs, as there were three floors, if you counted the basement.

They all walked through a set of doors and down a long, lit hallway, although it gave you the feel of a scary movie with the light bulbs flickering as they made their way to the morgue.

Sheriff White stopped just outside the door leading to the unknown child. "All we need for you to do is tell us if she is or isn't your daughter," White said. "Then we can proceed from there. Does she have any birthmarks or scars?" White asked.

Ashley nodded, "She has one on her forehead and one on her chest. They're small almost like a freckle, but there's one on her lower back just above the left butt cheek that looks like a butterfly."

Sheriff White nodded, "Okay, are you ready?"

Reece nodded and then Ashley. She knew she'd have to do this and get it over with. Within the next ten seconds her world could fall off its axis and forever be destroyed. Sheriff White opened the door and they all filed inside. Ashley stood beside the table that held a child's body. Reece stood beside her with his arm around her waist, pulling her close to him. She swallowed as she stared down at the white cloth covering the body.

"Are you ready?" asked Sheriff White.

Ashley took in a breath and held it before answering, "Yes."

Sheriff White singled to the medical examiner to pull back the sheet.

39

Lily's belly was hurting. She hadn't eaten since the banana earlier that morning. Her Uncle Dan hadn't come back in the room and neither had her so-called Daddy Rob. She'd been locked up since she was sent to her room. She'd had to use the pot a couple of times to pee in, but she didn't have to go as much because she hadn't had anything to drink and she was beyond thirsty.

She lay curled up in the blanket on the bed. The temperature had gotten cold throughout the day and she was freezing. No food, no water, and no heat for her growing body.

She heard the floorboards creak outside her door, but she didn't move. She knew no one was coming in to check on her; if they cared, they would've done so earlier, wouldn't they?

The lock clicked and the door opened. She couldn't tell which man it was because he was still behind the door, and the room was somewhat dark because of the curtains being closed.

He stepped forward, allowing the light from behind him to silhouette his body. She squeezed her eyes shut, but knew he'd probably seen that she was awake. He stepped towards the bed.

"What in God's name have you done in here? It stinks like piss. Did you go and pee the bed?" Dan shouted at her. "Didn't my sister teach you better than that? Leave it to Ashley to raise a child out of wedlock and not teach it some manners."

Lily tried to lie still, but her belly really hurt. Her body was still dirty from the fall and she was shivering. All she wanted to do was to see Mommy and Grandma Cat again. She just wanted to go home.

"Lily get up," Dan nudged her shoulder. "We need to leave before he gets back."

Leave? She wanted to ask. Was he taking her home? She didn't want him to get mad at her and leave her locked up in this room. She opened her eyes; he was standing there looking down at her. Then, like that day at Grandma Cat's house, he smiled that devious smile. The smile that scared her and made her realize he wasn't a good man. That he'd do bad things to her.

She wished Daddy Rob hadn't taken her from the zoo. She'd been having a great time with Grandma Cat. They were about to feed the ducks and then...then, she didn't remember what happened. She woke up here scared and alone until she came out of the bathroom and saw it was her Daddy Rob on that first day.

How many days had she been here? She didn't know, but to her it seemed like a really long time without her mommy. He'd promised her that her mommy would meet them here, but she hadn't shown up yet and now Uncle Dan wanted to leave.

"What about my mommy?" Lily asked.

"What about her?"

"Is she coming too?"

"Why the fuck would she be coming with us?" he snapped.

Lily flinched and sunk back into her blankets, pulling them tighter around her. She didn't like it when he got angry. There were times she'd hear him in the other room yelling at someone, but they didn't yell back at him.

"Come on, let's go cleanup your filthy body and get out of here."

Lily wanted to fight him, but she did need a bath. She hoped he had clean clothes to put her in, and then it came to her. He'd have to undress her and see her naked. Even Daddy Rob had never given her a bath before. Just Grandma Cat and Mommy.

Once in the bathroom, she hesitated before telling him that she could wash herself. He eyed her and then nodded and said, "Okay, but the door stays unlocked."

She thought about it and nodded in agreement. She closed the door and walked over to the bathtub. She'd seen her mommy many times pull up on the small metal lever to keep the water from draining out.

She turned on the water and held her hand under it, just like Mommy did, and turned the knob until it felt warm enough. When it did, she looked around for soap and shampoo. She found it under the cabinet next to the toilet paper. She placed them on the side of the tub, undressed, and climbed inside.

The water was amazing, and it made her smile. She wished she could stay in here forever, but knew that Uncle Dan wouldn't let her and besides, the water would get cold after a while.

After washing her hair and body, she rinsed off and pushed the lever down so the water could drain out. She looked around the room, saw that the towels were too far to reach, and she would have to get out of the tub to get one.

She held onto the side of the tub and threw her good leg over and then the leg she'd hurt falling down the hill, being careful not to slip and fall. She walked slowly over to the towels and grabbed one just as the door opened.

"Are you done in here yet?" Dan asked, not sticking his head in.

"Yeah, but I don't have clean clothes to put on. Did Daddy Rob bring me any clothes?" Lily asked.

"Let me go check," Dan replied before closing the door.

Lily quickly dried off and wrapped the towel around her body. A few minutes later, he opened the door. He stood half in the room, holding some clothes in his hand. She grabbed at them, but he pulled them away before she could get them.

Lily stepped back; he smiled again at her, then placed the clean clothes on the counter and shut the door. She wanted to go home really bad.

She dropped the towel to the floor and quickly stepped into her clothes. She pulled the shirt over her head just as the door swung open and Uncle Dan grabbed her.

"Come on, we have to go. He's on his way."

Dan placed Lily in the backseat of the car and buckled her in. He jumped behind the wheel and took off down the driveway, stirring up dust behind him. He knew he had about an hour to get out of the house, get her in the car, and drive as far away from here as he could, but he couldn't waste any more time. The sooner he left, the further away they'd be.

40

Rob slammed the trunk of his car before going back into his apartment to get a few more things. He had to look like he was taking a trip. He didn't really want to leave Ashley right now, but what other choice did he have? There were more important things to do that he had to take care of.

He locked the door to his apartment, went back down the stairs to his car, and got in. As he drove through town, he noticed Ashley's SUV sitting at the police station. He looked at the clock on the dashboard; he had some time and parked a couple of vehicles down from hers.

He'd just see if there were any new leads on Lily and then get back on the road. He didn't have time for mistakes. Mistakes that would cost him his relationship with Ashley, which he knew was probably too late. That Reece guy was here in town and Rob doubted that he was going to be leaving anytime soon. He had thought long and hard last night after leaving Catherine's house on what to do. He had to get Reece out of the picture. He had to get Ashley to see that Reece wasn't the type of man to stick around. He wasn't a father figure and would end up hurting her and Lily.

No, he couldn't have this stranger do that to them. He deserved Ashley, not some longhaired, muscle-toned man who was just passing through. He'd prove this to Ashley and make her choose him.

He jumped in his seat when there was a knock on the car window. He powered down the window to hear what the cop had to say. "You've been sitting here for fifteen minutes. If you're not going to get out of your car, then I'm going to have to ask you to leave," the overweight donut-eating officer said. "Just 'cause this is a small town doesn't mean that you're not some crazy white boy looking for trouble," the cop said.

Not many people knew who he was in this town. He worked long hours during the week and only came back on the weekends, except for the last two days. He'd had to take a couple of sick days so he could straighten things out with Ashley, but that hadn't worked to his advantage. He worked out-of-state where no one knew him and what he did for a living.

Rob debated whether to cause a scene or just leave. Show this cop a crazy white boy. He really wanted to see what Ashley was here for, but thought better of it. He powered up his window and backed out of the spot.

He drove towards the highway, stopping only to fill up the gas tank and get back on the road. He had to take care of what he'd started. He needed to get rid of Dan because he was causing too much shit between him and Ashley. That was why he decided to text him about going to the cabin.

There would be no more mister nice guy. No, he had to show everyone what he was capable of. Even if that meant putting Dan back in the room where he couldn't see anyone or hear anything. He would need another treatment, but this time he'd turn the switch up as far as it could go.

Rob turned onto the dirt road and drove up to the cabin. There were no other cars, which told him that Dan hadn't arrived yet. He stepped out of the car, looking down at the lake that had almost ended his life when he was eight years old. He turned his eyes away from the lake and made his way up the stairs to the cabin. He punched in the code and opened the door. Once inside he was shocked at the mess in the kitchen. "What the hell?" he mumbled. The place smelled of piss and the beginnings of rotting food in the kitchen.

Dirty dishes were piled high in the sink and food obscured the counter. "Who the hell was here?" he said into the empty room. He heard a floorboard creak behind him, then everything went black…

41

Catherine had just finished putting the pot roast in the oven when the phone rang. She closed the oven door and grabbed the phone before it rang again. "Hello," Catherine sang.

"Mom, it's me, Ashley."

Catherine could hear the faint hitch in her voice. "What's wrong? Is everything okay?" She could go on and on with questions, but she knew better than to push her daughter. She was beyond exhausted with Lily missing, and Catherine throwing out questions would just make it worse. Make her daughter pull away.

"I received a call from Sheriff White an hour ago," Ashley said.

Catherine gasped, "What? Is everything okay? Did they find Lily?"

As if Ashley hadn't heard the questions, she said, "He wanted me to come down to the station. There was some new evidence that had surfaced," Ashley replied. "They found a child's body and Reece and I had to identify it."

Catherine grabbed the wall; afraid she might fall over from the news Ashley was about to tell her. *Oh, dear God, don't let it be true,* she thought to herself. *Not my grandbaby.*

"Mom, it wasn't her. It wasn't our Lily, but…" Ashley paused. "It was Jeanne Miller's little girl, Sierra."

"Oh, my dear Jesus." Catherine sat down in the chair shocked by the news. "Did they say what happened to her? Did someone? Was Jeanne there? Oh, my heavenly

God, why would someone hurt that little girl?" Her eyes began to water as she stared out into the room. *Poor Jeanne. How was she going to get through this? The news will just destroy her.* Catherine thought.

"Mom, are you still there?" Ashley asked.

"Yes, I'm here," Catherine replied, blotting the tears away with a dishtowel that she held in her hand.

"They didn't tell me what happened to her because it wasn't Lily, but I could see the mark on her head. I don't know if someone used a rock?" Ashley choked out the words.

"Oh, no!" Catherine shrieked.

Who would do that to her? To a child? Catherine thought.

"Lily and Sierra were friends. She was just over here playing with Lily while you were gone," Catherine stated.

I just can't believe it. I mean, I'm relieved it's not our Lily, but oh my, poor Jeanne. Catherine hoped she wasn't talking out loud. Some things needed to be kept private.

"Her husband Paul just left you know? Headed off to serve his time in Afghanistan. Now she's left to deal with her child dying and being five months pregnant too. What will she do? I should go be with her. See if she's alright," Catherine said.

"Mom, she's here at the police station now. She was walking in when we were walking out. I just wanted to let you know what was going on," Ashley replied. "Once we got back to my place, I thought I'd call and let you know. I didn't want you to hear it from someone else."

"No, I understand. Thank you. Will you be coming to my house soon? I have a pot roast in the oven. Should be ready by five this afternoon," Catherine said.

"Sure, yeah. Reece and I will be there for dinner."

"Did Sheriff White say anything else to you about the whereabouts of Lily? Are they still looking for her?"

"No, he hasn't said anything about Lily. Sheriff White did say he pulled his men off the search party when they found the body of Sierra," Ashley replied, sounding defeated.

"Oh? Are they not going to keep looking for Lily?"

"He didn't say," Ashley replied. "We'll talk about this later when we come over for dinner."

"Well, I guess so. I'll see you both a little later then?" Catherine asked.

"Yes, see you soon."

Catherine sat back down in the chair after hanging up the phone. She couldn't shake the news Ashley had told her. Many times, Catherine had felt worried about that little girl walking through those woods by herself to get here and back home again. All these years you wouldn't think someone would do such a thing in a small town.

As much as she didn't want to think it, these things hadn't happened until her son showed up. As a mother, we stand by our children through the good and the bad, but hurting or even killing a child or a person was something she wasn't willing to live with. If her son Dan did this, she couldn't protect him. She wouldn't allow him to get away with this.

Although they are innocent until proven guilty, there was just something off about him since he'd come back into town. Deep down, it was what her gut was telling her. As hard as she fought the feelings, she believed her own son was behind Lily being missing. If that was the case, then he probably had something to do with Sierra's death as well.

42

Dan glanced down at his gas gauge and was thankful he had three-quarters of a tank. He didn't know exactly where he was going, but would figure that out as he drove. Earlier when he left the cabin, he had turned in the opposite direction because he knew he'd be spotted if he went left instead of right.

When the text came in from Rob saying he wanted Dan to meet him at the cabin, he almost texted him back that he was already there, but wouldn't Rob know that already? Dan couldn't make sense of Rob lately. One minute everything was fine and the next he didn't remember a damn thing.

Dan looked in the rearview mirror and saw Lily fast asleep on the backseat, sucking her thumb vigorously. She was probably hungry as he remembered doing the same thing when he was younger. His mom would put cayenne pepper on his thumb right before he'd fall asleep to get him to stop sucking his thumb. He had to agree that it worked. Although, now, he didn't much care for spicy foods.

He turned on the radio, but only loud enough for him to hear. He didn't want to wake up Lily. He was hoping to make it to another state before having to stop somewhere and rest for the night, but he could probably make it another four or five hours.

~ ~

It had just started getting dark when they'd left the cabin and now night had fallen as Dan continued to drive south through West Virginia and into the state of Virginia.

He saw the sign for Lexington and decided they would rest there for the night. He wasn't sure where they would go next. Maybe end up in Georgia somewhere, possibly Florida, which seemed to be a popular state where people went to disappear and start a new life.

He heard Lily stir from the backseat and looked over his shoulder. "Are you hungry?" he asked.

Lily nodded.

He turned back around saw a McDonalds sign up ahead. "Do you like McDonalds?" he asked, looking in the rearview mirror this time.

She nodded again.

"You can talk to me you know. I don't bite," Dan said.

"Well, we do," said the voice in his head.

"Don't start with me," Dan mumbled under his breath.

"Oh, don't cry about it, Danny boy. You fucking pathetic loser. Like you think, you're going to get away with taking her. They'll catch you, you know. You'll screw this up and go right back to that looney bin you came from," the voice replied.

Dan hit the side of his head with the fist of his hand. "Stop it, stop it, stop it," he shouted. "I'm not going back there. You can't make me go back," he started arguing with himself.

"And just how can I make you go back? I'm all in your head. It's you who will put yourself back in that place."

180

"No! I'm not going back there. I won't let them strap those wires to my head again." Dan's eye started to twitch. He yanked the wheel to the right, almost missing the exit.

The jolt knocked Lily over onto her side. Her screams emerged from the backseat as pain soared through Dan's head, causing him to veer off the road and into a guardrail. The car flipped up in the air and over the embankment, crashing down on its hood.

If someone were to drive by a few minutes after the accident, they wouldn't be able to see the car flipped over or the smoke coming from the damaged engine. Without streetlights or highway lights in the surrounding area, it was completely dark.

If anyone was driving by at that particular time of night with the windows up and the radio on, they wouldn't have heard the faint cries of a child trapped inside the overturned car.

Part 2

I take one breath, then two, and
think if only there was peace
within me, only then will I have
peace from you.

Donna M. Zadunajsky

43

Sheriff White called Ashley the following morning; the day after the body of Sierra Miller was found and identified.

There was still no news about Lily. His call was to suggest a nationwide news broadcast about her missing daughter since Lily's body nor any new evidence had been found. He figured with the amount of days that had gone by, he was sure that whoever took her was no longer in the state of Ohio and decided it was time to call in the FBI.

With Reece in her life, Ashley had decided to stay at her apartment instead of at her mother's house. Although she felt guilty for leaving her mother alone while Lily was still missing, she also felt uncomfortable having Reece sleep in the same room since her mother was an old-fashioned woman with religious views.

She finished getting ready and was waiting on Reece in the living room. They had stopped at a consignment store after breakfast yesterday and found some clothes for Reece to wear. When he was released from prison, he had nothing but the shirt on his back. After days of wear, the clothes smelled a little too ripe.

They were headed to the police station to give a broadcast. Ashley made sure that the TV station had a recent photo of Lily to air along with the speech she and her mother would be giving.

Fifteen minutes later, Reece and Ashley pulled into the parking lot. Reece grabbed her hand and squeezed. "Everything will be alright. Someone will see her picture and we'll get her back," Reece reassured.

Ashley nodded, "I hope so."

"We need to stay positive. We'll find her," Reece insisted.

"I'm trying to, but after Sierra…" she paused, choking back her tears. "I'm scared. I don't want her to be the next…" she couldn't say it. She wouldn't say it.

He was right, they needed to stay positive that Lily would be found and they would have her back soon. Once the photo of Lily was broadcast, everyone would see it and call the station. She couldn't let herself think that whoever did this to Sierra would do the same to her Lily. She thought with all the love inside her, she'd know if something had happened to her daughter, wouldn't she? Like her mother said, she'd feel it in her bones if Lily was gone from this world.

Reece leaned over and kissed Ashley gently on the lips. When she slowly pulled away, she looked into his deep blue eyes. "I wish I'd never been without you," Ashley whispered.

Reece smoothed his hand along her cheekbone. "I wish the same. I missed you before you were even gone." He kissed her again before they exited the car.

Although the thought had entered her mind from time to time, *"Then why had he left me the following morning?"*

He met her at the front of the vehicle and they walked hand in hand to the entrance. Once inside, they were escorted to the briefing room where they were to give the speech. Catherine was waiting just outside the door for them.

Ashley hugged her mom. "Thank you for coming."

"I wouldn't miss this. I want to tell Lily how much I love and miss her and that we are thinking about her and looking for her. And I want the person who took her to know that she needs to be home with us."

Ashley nodded before giving her mom another hug and then they all walked through the set of doors to the front where Sheriff White was waiting for them.

Ashley glanced around the crowded room. News stations from Cleveland and Columbus were here and the surrounding cities. NBC, CBS, FOX 8 and ABC were all here to cover the story of her missing daughter.

She never thought she'd be on the news, much less the local news about her daughter being missing. She prayed that it was all a dream, but she knew it wasn't. Then Reece wouldn't be here by her side. He wouldn't be real to her. But he was here with her, and he was looking for his daughter too.

After shaking hands, Sheriff White spoke, "First, I'll go over what happened at the zoo and where we are now. Then, Ashley, I'll have you speak to the public about Lily. The News stations will be showing a photo of your daughter as you are speaking. Then if anyone else wants to speak to the public they can." He cleared his throat. "We have ten minutes to let the world know that we are looking for your daughter. I wish we could have more time than that, but they said that they will air the news clip every hour so that'll do us some good."

Ashley and Catherine both nodded. Reece, who was still holding Ashley's hand, gave it another squeeze and smiled at her. Sheriff White stepped up behind the podium and began his speech:

"Good Morning, I'm Officer Richard White of Craven Falls, Ohio. As of Sunday March 22nd, a little girl by the name of Lily Rose Teodora age 5 was taken from the zoo here in town at approximately 3 p.m. The grandmother, Catherine Teodora, had turned for a few seconds to get some food for the ducks and when she turned back around Lily Rose Teodora was nowhere to be found," he said.

"After searching the area by herself, she then stopped one of the zoo workers and told them about her missing granddaughter. From there, a search was conducted at the zoo, closing all the exits. The local police were contacted and everyone in Craven Falls was informed of the missing girl as well. It has been three days and there have been no reports of the child even being sighted," Sheriff White concluded.

"I have Ms. Ashley Teodora here to speak to the public about her missing daughter and a photo of the child will be broadcast across all cities and states until she is found and brought home safely."

The room lit up with bright flashes and sounds of cameras clicking. Sheriff White raised his hand to signal that he was going to speak again.

"If you have any questions, please save them for the end of our broadcast and we will try to answer them as best as we can," Sheriff White stated.

Ashley's stomach flipped, she swallowed, and took in another small inhale through her nose. When she felt somewhat better, she moved towards the podium. Cameras flashed in her face as she stood frozen in her shoes. She wasn't sure if she could do this. The world was seeing her for the first time as a vulnerable woman who was helpless in the search of her daughter. Maybe they blamed her too. Maybe she was a bad mother for working all the time and getting a better education. Maybe she did deserve to have her daughter taken from her.

She swallowed, bile rising up into her throat. She couldn't get sick now, not in front of all these news people. They'd air it, for sure, on the news for everyone to see.

She jumped when Sheriff White touched her arm. She turned towards him and noticed a concerned look on his face. Both her mother and Reece looked concerned as well.

She turned back towards the front and cleared her throat. She could do this. She had to do this for her Lily Bug. She breathed in through her nose, exhaled and spoke:

"Good Morning, I'm Ashley Teodora and I'm here today to help find my little girl who was taken from me."

Tears sprung instantly into her eyes, she wiped them away and continued with her speech.

"Her name is Lily Rose Teodora, she has long black wavy hair and deep blue eyes. She's at least two-feet tall and weighs thirty-eight pounds. She loves to plant flowers and play with her dolls. She has a pink blanket that she carries with her everywhere."

More tears escaped and ran down her face, but this time she didn't wipe them away.

"Please, if you see her or hear anything, please call your local police department or the phone number on the screen. And to Lily, if you are watching or you can hear me, please come home. Your Grandma Cat and I miss you so much, and we want you home with us Lily Bug."

Ashley stepped away and nearly fell into Reece's open arms, her face buried in his chest as she wept.

Catherine took small hesitant steps over to the wooden podium. She placed one hand on each side of the stand and spoke:

"Hi, Miss Lily, it's your Grandma Cat. I'm so sorry that I wasn't watching you when I should have. I just want you to know that you're not in trouble if you wandered off and got lost. We just want you home with us, safe and sound. Your momma and I miss you so much. We have a wonderful surprise for you when you come home."

Catherine looked over her shoulder and smiled at Reece. He smiled back at her.

"I have lots of flowers that need some planting, but I need your special touch to get them growing. Please, whoever you are, please bring our little girl home."

Catherine choked up on the last few words she said before stepping back and away from the podium.

Sheriff White immediately took the stage as questions were thrown at them. He held up his hand. "We will answer as many questions as we can, but only one at a time," he stated and pointed to a woman with brown hair, wearing a dark blue skirt and matching suit jacket.

"Do you have any leads as to whom might have taken the little girl?" she asked.

"As of right now, we believe it was someone she knows. Someone possibly close to her," Sheriff White answered.

"Did you question the mother's whereabouts at the time of the child's abduction?" A man asked near the back of the room.

"Yes, we did a thorough investigation. Ms. Teodora was nowhere near the victim when the kidnapping took place. She has not only supplied us with proof of where she was, but we also had eyewitnesses that place her at the time indicated."

"Could she still have had something to do with the child's abduction? Maybe planned the whole thing so it would make her look innocent?" A woman from CBS asked.

"No, Ms. Teodora is exonerated from the case. There is no proof that she could've had anything to do with the kidnapping."

"What about other family members? Did you question them as well?"

"As of right now, we cannot locate Rob Mahan who was in a relationship with Ms. Teodora before the time of the abduction. We do have some knowledge that make him a person of interest, but at this time since we cannot locate his whereabouts, there is no information to report; the same goes for Dan Teodora, the Uncle of Lily Rose Teodora. He was said to be visiting in town when the kidnapping happened, but has vanished as well.

"We are still looking into the two men who may or may not be involved in Lily's abduction. That's all the questions we're going to answer for now," Sheriff White said before stepping away and ushering Ashley, Reece, and Catherine out the doors at the back of the room.

44

After cautiously flipping the car over, the firefighters cut Dan out of the car and rushed him to Bluegrass Hospital in Lexington, Virginia.

A passenger in a pick-up saw the overturned car around 6:30 the following morning and had her husband pull over. She stated to the state trooper that after pulling over to the side of the highway they approached the car to see if there was anyone in the vehicle before calling 9-1-1.

Other than Dan, there was no one else in the car, but they did find a child-sized pink blanket; no other bodies were found near or around the accident. A search was issued of the surrounding area, just in case someone else might have been in the car with the driver.

Once the ambulance arrived at the hospital, Dan was rushed into surgery to stop the bleeding in his abdominal region, which seemed to have been caused by the gearshift puncturing his right kidney.

After six hours in the operating room, the surgeon had no other option but to remove the damaged kidney. An MRI scan was then given to rule out any possible head injuries, like a concussion, but to their surprise they found a mass on the Lateral orbitofrontal part of his brain.

The Lateral orbitofrontal manages emotional impulses in socially appropriate ways for productive behaviors including empathy, altruism, and interpretation of facial expressions, which can also cause a person to hear voices that aren't really there. A surgery was scheduled in two days to remove the mass.

Dan remained unconscious in Bluegrass Hospital. The state police found no identification in the car or on Dan's body; he is currently considered a John Doe.

45

Lily had been walking all night in the dark with the moon as her guide. Now the sun was slowly making its way above the hilltops. She entered the woods in front of her, using the shooting beams of light that cut through the budded tree limbs to guide her.

She stopped to rest her hurt leg and feet as she picked berries off a bush and popped them in her mouth. The tangy fruit squirted juice between her teeth when she bit down. She couldn't remember the last time she'd eaten. She picked another one and another until her belly started to hurt, then vomited up all the red berries she'd just eaten.

Tears cascaded from her tired and bloodshot eyes. She wanted to go home, but she didn't know where that was. It'd been so long; at least that's what it felt like to her. Was it days, weeks, or months? She wasn't sure, but she wished someone would find her and take her to her mommy and Grandma Cat.

Lily wiped the snot coming from her nose with the sleeve of her once clean shirt, now caked with dirt and blood. Her belly hurt really bad and she was so exhausted. She needed to find a place to rest, maybe even sleep for a while. She wished she had her *blankie,* but she'd left it in the car when she crawled away from the wreckage.

It had been dark out and she wasn't sure where it was. All she wanted to do was to get away from Uncle Dan who was scaring her to death. He'd been yelling at himself, then they flipped over, and Lily's body hurt all over. She was glad that she was given two arms because her left one hurt like it did last year when she'd broken it.

The day had passed and the night crept in as Lily walked a little further. She saw an old decrepit shed. The boards looked like they were about to fall off with its white paint peeling and edges curling up.

She walked towards it, almost with a bounce in her step. When she approached, she looked up at the door. There didn't seem to be a lock on it, just a rusty old knob and hinges. She grabbed the handle. The door squeaked open as she pulled it towards her. She wrinkled her nose when a musty dingy smell entered her nostrils.

There was a small window near the back, shedding light into the room just enough for her to see. Tools and pots lay on the table that was pushed against the wall. It reminded Lily of Grandma Cat's greenhouse, but much smaller and dirtier. Grandma Cat had lots of plants in hers. This place had no plants.

She looked around and saw a string hanging from the ceiling. Lily slid a wooden stool over from where the table was and carefully climbed up on it.

She pulled the string; a light flickered on, flashed, and went out. She wasn't in total darkness. She still had some light beaming in from the window and would have to make do with what God gave her.

Grandma Cat always talked to God and Jesus. She told Lily that They would protect her from harm and keep her safe. Lily didn't know about that. She didn't think They were keeping her safe since Daddy Rob took her from the zoo or with Uncle Dan. No, she didn't think They were helping her. She'd tell Grandma Cat that when and if she saw her again. Lily tried not thinking about seeing Mommy or Grandma Cat again. It made her sad and sick to her stomach.

Lily made her way around the many obstacles and found an old wadded up blanket in the corner on the floor. She picked it up. It smelled horrible, but she was tired and cold. She laid the blanket on the floor and folded it in half so she could cover herself with it. Her mommy had shown her how to do that.

One time, Mommy and she made a tent in the living room with blankets and pillows. It was like their own fort where they had slept a couple of nights. Then Mommy's back had hurt and said she couldn't lie on the hard floor anymore so they moved the fort to Lily's room.

Lily crawled under the blanket, using her good arm as a pillow and instantly fell asleep. She was so tired that she didn't hear the door squeak open and the footsteps walking towards her.

46

Back in Craven Falls, Reece hadn't heard Ashley yelling his name. It was the frantic arm-waving that she was doing that got his attention. He turned off the lawn mower and walked over to her. After the news report, Ashley and Reece had decided to go to her mom's house. Reece was outside mowing the yard when Ashley came running out of the house.

"What's wrong? Is everything okay? Did something happen to your mother?" Reece asked his eyes looking past her towards the house.

"The phone rang. There was an accident. We have to go," Ashley blurted out, not making any sense to him.

"Wait… what?" he said, grabbing her by the arms to settle her down. "Start over and tell me what happened."

Ashley took in a deep breath and then spoke, "A hospital in Lexington, Virginia, called the number we left on the broadcast. They said there was an accident and that they have a John Doe in the ICU that fits the description of my brother Dan. We have to go there and see what he's done to Lily."

"We don't know that he took her," Reece said.

"He did, I'm sure of it. Besides, why would he be driving through Virginia? Why would he be in such a hurry to leave?"

"I don't know, but we'll find out. What did Sheriff White tell us to do?"

"He said to meet him at the hospital," Ashley replied.

"That's what six or seven hours away? We wouldn't get there until this evening; maybe by nine, the latest."

She nodded, "I don't care. But if we leave now, we'll get there before it's too late at night."

"Alright, let's go. I just need to put this away for your mom and we'll leave," Reece said as he walked away and started pushing the mower towards the shed.

~ ~

It only took six hours to drive to Lexington with Reece behind the wheel. Ashley had spent most of the time staring out the window, while holding onto his hand.

Catherine sat in the backseat with her bag of yarn to crochet more winter hats for the children in need. Something she loved to do for the church.

Reece sat behind the wheel, keeping his mind focused on the highway. He wanted to get there fast, but also safe. There was no reason to drive like a maniac and get into an accident. Then, what good would they be to Lily if she were waiting there for them?

Since he'd found out that he had a daughter, he couldn't stop thinking about her and wished that it weren't under these circumstances.

He wasn't a bad guy. That's not why he ended up in prison. He'd just been at the wrong place at the wrong time. Not to say the judge wasn't being a prick that day, giving him five years without parole for fighting at a bar. It was technically self-defense, and Reece wasn't the kind to back down and let someone kick his ass. Apparently, the judge was having a bad day as well and took it out on him. So, he did his time and now…now he had a chance to start a life with the woman that kept him going while in prison.

He looked over and couldn't help but smile. She was so breathtakingly beautiful sitting there looking out the window. He wanted to spend the rest of his life with her and hoped that she felt the same—that she loved him as much as he loved her. Granted they hadn't really known each other long, but that one passionate night with her grabbed ahold of his heart and wouldn't let go.

He never forgot the morning after their night together. He woke up beside her. She was just as beautiful sleeping as she was awake. He had to fight off the urge to touch her, not wanting to wake her from slumber. He gathered his clothes and left for work, hoping that he'd see her again. He had no phone number to leave behind for her to contact him, nor was he from the area.

He came back that evening and she was gone. No one was at the house to tell him where she'd went and if she'd be back. His heart ached for her, but he'd kept himself busy with odd jobs in town, hoping to run into her again. He'd asked around town, but no one knew her name. He hadn't found her and it took a toll on his heart. He'd then moved on to another town and then another, never seeing her again.

Who would have thought that going to prison, getting out five years later and taking a bus to Craven Falls, would answer all his prayers? That the woman of his dreams was only a bus ride away the whole time. And just think, he was about to move on and leave this town behind?

~ ~

Reece took the next exit, following the Google map to the hospital. He parked the car and killed the engine.

Ashley looked at him and then at her mom. "Let's go bring our baby girl home," she said with a faint smile.

Reece could tell she was trying to be strong, but she didn't have to be around him. He was strong enough for the both of them.

They all climbed out and walked to the main entrance of the hospital. Reece didn't see Sheriff White anywhere in the lobby.

"I'm going to go ask to speak to whoever's in charge of the hospital. See what we can find out about Dan and Lily," Reece said before walking away.

He approached the receptionist's counter where an elderly lady sat talking on the phone. She finished a few seconds later, then spoke to Reece. "How may I assist you?"

"Hi, I received a call from your hospital about a patient here that could be involved in a kidnapping."

The woman's eyes widened, her face registering shock. She swallowed. "I'm not sure what you're saying."

"My name is Reece Garran and I need to talk to someone that's in-charge here. Like the Chief of Staff or someone like that," Reece said.

The woman picked up the phone and punched in a few numbers. He could barely hear her as she whispered into the phone as if afraid that someone would hear her. She placed the phone down in its cradle. "Someone will be right with you," the elderly lady said. "You can wait in the waiting room."

Reece nodded and walked back to where Ashley and Catherine were sitting.

"What did she say?" Ashley asked.

"She called someone in-charge here at the hospital and then said to wait over here until they arrive," Reece replied.

He sat down next to Ashley and wrapped an arm around her, pulling her in close to him. He felt her take in a deep breath, and then exhale. Her body melting into his as he held her tight. Again, he thought about the way they'd found each other, and wished it weren't under these circumstances. He knew there was always a reason why things happened the way they did, and he had no choice but to see where it would take him.

Reece looked up to the sound of high heels clapping against the tile floor and then stop in front of him.

"Mr. Garran?" A woman with long slender legs and brunette hair asked.

"Yes, I'm Mr. Garran," Reece said as he stood.

"Hi, I'm Miss Aria Traverse," she said, holding out her hand. They shook hands and then he introduced Ashley and Catherine.

"Follow me, I have a place where we can talk in private."

47

An hour after the people phoned 9-1-1, Tate drove past as the fire department was flipping a car over. When he saw the make and model of the car, he knew it was Dan's.

He would've been here earlier if he hadn't had to take care of a much-needed problem at the cabin. He wasn't sure when the crash had happened. Otherwise, he would have seen Lily crawling out of the shattered rear window and walk away from the wreckage, but he hadn't.

He turned around and pulled off the side of the road and watched from afar as they pried the front and rear doors open, but they had only pulled out one body, Dan's.

"Serve's you right, you conniving bastard," Tate mumbled.

He got out of his car and walked up to a police officer to find out more information. After asking several questions and learning that there was a pink blanket in the backseat but no other signs of a child, Tate knew that Lily was probably roaming around out there lost and afraid and that he needed to be the one to find her.

He drove a little further down the highway away from the cleanup crew and found a place to stash his van. He had kept his van hidden behind the cabin and used the black convertible that matched Rob's when he drove to and from Craven Falls.

He realized too late that he should have taken Lily when he had the chance, instead of leaving her with that lunatic Dan at the cabin. Now, he had to walk through the hills of fucking Virginia to find her before someone else did.

The thing was, he was good at not only finding people, but manipulating them too. All he had to do was watch them like a hawk and then—*be* them.

He would find Lily, a little girl who had no clue where to go. She was probably slow and stopped a lot. Tate would do whatever he had to and find her.

By the time he entered the woods night had fallen, which made tracking her more difficult. He glanced at his watch, 8:59 p.m. He contemplated on whether to rest for the night or continue to search for her, knowing that she wouldn't be wandering these woods at night. No, she would be too afraid of the woods, the dark. He decided to walk a little further, and then he would rest.

He stopped walking and listened to the sounds around him. He thought for sure that he'd heard a squeak, like a door on rusted hinges, but he wasn't sure. He took cautious steps, trying not to step on any branches. Up ahead in the distance he saw a cabin, but in front of that cabin was an old worn out shed, and going in the shed was Lily.

Once she entered the shed, it wasn't but five minutes, maybe less, when an old man with white hair came out of the cabin and went inside after her.

If she would've looked past the shed, she would've seen a light on in the cabin where someone was living, but she hadn't.

He watched as the old man carried her from the shed and into the house. He crept up to the window and peered inside. The man went into a room, placed Lily on a bed and covered her up, flicking the light off as he left the room.

Tate wasn't sure what he was going to do now. He had his revolver, but in all honesty, he didn't really want to go killing anyone. Hurt them maybe, but not kill them. This whole plan he had in taking Lily hadn't exactly gone his way. All he wanted was to get Ashley to see that he was the right man for her, not Rob.

He would listen each time Rob talked about Ashley. The way he described her made his cock stiffen in his pants. He fantasized about her each morning when he woke up, for almost two years.

After months and months of planning, this Reece guy entered the picture and fucked it all up. No, it wasn't supposed to play out this way at all.

If he were the killing type, Dan would be first on his list. He hoped that he was dead from the wreckage. At least when he saw Dan before the ambulance took him away, he didn't look too good.

Tate saw the blood seeping out from his abdomen, but he didn't care if they saved him or he died, not after what he did. Not after taking Lily and running off with her.

Tate quietly walked away from the window and went around the house to where Lily was sleeping. He tried to lift the window, but it was locked.

"Shit," he swore. What was he going to do now? How was he going to get her out of the house without being seen by this man?

He was sure he could overpower the old man, but he had to come up with a plan. He always had to have a plan. There was still so much more to do before he was ready for Ashley and him to be a family.

48

Ashley stood at the glass sliding door in the ICU, looking at her brother Dan. His left leg was elevated and in a cast. His head was bandaged, covering half his face.

Dan was still unconscious due to the head trauma he had suffered in the car accident, and he was heavily sedated. The doctors also told them about the mass on his brain and that surgery was needed to help save him.

She slid the door open and stepped inside. The hairs on her arms stood straight up. The room felt chillier than the rest of the hospital. She rubbed both hands along her forearms, trying to produce heat, but it didn't seem to work.

She glanced around the enclosed room as she hugged herself. The pale walls and florescent lighting made her feel even more depressed.

The sheets smelled over-bleached as she inhaled, making her nose crinkle from the scent. A metal IV stand with a saline bag stood next to the bed. There was no array of get-well cards or flower arrangements in the room. He had only his family who knew he was in the hospital. Dan hadn't talked about a girlfriend or should she say boyfriend?

She hadn't thought about Rob and wondered if he had left town as well. Did she even care? No, not really. She was glad that he was leaving her alone and not begging for her to come back to him. She couldn't even believe he had denied sleeping with her brother.

She shook her head to dislodge the thoughts entering her mind. She didn't want to think about what had happened. She just wanted to find her daughter and bring her home.

She walked to the side of the bed and peered down at her brother who seemed at peace. Evil thoughts entered her mind and she wanted to strangle him in his sleep or maybe just shake him until he woke up, whichever came first.

She wanted answers. She wanted to know why he took her daughter. Ashley knew he had taken her because she had Lily's pink blanket in the belt loops of her pants.

She held the cotton fabric between her thumb and forefinger and rubbed them together. It still felt soft on her skin, although it was dirty from the wreckage.

Sheriff White had given her the blanket after arriving at the hospital an hour ago. Both Ashley and her mom hugged and cried for their missing Lily. The blanket only proved that Dan had Lily at one time and now she was missing, again. She was out there somewhere alone and afraid, and maybe even hurt.

Reece had been so kind and supportive, but she could tell once she regained her composure that he was just as upset as she was. His jaw was tense. The muscle was twitching near his ear, and you could see the veins in his neck had become enlarged. She wished she could comfort him in the same way he did her, but she wasn't sure how.

Did he hurt like she hurt? He hadn't known about Lily but a few days. Actually, he didn't really know her at all. No home videos could fill the empty spaces of a daughter you never knew you had. He had never played with her or helped take care of her. Was she trying to find negative things about Reece? No, she cared for him; she might even love him. No, she knew she did love him and had always carried a place for him in her heart.

Years ago, she'd tried looking for him. Especially after she'd found out about the baby she was carrying, but he was nowhere to be found. She even went around asking friends that were at the party where she'd met him if they'd seen him, but no one had known whom she was talking about. He was like a ghost who had vanished into thin air.

An alarm pierced through the room, bouncing off the walls around her. She stepped back, away from the bed as several nurses came bursting into the room, pulling the crash cart from the opposite wall towards the bed.

Ashley pressed herself against the glass slider behind her, listening as the doctor called out orders. She watched as the doctor placed the paddles on Dan's chest and his body jolted up off the bed.

Once, twice, three times.

Tears instantly stung Ashley's eyes as she stood trapped inside the room when the doctor called time of death at 10:19 p.m.

49

Catherine looked up when Ashley walked into the lobby down the hall from ICU. She knew right away that something was wrong. It didn't take a scientist to know she'd been crying. Not that Ashley wouldn't be crying over her brother being in the hospital, but what if it had something to do with Lily?

She stood and walked to her daughter. "How is he doing?" Catherine asked. "Did he say anything to you? Did he tell you where Lily is?"

Ashley swallowed before speaking. "Mom he…" she paused, trying to gather the strength to tell her mom. "Mom," Ashley's mouth became dry. "He died," Ashley whispered.

"What?" Catherine gasped. "What are you saying?"

"I was in the room and the next thing I know the alarm is going off and they started working on him, but…" she breathed in and hiccupped a cry.

"He died?" Catherine asked, almost in a whisper.

Ashley nodded.

"Oh, my sweet Jesus, not my baby boy," Catherine said. "Oh, my sweet Jesus."

Catherine began to feel lightheaded. Reece must have noticed and came up beside her, helping her to the chair. Ashley knelt down in front of her, placing her head in her mom's lap.

"Were you able to talk to him?" Reece asked.

"No," Ashley's voice squeaked as she cried. "He was still unconscious while I was in there, and then the alarm sounded. It happened so fast. They tried to revive him, but… but his heart stopped."

Reece smoothed his hand down Ashley's back, moving her hair from the crevice of her neck.

"Mrs. Teodora?" a doctor in a white coat asked as he stood in the doorway.

Both Catherine and Ashley raised their head, "Yes," Catherine spoke.

"I'm sorry, but I have some bad news. I'm afraid your son Daniel has succumbed to his injuries. The head trauma and internal bleeding were just too intensive; he didn't make it, Mrs. Teodora," the doctor said.

As if Catherine hadn't already known what happened, she broke down in her daughter's arms.

"Would you like to have a minute or two with your son before we take him away? Do you have any questions for me?" the doctor asked.

"What happened?" Catherine asked, wiping the tears from her eyes.

"I'm afraid he had a cardiac arrest. We tried everything we could. I'm so sorry for your loss," he said. "If you would please come with me, I'll show you back to his room."

"Mom? Do you want me to come with you?" Ashley asked.

Catherine nodded. "We should all go together and say goodbye," Catherine whimpered.

Reece and Ashley both stood, helping Catherine to her feet. Reece slid his arm around Catherine and helped her down the hall to the room Dan was now resting in; finally, at peace from his inner voices and demons.

A white sheet was pulled up to his chest. The bandage around his head and half of his face was still in-place. The leg that had been elevated was underneath the sheet.

Catherine cried harder as she knelt over the bed, holding Dan's face in her hands and kissing his forehead. She grabbed his hand and squeezed, noticing how cold it had become in such a short time.

"My baby boy," she whispered by his ear. "I will always love you, my son." She kissed him again before standing and hugging Ashley.

Ten minutes later, a nurse came in to take Dan away. Catherine was thankful that Ashley was there and hugged her tighter until she could stand on her own.

Before they climbed into the elevator, Catherine let the hospital know where to send Dan's body. She would have him taken back home and buried beside his father in the Craven Falls cemetery.

Catherine had plots for all her children, although Ashley insisted that she wanted to be cremated when her time came. It was something Catherine and Ashley's father had decided on when the kids were younger.

After leaving the hospital, Reece drove them to the police station where Sheriff White was talking to Chief Clarkson. The Chief informed them that a search was conducted, but nothing was found.

"I'm going to get our team together and widen the search. If the little girl left while it was still dark, she could be further than we expected," Chief Clarkson stated. "We'll find her. She can't be more than a couple of miles; that's if she walked all night. We have only checked the surrounding area near the accident. We'll not only have eyes on the ground, but also in the sky. I have informed the local news stations and they will be broadcasting about the missing girl as well."

Catherine had been sitting in the chair as she listened to them talk. She was exhausted by the drive and wanted nothing more than to rest her weary eyes for a while.

She looked up at the clock on the wall. It was nearly midnight. They wouldn't be doing any searches tonight. They'd wait until first light.

As if the Chief had read her mind he spoke, "We're heading out at 6:00 a.m. It will just be getting light out, and if she's out there, she may be getting hungry and searching for food," Chief Clarkson said.

"We won't stop until we find her. *But*, by chance this man Dan didn't take her, then I'm afraid we're back to square one. I'd like to go and talk to Dan once he wakes up," Sheriff White concluded.

Ashley swallowed. "He passed away about an hour ago. Cardiac arrest," Ashley said.

"Oh," Chief Clarkson paused. "I'm sorry for your loss Mrs. Teodora," Chief Clarkson said as he took off his cowboy hat and placed it over his heart, looking in Catherine's direction.

She hadn't paid him any attention with her head bowed down, looking at her lap.

Reece cleared his throat to break the silence. "I think I saw a hotel about a mile or two down the road when we came into town," Reece said.

"Yes, there's a couple of them," Clarkson replied.

"I'd like to go with the search party in the morning," Ashley informed the two police officers.

"Sure, that's no problem. We have quite a few locals helping in the search," Chief said.

"I'll be there along with you," Reece confirmed.

Catherine wanted to go, but she wasn't sure she'd be able to do the walking. Maybe it'd be best she stayed at the hotel and wait for word that Lily had been found. She still had to call the rest of her family and let them know about Dan. Something she wasn't looking forward to. She was glad that Ashley had talked her into getting a cell phone and programed all of their phone numbers into it.

"Mom, are you ready?" Ashley asked, touching her shoulder.

Catherine lifted her head, her eyes bloodshot and puffy from all the crying she'd done. She nodded and pushed herself off the chair.

When they got to the hotel, Ashley and Reece went together to get a couple of rooms, leaving Catherine to her thoughts which were of Dan.

He'd been a troubled child, but she'd worked with him as often as she could. She believed he had ADHD, but never had him tested. She had even considered him as having bipolar disorder. His learning abilities were at a lower standard than the rest of his peers, and it made him feel left out at times. Kids his age made fun of him because he was slow at learning and they called him names.

When he informed her about joining the Army, she had concerns that they would disqualify him if they had him tested for such disorders. But, since she hadn't taken him when he was a child, there was no record of him even having a learning disability or mental condition, and they apparently didn't check. She blamed herself for not being there for him and getting him the help he apparently needed.

Catherine couldn't shake the sadness that flowed through her body. Of course, she had every right to be sad; her son had just died. He was her last baby born, right after Ashley, but she felt at peace because she knew he'd be with his father again.

50

Lily opened one eye and then the other. It only took a second for her to realize that she wasn't in the dingy old shed that she had found and went to sleep in. No, she was in a bed. Not her bed at her house or even Grandma Cat's. That would mean she was home. She'd actually slept through the night without feeling someone carry her into this place, a house she had no idea where it came from. Was she finally rescued from the nightmare that had taken over her life? She was only five years old and shouldn't ever have to go through something like this.

Sunlight beamed through the faded blue curtains hanging over the square-framed window. She looked around the room. It wasn't the same cabin Daddy Rob or her Uncle Dan had kept her in. It was a different place. There were no pictures on the walls, and it didn't have the fake potted plant she'd had to use as a toilet.

Uncle Dan had driven for a long time on the road and then crashed the car. She'd walked forever when she came upon the old shed, hungry and tired from all the walking she'd done in the heat with no water or food.

The door to the room creaked open and a furry brown spotted dog came walking in. The dog came to the side of the bed and looked up at Lily, then jumped up on the bed. Lily laughed and laughed as the dog licked her face.

"Shadow get off there right now," said the old man. "You don't go jumping up on beds, you know better."

Lily let out another giggle before the dog jumped off the bed and stood next to its owner. She looked up at the old man and pulled the blankets up to hide her face.

"I'm not going to hurt you, little one," the old man said. "Can you tell me your name and where you're from? Can I call your mom or dad?"

Lily peeked over the blanket and up at the old man who stood inside the doorway. His hair was white and cut short above the ears; he wore glasses and had a white mustache. She couldn't see the color of his eyes, not that it mattered.

She pushed herself up and against the headboard of the bed. "You would call my mommy?" she asked with excitement in her voice.

"Yes, is that okay?" the old man asked. "She's not the one you're running from, is she?"

Lily shook her head. "No," she said as happy tears sprung from her eyes. "I want to call my mommy. I want my mommy," she repeated several times.

The old man walked over to the bed and sat down beside her. "It's okay, sweetie. Come with me into the kitchen. Once you've had some breakfast, we'll call your mommy."

Lily nodded in agreement and her belly growled at the mention of food.

"You sound hungry to me," said the old man. He stood and walked to the door, Shadow following right behind him.

Lily slipped out from under the blankets and followed them towards the kitchen. She looked around as they made their way into the other room. "Do you have a bathroom?" Lily asked.

"Down the hall, third door on your left," the man said.

Lily looked down the dark hallway. She could see, but was scared because she hadn't been in this place before and didn't know what to expect. She kept her hand on the wall as she made her way down the hall. She counted as she passed the first room, one. She took a few more steps, two, and then stopped at the third door.

She pushed the door open, light poured out of the room. She saw a sink, tub, and on the opposite side of the room was a toilet. She went inside and closed the door. She went to lock it behind her, but there wasn't a lock on the door. The urge to pee surfaced and she ran quickly to the toilet.

Once she was done, she hurried back down the hallway and followed the sound of bacon sizzling in a pan on the stove. Her stomach growled and her mouth watered.

She walked to the table, pulled out a chair, and climbed up. The dog named Shadow stood next to the old man as if waiting for something to fall to the floor.

"Why did you name your dog Shadow?" Lily asked.

"Well," he said as if he had to think about it for a moment. "One day I was driving back from the grocery store, and I saw this small brown-spotted pup on the side of the road. She was limping on her front paw, you see, so I stopped and picked her up," the old man smiled down at the dog and gave her a piece of bacon. "She had no tags and there was no one around, which there never is on the back roads here in Chesterton County. I began to believe that someone had abandoned her so I took her home. The moment she was able to walk again she followed me everywhere I went. So that's how she got her name, Shadow."

"Shadow," Lily repeated, and the dog looked over her shoulder at Lily.

Lily giggled.

"Do you have any dogs?" the old man asked.

"No, my mommy said that they're a lot of work, and she's too busy with school and work to take care of a dog."

"What about a cat?"

"Nope, Mommy's allergic to them."

"Oh, well, maybe once you get older you can get a dog of your own," the man said as he flipped the bacon over in the pan. The bacon popped and oil splattered on his shirt, and he jumped back a little.

"Did that hurt?" Lily asked.

"No, luckily the shirt caught most of it. It's mostly just a reflex."

"My mommy got burnt once and now she has a scar on her right arm. She said it made a bubble and it popped. It was filled with liquid, but once it popped, it healed and made new skin," Lily said matter-of-factly.

She watched as the old man placed the remaining bacon on a plate and turned off the stove. He placed the plate on the table and brought over another pan filled with scrambled eggs. Her mouth began to water again from the smell. She licked her lips and swallowed.

He scooped some eggs onto her plate and handed her the bacon. "Take what you want and only what you'll eat. I'm not sure how long you've gone without food, but you don't want to eat too fast because you'll make yourself sick," he said.

Lily took two pieces of bacon, placing one on her plate and eating the other. Everything smelled so good.

The old man placed some toast on the table and then took a seat across from her. "Eat slow and you should be fine."

Lily nodded and chewed every bite slowly. Her stomach growled loudly as she chewed and swallowed. She wondered if it would ever stop.

"What's your name?" Lily asked.

"Jed Roberts," he replied.

"What's your name?" he asked.

"My name is Lily Rose Teodora. I'm named Lily because it's my mom's favorite flower and Rose because it's my Grandma Cat's middle name," she said in one breath.

He nodded. "Nice to meet you Lily Rose Teodora."

"Nice to meet you too, Jed," she said with a smile.

When they finished breakfast, Jed placed a plate on the wooden floor for Shadow. Lily helped take her plate to the sink and then sat on the floor next to Shadow, petting her.

"When can I call my mommy?" she asked as someone knocked on the front door.

Jed grabbed a dishtowel, drying off his hands as he walked to the door and opened it.

Lily looked up as the door creaked open and her face froze with fear.

51

Reece washed up and met Ashley downstairs in the hotel. Their plan was to have something to eat and then head to the police station where they would go over the layout of the area. He knew they'd start at the wreckage and then spread out from there.

Last night before falling asleep, he prayed that this would end today. That he will find his daughter and bring her home, even if it took him through the dark hours of the night, he'd find her.

Ashley and Reece said their goodbyes to Catherine and drove towards the station. Ashley assured her mom that she'd call her as soon as they found Lily. Catherine had nodded and hugged them both.

The sun was just starting to rise when they arrived at the wreckage. Reece squeezed Ashley's hand before exiting the car. They walked to where a group of at least forty people from the town were waiting.

After checking in, both Reece and Ashley headed towards the woods. Chief Clarkson handed out walkie-talkies and told everyone to check in every half hour or if they found the missing girl. A photo of Lily was also handed out to the local town's people.

Reece and Ashley stood twelve feet apart, checking behind bushes and huge boulders and calling out Lily's name. There were also a couple of caves that Reece had stumbled upon and checked out, but came up emptyhanded. He'd look over and shake his head at Ashley, letting her know he had found nothing.

They listened as people reported back also emptyhanded. Several hours after starting Ashley told Reece that she needed to rest for a few minutes and find a place to empty her bladder. He helped her into one of the small caves and stood guard outside as she relieved herself.

An hour later, they came to a stream. Reece looked around the area, hoping to find tracks small enough to be human and Lily's size, but found nothing.

The sun rose with each passing hour and was now at high noon. The temperature was warm, but would get hotter as the day passed, reaching the high eighties.

The deeper into the woods they went, the more Reece tried to keep a positive attitude. He was afraid that at night these woods not only were pitch-black, but animal predators came out as well. With Lily being little and having no experience with the wild, he was scared for her. *How would she defend herself? What if she was hurt and couldn't walk?* He didn't want to think negative thoughts, but they seemed to find their own way into his mind.

"Reece, I think I found something," Ashley hollered.

Reece ran over to where Ashley stood and followed her finger to a faded white shed in the distance.

"Let's go," he replied.

Reece led the way through the woods and stopped at the shed. Without opening the door, he walked around the decrepit building and towards the cabin. He figured if she was here, she'd be in the house and not hiding out in a shed. He'd think Lily would want to get help, not hide.

He stopped at the foot of the wooden steps. Ashley hadn't been paying attention and ran into the back of him.

"Sorry," she said.

He led them up the steps and stopped in front of the door. Reece knocked, waiting for someone to answer.

After a few minutes with no response, Reece walked over to the window and peered inside. He could see a table to his right and the kitchen beyond that. A living room with a sofa and a couple of chairs was to the far left, but a wall was blocking what he couldn't see. He figured the bedrooms were on the other side of the house. Other than what he saw, there seemed to be no one at home.

He heard rattling and saw that it was Ashley trying to open the door.

"I think it's either locked or stuck," she said.

"I'm going to go around back and see if I can see inside the other rooms," Reece said. "Stay here."

Ashley nodded.

He stepped off the old rickety porch and went around the side of the house. He looked in the first window he came to, but other than a messy bed and a dark brown dresser, the room was empty. He walked to the next window, but it was higher off the ground, which told him it was probably the bathroom.

He turned the corner of the house and saw another window. He trotted over and peeked inside. He saw a man with white hair lying on the bed with a gag in his mouth and his arms and legs tied.

Reece looked around the room, but didn't see anyone else. He tapped on the window. The old man turned and looked at him, his eyes went wide. Reece wasn't sure if that was from fear or relief.

The man's eyes shifted towards the door as if trying to tell Reece that someone was outside the bedroom door. Reece pulled up on the window, but it was either locked or painted shut. Reece mouthed to the man that he was going around the house, making a circle in the air.

The man nodded.

Sticks and broken branches layered the ground beneath his feet. He tried not to step on anything that would make a sound as he crept around the west side of the house and stopped short of another window.

He lowered his body and peeked in near the bottom. On the floor of the living room sat Lily with her hands tied behind her back and her feet bound, probably so she wouldn't take off running.

His eyes sketched out the rest of the room. He saw a shadow of a man holding something in his outstretched arm. The shadow moved and that's when he saw Ashley.

52

It happened so fast. Ashley was standing with her back to the front door when she was grabbed from behind, a gun pressed against the temple of her head and forced into the house. She couldn't scream because there was a hand over her mouth.

At first she tried to fight, but the man was stronger than her. She hadn't seen his face until he pulled her into the living room and flung her down onto the sofa. She sucked in a quick breath when she saw his face. "Rob," she whispered.

He shook his head.

She looked confused. *If it wasn't Rob then who was he?* Ashley heard a muffled sound and turned towards it. Lily was on the floor, her hands tied behind her back and a gag in her mouth. Ashley reached down and pulled her daughter to her, removing the cloth in her mouth.

"Oh, sweetie," Ashley whispered. "You're okay. Mommy's here now," Ashley said into her daughter's ear as her eyes stared at the man who *supposedly wasn't* Rob. Ashley was really confused...

Ashley sat Lily up, untied the gag from her head and started to untie the rope tethered to her hands.

"Leave the hands and feet tied. I don't want her thinking she can run away from me," Tate said.

"But my arms hurt," cried Lily.

"Fine!" Tate growled. "Just the arms."

Ashley quickly untied Lily's arms. "Who are you, if you're not Rob?" Ashley asked.

"My name is Tate and I've been watching you for quite a long time."

"Do I know you?"

He shook his head.

"Do you mind telling me who you are then and what you want with us?"

He seemed to hesitate for a minute or two before speaking. "After you met your fiancé Rob, he would check himself into a psychiatric facility in Pennsylvania. He would stay anywhere from a few days to two weeks at a time. It was there that he met your brother, Dan Teodora," Tate said, lying. "I was working there as an orderly, helping the nurses restrain the patients when they fought not to get their daily shots. Rob had checked himself in and quickly became friends with Dan. I spent a lot of my time in the social room and would listen to their conversations, learning everything I could about Rob," Tate said with a devious smile on his face. "There was just something about him that intrigued me. When his scheduled time was up, I followed him to Craven Falls and that's when I spotted you," he said with a shit-eating grin on his face. "I spent the last year changing my appearance. My face had to look exactly like Rob's before I did the switch. Our height and body figure were almost identical, so that was an easy fix, but the face took time and many surgeries to get exactly right."

Ashley gasped at his words. *This was all news to her. She would have known if Rob had been mentally ill, wouldn't she? Although he hadn't told her about his check-ins at the mental hospital, she thought back to the many trips he'd made out-of-town, and it all seemed to click together. Everything this Tate guy was saying started to make sense. She didn't know that Dan had ever been in such a place. Her mother had never told her. Had she? No, she'd have remembered something like that. She could see her brother being in a place for his behavioral issues when he was a kid. Would he have done so without their knowing? Yes, she was sure that he wouldn't tell his family that he needed psychiatric help. She wouldn't tell her family either if she felt like she was losing her mind.* Her thoughts raced inside her head, going every which way. There was no way of shutting her brain down once it got started.

"Got you thinking, don't I?" Tate said. "You were always one to analyze everything that went on around you. God forbid that you'd screw up your life like you did getting pregnant with her," he said, pointing at Lily. "What a fucking mistake that was! But after I thought about things. I could actually see myself as a father. Her father," Tate said with a smile.

"You will never be a father to her!" Ashley yelled. "You won't come anywhere near her."

"Tsk, tsk," he said, moving his finger back and forth. "I see that you have already forgotten that I did take her from you once. It was comical if you ask me. The moment your mom turned around, I slid in and grabbed her. It was way too easy. No one around us thought anything of it. After I placed the rag of chloroform over her face, she went limp as if she were a sleeping child. Many other families at the zoo were carrying a child in their arms so one more didn't make me look conspicuous," Tate said with a strong posture, holding his hands loosely behind his back as he paced.

Ashley wrapped her arms around Lily and pulled her in close to her. She needed to protect her and keep her safe. She wasn't there for her when she was taken the first time and she'd be damned if she'd let something happen to her again. *No!* She screamed inside her head. She'd be strong and never let anything happen to her daughter again.

She couldn't believe what she was hearing or seeing. This man looked exactly like Rob, but was nothing like him. He wasn't kind or sweet. Tate was a killer. A kidnapper. How hadn't she'd known the difference between him and Rob? Then a question plagued her. "What after all this time did it take for you to come out? Why be Rob Mahan? Why take over his life?"

He smiled his conniving smile. "Ask Rob," he replied.

"What does Rob have to do with this?" Ashley asked.

"Oh, you'll soon find out."

53

Reece could hear every single word they were saying from his perch by the window. His knees were starting to cramp from being in the kneeling position too long. He took a step to his right and slowly stood up, resting his back against the side of the house.

He lifted a leg and shook it, and did the same to the other leg. He needed to think of a way to get into the house without this Tate guy knowing or hearing him.

The walkie-talkie radio on his hip started to chirp; he placed his palm over it to shield the voice and with his other hand turned the volume down. He took a quick peek inside the house through the window to make sure that Tate hadn't heard the noise and done something to Ashley and Lily. He hadn't.

Reece walked around the side of the house and made a call to Chief Clarkson on the walkie-talkie. He explained where he was and what was happening and that Clarkson should send in an army of men to surround the cabin. He also let the Chief know that Tate was armed with a gun and that he had Ashley and Lily as hostages inside the cabin.

The Chief told him to stay low and to inform him if anything changed before they got there. Reece complied, finished his conversation, and then went back to the window.

Tate had his back towards Ashley, but then turned back around. He was asking her where her boyfriend was.

"I know you didn't come out in these woods by yourself so where is he?" Tate asked.

Lily looked up at her mom as Ashley looked down at her. "Shh, it's okay sweetie. We'll be okay," Ashley reassured Lily. She kissed the top of Lily's head and squeezed her in tighter.

"Tell me where he is?"

"I didn't come with anyone. I came searching for Lily on my own," she said.

He studied her face.

"I got the call that there was an accident and that the man in the crash fit the description of my brother. So, I drove down here and went to the hospital where Dan was taken and also where he died," she choked up. "I overheard the police officer say where the crash had taken place and drove over here to search for my daughter. They said that there was a pink blanket at the scene of the crash. I knew it had to be Lily's *blankie*. That's the truth. I'm not here with anyone else," she lied.

Reece was amazed at her comeback and how believable it sounded. He was sure that she was probably praying that he was coming up with some kind of plan to save them both. But, that was the problem, he didn't have a plan in progress other than the Chief and the cops coming to the house. He hadn't yet figured out how to save Ashley and his daughter.

That's when he heard a loud thump at the other end of the house and knew it had to have been the old man. He looked through the glass window and saw Tate whip his head towards the sound. Then Tate said, "Stay here and don't get any ideas about running."

Once Tate left to go see what was happening in the other room, Reece tapped on the window. Ashley turned around and gave him a smile of relief.

Reece pointed to the door and then made a circular motion with his finger, hoping she understood that the house was being surrounded by Clarkson's men. She nodded and quickly turned back around when Tate came back into the room.

Reece ducked down before Tate could see him. He didn't want to wait for the police to show up, but he didn't have a gun or any kind of weapon on him. Then, he remembered the shed they'd seen when they'd first arrived.

He lowered himself and crawled beneath the window until he was clear of the frame and wouldn't be seen, and then stood. He made his way to the shed, trying not to make any noise by stepping on branches and dried leaves leftover from winter.

The door squeaked as he opened it and cautiously slipped inside. Although there was a little light beaming in through the small window and cracks of the walls, he waited a few seconds for his eyes to adjust before moving around. Once he could see in front of him, he walked to the table and searched for any kind of weapon he could use to save his daughter and the love of his life.

He moved things to the side and lifted empty flowerpots out of his way. He saw a rusted old hammer and grabbed it. There were two screwdrivers; he stuck them in his back pocket. He had to stop and think for a moment what he could use, which reminded him of his days in Afghanistan. There were times he'd had to make his own weapons to defend himself when he was out of ammo. He got good at throwing things like steak knives and butter knives when he was in some of the houses over there.

He was hoping he didn't have to kill anyone, but if it came down to someone hurting the people he loved then he'd have to do what he had to do—end of story.

He stopped moving when he heard footsteps. Lots of footsteps, which meant that the police had finally arrived. He walked to the door and peeked out, not wanting to get himself shot in the process. The moment he stuck his head out the shed door, there was a rifle pointed at his chest.

"It's me, Reece Garran," he said in low voice. "I came with Ashley Teodora to find her daughter."

Chief Clarkson walked up beside the man holding the gun. "He's with us," Chief said, nodding towards Reece. "You almost got yourself shot," Chief Clarkson informed.

"Yeah, I guess I did," Reece replied, filling the Chief in on how many were in the house and where they were located.

Chief Clarkson motioned for them to split up and to keep their eyes open. "We don't want any causalities today, if we can help it. Let's make sure we get those people out of the house safely."

"What do you want me to do?" Reece asked.

"Stay put. We'll take care of this and get them out of the house."

"What?" Reece mumbled. "I need to help get them out."

"I understand your concern, but we have this under control," the Chief replied before walking away and joining his men surrounding the house.

Reece was not going to sit back and wait for something bad to happen. He waited until Chief Clarkson was out of the way and made his way to the back of the house where he'd last seen the old man.

He cautiously looked inside the room and saw the old man lying on the floor. Reece couldn't tell if he was still breathing, but he didn't see any blood and prayed that he was alive.

54

Lily was scared as she leaned into her mommy. Her hands were still sore from the ropes, but also was her arm that she'd hurt in the accident.

She tried to tell this man whose name was Tate when he'd first tied her arms behind her back that it hurt, but he'd told her to shut her trap and be good. When she refused, and whined about her arm hurting, he put a gag in her mouth.

She didn't know if her mommy knew, but she'd seen a man watching them from the outside window, and then he disappeared. She wished he'd come back and save them from this man named Tate.

When Lily was at the other cabin and she'd seen this man Tate for the first time, she could have sworn that he looked exactly like Daddy Rob. That's why, at first, she'd been so comfortable around him, but now that he'd told her mommy how he'd changed himself to look like Daddy Rob—Lily didn't quite understand it all—it explained his moodiness when he was trying to work the cell phone and that he could swim, unlike Daddy Rob who was afraid of the water.

Lily looked up at her mommy, who was looking at Tate. Was her mommy thinking about how she could save them both? Lily hoped so. She wanted to leave this place and go home where she could be with Grandma Cat and her friend Sierra, who lived next door to Grandma Cat through the woods.

Lily wasn't allowed to go in the woods alone, but Sierra's mom let her go by herself and Lily would meet her where the grass edged the trees. They played on Lily's swing set almost every day.

Lily heard a sound outside the window and quickly looked up at *Tate*. He must not have heard the noise because he was still pacing back and forth. Maybe she'd heard him and not something outside.

She watched as this man Tate took a step, and the floor creaked and moaned beneath the weight of his big brown boots. Yes, it was possible that had been the noise she'd heard, but if not she didn't want *Tate* to know about the man outside the window. It made her turn back around and bury her face in her mommy's chest so the bad man named Tate wouldn't know she'd been watching the man outside. *Who was this other man? Was he a bad man too or someone good who could help her and Mommy?*

The room fell silent, which meant that he had stopped pacing the room. A screeching sound pierced her ears, and then someone was talking in a loud-echoed voice.

"Tate Lanier, we have the house surrounded. There is nowhere for you to run. Let the hostages go so we can talk man-to-man." Chief Clarkson demanded.

"Shit," Tate said. "How in the hell did they know I was here? Did you call them?" he said, waving the gun at Ashley.

Ashley shook her head no and pulled Lily in tighter.

Lily sucked in a quick breath and tried to wiggle from her mommy's grasp, but it was as if she had a death grip on her.

"Mommy, you're hurting me," Lily yelped. Ashley loosened her hand, but only a little.

With her ear pressed against her mommy's chest, she could hear and feel the heartbeat pulsing hard and fast. Lily looked up, her mommy's face was still and her eyes were wide with fright. Lily turned back around to where Tate was standing and saw the same man she'd seen outside the window.

He had black wavy hair like hers and when he looked right at her, she froze. She'd spent many hours just staring into the mirror at home and wondered if her daddy had her eyes too. She knew her eyes well and the curve they made when she smiled. The same curve this man had when he smiled at her. But, she knew he wasn't her daddy. Her daddy was dead; at least, that's what her mommy had told her.

The man with long hair quickly slipped his arm around Tate's neck and slowly laid him down on the floor unconscious. Lily beamed with excitement and flipped around so her mom could untie her.

Once her feet were free, Lily stood and ran to the man. "You saved me, you saved me," she hollered, wrapping her arms around his legs. He was her hero.

Reece knelt down and pulled Lily up into his arms, hugging her tight, and then went to Ashley, gathering her into his arms. They held each other until the front door burst open and Chief Clarkson stood in the doorway.

55

Catherine could feel the tightness in her neck from not sleeping well the night before. She'd tried to massage it the best she could, but gave up. Maybe some aspirin would help.

She hadn't brought an extra change of clothes with her, mostly because she'd wanted to get here and see her son. "God rest his soul," she mumbled into the empty room.

Early this morning after Reece and Ashley left to join the search party, she'd gone back to bed.

She ended up falling to sleep, but only to wake a couple of hours later to her stomach growling. She hadn't eaten anything since they'd all left her house the day before.

After a shower and redressing into the clothes she'd worn the day before, she walked to the lobby of the hotel. She asked the hotel manager, who was working the front desk, where they kept food and refreshments.

She walked across the hall, pushed open the door, and entered a room. The smell of aromatic blend of coffee enticed her nose. The small room was filled with tables and chairs. She spotted a counter along the wall which held three coffee pots, a basket of assorted bagels and bread, a basket of fruit, and a chrome toaster.

She grabbed a cup, poured herself some coffee, and added two sugars and cream. She grabbed a spotted banana from the woven basket and sat down next to the window.

The blazing sun was a yellowish-orange that reflected through the window, casting a prism of colors. The warmth helped relax her. She took a sip of her coffee, swallowed, and closed her eyes as the heat ran down the back of her throat.

When she opened her eyes her thoughts went to her daughter, and she wondered how the search was going and if they'd found Lily yet. She had her cell phone on her, but wasn't sure if she should try calling or texting her daughter.

Catherine glanced up at the wall; it was 11:13 a.m. She peeled her banana, took a bite, and chewed. Now that she was eating, she didn't feel very hungry anymore.

She wasn't one to waste food, but she knew if she kept the banana, it would just get rotten. She tossed the rest of the banana in the trash can and went outside.

She had to keep herself busy or she'd go nuts just waiting around to hear any news about Lily. She decided she'd walk into the small town and see what shops they had. She'd find something nice for Lily. She couldn't let herself think that they wouldn't find her.

She saw a bench in a park ahead of her, strolled over, and sat down. She glanced around spotting several dog walkers and a couple lying on a blanket near a huge oak tree. It was a peaceful place to relax and watch the squirrels dig in the grass looking for nuts.

A beautiful butterfly fluttered around her and settled on the arm of the bench. She pulled her cell phone from her purse and called each of her children, starting with the oldest, which was Paul, then Matthew, Kevin, and Saul, letting them know what had happened to Daniel and that she'd keep them each posted on when the funeral would be held.

Ashley was the only one who'd stayed living in Craven Falls. Paul and his wife and two daughters lived in Warren, Ohio, where Paul had his own Veterinarian Clinic.

Matthew and his wife, who had one boy and one girl, lived in Youngstown, Ohio, where Matthew taught eleventh grade American History.

Kevin, who had never married, lived in Akron, Ohio, and had become one of the top surgeons in the Northeast.

Then there was Saul, who was married with three boys, and the only one to move out-of-state. Saul resided in Pasadena, California, where he worked for Paramount Studios.

Catherine had thought about going to see him, but she'd never been on a plane before. Saul said he'd fly her out there and even invited Ashley and Lily to accompany her so she wouldn't be so nervous on the plane, but she hadn't made the time and now she wished she had. Not that she couldn't still fly out and see him. After yesterday, she would definitely put it on her to-do list.

Life is too short to be putting things off. If you continue to wait for the right time, then you'll never do it, she thought.

"Isn't that the truth?" she muttered.

After finishing the last call, she placed her phone back in her purse, wiped the tears from her cheeks, and stood. She walked along the path that connected to the sidewalk.

There were a few cars parked on the street as she walked down the stoned sidewalk. She looked into the window of the first shop. Her eyes sketched over the welcoming display, but didn't see anything worth entering the store for.

The next one was a bakery. A red and white striped awning hung overhead. She strolled past it, not thinking twice about what was inside; although she smelled the yeasty bread baking through the open door. She didn't need to stop and eat the bread and sweets the doctor had told her to stay away from.

She stopped at the next window when she saw a pretty pink dress with lace around the edges displayed on a child mannequin.

A bell rang as she pulled open the door.

"Good morning," said a lady at the register. "Is there something I can help you with?"

"Yes, I'd like to know if you have a size five in the dress displayed in your window?" Catherine asked.

"Well, let me see," the lady sang as she walked from behind the counter to a rack along the opposite wall.

Hangers clanked against the metal pole as the woman checked for the size Catherine wanted.

"Here we go." The slender woman held the dress out for Catherine to see.

Catherine smiled. "Thank you so much," she replied, holding her hand out to grab the hanger. Catherine held out the dress imagining her granddaughter in it. "Ah, she will love this. Do you have any shoes that will match?" Catherine asked.

The clerk's arms flew up in excitement as she clapped her hands in front of her. "Yes, I do. Follow me this way," she chimed.

Catherine followed the overly excited woman to the back of the store where several racks of shoes stood.

"I think these are just darling, don't you think?" the lady asked as she held up a pair of white dress shoes with a pink bow on the top.

Catherine smiled, "They're absolutely beautiful, do you have a size four?" She was ecstatic with joy. After selecting the shoes, they both walked to the counter.

Several minutes later, Catherine walked out of the store with her purchase. She hadn't taken but three steps away from the door when her cell phone rang in her purse. She quickly searched for it and answered the call. "Hello," she said.

"Mom."

"Ashley, is this you? Did you find Lily? Please tell me you have some good news," Catherine prayed.

56

Ashley filled her mother in on what had happened as Reece, Lily, and her rode to the hospital with Chief Clarkson.

Lily had been missing for almost a week, and she looked thinner than she had the last time Ashley had seen her. She kept her daughter close to her the whole ride. She was never going to let her daughter out of her sight again, but then that would cause some conflict when Lily started school in the fall.

When she hung up the phone with her mom, she listened to Reece and Chief Clarkson's conversation about Tate Lanier.

"How many years do you think he'll get for kidnapping?" Reece asked.

"Don't know. It'll all depend on the judge, which is usually the case," Chief Clarkson replied. "He'll be tried in Ohio for the kidnapping of Lily and in Virginia for taking Jed Roberts hostage in his own home."

Ashley thought about her brother Dan and wondered what would have happened with him if he was still alive. Would he be tried too for the kidnapping? Lily was in his custody when he had the car accident. She didn't know, and she would never know because he was dead.

A single tear escaped from her eye and ran down her cheek. Even though he'd taken her daughter, she still loved him as her brother. Her mind slipped back to that day three weeks ago when she saw Dan in bed with Rob or could she have been mistaken and it was really Tate?

She'd have to ask that question the next time she saw Rob. She still couldn't believe that they were, in fact, engaged to be married after everything that had happened. There wasn't going to be a wedding. Would she ever get married?

She glanced up and over at Reece who was sitting in the front seat next to Chief Clarkson. Maybe, if things worked out with Reece. She had thought about him all these years and when he showed up out of the blue, it was like she'd fallen back in love with him. It was that simple.

When Lily started talking at the age of two, she'd asked about her father. Ashley couldn't think what to tell her and just said he had died. She hadn't even told her daughter how, and she hadn't asked.

"Mommy," Lily whispered.

"Yes, sweetie," Ashley replied.

"When can we go home? I want to see Grandma Cat," Lily said with a frown.

"You'll see her soon," Ashley said, knowing that her mom would be waiting at the hospital when they got there. She hadn't wanted to tell Lily, but rather to surprise her. After everything Lily had been through, a surprise was just what she needed to cheer her up.

The men chatted, while Ashley looked out the window watching the houses go by. They were leaving the countryside and driving into the urban part of town now. Soon they'd be at the hospital and then they could go home and start living the rest of their lives. She smiled to herself, praying that Reece would be a part of that life. She'd have to sit down and talk to him about what they were going to do and how they were going to tell Lily that she was his daughter.

She bit the inside of her lip thinking that she shouldn't have told her daughter he had died. Now, Ashley would have to tell her the truth and hope that Lily would be okay with Reece.

A thought from earlier flashed into her mind of Lily running into Reece's arms and saying that he was her hero. A smiled planted itself on her lips. She knew it wouldn't be a problem at all with Lily. Because who wouldn't want a hero as a father.

57

Reece came into the hospital room after talking to the Chief out in the hall. He had received some disturbing news about Tate and didn't know how to tell Ashley.

Every time Reece looked at Ashley, he fell more in love with her and didn't want anything to happen to her or his daughter. He would make sure they were safe.

The Chief ordered an officer to watch over them until they left the following morning to drive back to Ohio. From there, Chief Clarkson had informed Sheriff White to have an officer watch them the moment they arrived home.

Reece knew Ashley would notice the officers and start asking questions, but he wasn't sure how to tell her that Tate had escaped the police and was now out there somewhere roaming the area, probably planning his next move.

The doctor suggested that Lily spend the night in the hospital so she could get fluids and antibiotics. Several CT scans and X-Rays were done on Lily, which found her left arm fractured in two places, and she was being fitted for a cast. Luckily, her right leg was just badly sprained and bruised, and not broken.

Reece stood beside Ashley with his arm around her waist, pulling her in close. He saw Lily looking at them, but she never said a word. She would look at the doctor wrapping her arm with a pink cast, and then look towards them.

When the doctor finished, he left the room, promising that he'd be back later before his shift was over to see how she was doing.

Ashley slid onto the bed next to Lily and put an arm around her, hugging her. Reece sat in one of the two chairs next to the bed.

"Mommy?"

"Yes, Lily Bug," Ashley replied.

"Who is that man?" she whispered, pointing a finger in Reece's direction.

If Lily was trying to be quiet and not have Reece hear what she was asking, she didn't do a very good job at it. Or maybe he just had very good hearing.

Ashley looked at him for a measly three seconds, then looked away. If he was telepathic and could read her mind, he would, but he wasn't and he couldn't. He knew she had to decide right now if she was to tell Lily that he was her father.

"He's a friend of the family," she said without turning and making eye contact with Reece.

The words stung as they pierced his heart. He even held his breath, but only for a second before exhaling. He stood and left the room without saying a word. He needed some space to think, to breathe, because his heart was breaking.

~ ~

When he stepped outside the hospital, he hadn't realized how fast the day had gone by. The sun was making its way down the horizon, but still visible through the trees in front of him.

He spotted a bench a couple hundred feet away in an area designated for smokers and sat down. There was no one in the area smoking; besides he wouldn't care if they were, he'd been around plenty of people in the military and in prison that smoked.

He rested his face in his hands, and then used the heel of his hand to rub his eyes. He was crying. Not bawling like a child or a woman would, but like a man allowing some of the sadness in him to be released.

He only cried after holding things in for a long time, and he needed to release some of the pressure building up inside him. Would he have allowed himself to cry if he'd known someone was watching him? Probably not, but the tears would come eventually.

"Reece, are you all right?" Catherine asked, standing above him.

He quickly sat up, his vision blurred. He wiped his eyes again, this time using his shirt. "Hey, Catherine. I didn't know you were here?" he said, trying to act like nothing happened.

She sat down next to him. "Don't be ashamed to cry. All men do it at some point in their lives. They may say they don't, but I can guarantee that they do when they're alone," Catherine said matter-of-factly.

Reece took a deep inhale through his nose and blew out through his mouth. He did this a couple more times before opening up to Catherine. He knew she was someone special. Someone he could talk to openly without being judged.

"I wanted her to tell Lily that I was her father, but I know it wasn't the right time or place."

"No, probably not, but you both need to sit down and figure out what's going to happen next. I can see it in your face how much you love her," Catherine said, smiling.

"But… but with Ashley you have to understand that she has raised this child on her own. She's head-strong and will put up a fight if she knows she's right," Catherine continued. "She reminds me so much of her father. He did things his way, and God forbid if you proved him wrong. But I loved him more than I have ever loved anyone," she smiled. "Don't get me wrong, I love my children, but as a man, as my husband, he was my world, my life. That kind of love doesn't happen very often. You'll have to grab on with both hands and hold on tight," she nodded. "There'll be hard times and good times, but if you love her as much as I believe you do, then don't give up on her."

"Mom, what are you two talking about?" Ashley questioned with her arms folded in front of her as she stopped behind them.

Reece's head shot up when he heard her voice. To him she sounded like an angel. He could listen to her talk forever if she let him.

Catherine turned towards Ashley. "Talking to him like you should be doing, young lady. Now sit down here and get things straightened out while I go and spend some time with my beautiful granddaughter." Catherine stood and winked at Reece before giving her daughter a hug and asking what room Lily was in.

Ashley stood shell-shocked by what her mother had just said before finally taking a seat next to Reece. "I'm… I'm sorry for what I said upstairs. I just…" she paused. "It wasn't the right time to tell her."

"When will the right time be?" Reece asked, looking at Ashley.

Her mouth hung open, and then closed. "I'm just afraid, that's all."

"Afraid of what? That I'll leave you? That I won't be there for you and Lily?" he questioned. "I love you, Ashley. I have loved you since the first day I set my eyes on you at that party. And I'll love you until the day I die," he said, his eyes glistening.

Ashley swallowed, "You love me? But you don't even know me?"

"I want to, if you'll let me in. I want to know everything about you. What you like to eat, drink, wear, even your favorite color. Tell me everything. Let me be a part of your life and Lily's," he said in one long breath.

A tear slid down her face, he wiped it away with his thumb and held her chin in his hand. "I need you to survive. You are my world. If I hadn't have met you all those years ago, I would've never survived prison."

"Yes, you would have," she said, knowingly. "You've made it this far without me in your life."

"But I don't want to live the rest of my life without you. Don't you understand? My heart would be empty— you make it whole."

With those words came tears from both of their eyes, and he kissed her and she kissed him back. The kiss was so intense, like a fire burning deep inside him. His heart beat faster with each kiss, and their breathing was like two rhythmic hearts beating as one. If he could make love to her right now, he would.

When the kissing slowed, she leaned her forehead against his. "I love you," he said.

Ashley pulled back, looking into his eyes. She smiled, "I love you too," she said with a small laugh. "I love you too, Reece."

They hugged, laughed, and kissed each other. "There's so much we need to talk about. We need to know what and how we're going to tell Lily. She's been through a lot and this will just confuse her."

"How so?" he asked.

Ashley looked away and down at the ground. She whispered, "I told her you were dead."

Reece didn't say a word. He just sat there thinking about what she'd just said. *Why would she tell Lily he was dead? Had she even gone looking for him?* So many questions plagued him.

"I went asking my friends and other people at the party, but they said they didn't know who you were. I didn't think I'd ever see you again," she explained.

He sat quiet, trying to figure out what to say. Then pain struck his chest and he started gasping for air.

"Please, say something," Ashley said, turning to face him. That's when she saw the blood on his shirt, coming from a small area on his chest, which grew larger.

She looked up at his face and into his eyes. He was trying to say something to her as he gasped for more air, but she couldn't make-out what he was saying.

"Run, Ashley," he stuttered in a haggard voice. Reece looked at her, then his eyes moved beyond her shoulder and grew wide. She turned to see what he was looking at when a hand came from behind her and all went black...

58

Ashley woke hours later, her head foggy. She rubbed her eyes, trying to get rid of the blurriness. When she could see, she looked around the room.

She was lying on an old ratty cot, her hands restrained behind her back. She tried to move her feet, but they were also tied together at the ankle.

Ashley swallowed and her throat was parched. She licked her lips, which were becoming dry and cracked. The floor creaked somewhere in front of her. She looked in the direction, but it was too dark to see whom or what it was. Then, the person spoke as he came closer to her.

"Ashley, so glad you're awake. Was getting a little worried that I might have given you too much chlorophyll," Tate said as he knelt down in front of her.

"Why are you doing this to me?" she asked.

"I told you at the cabin. I love you and we are meant to be a family—you, Lily, and me. It breaks my heart that you don't feel the same. What does a man have to do to get a woman to see what she means to him?" Tate asked.

Her temper was rising inside her, which didn't happen often, not if she could help it. "Let me put it to you this way, asshole. Women don't appreciate being taken against their will or hog-tied as if they are about to be cooked over an open fire," she hissed.

He laughed loud and deep as he stood and made his way to a chair by the wall and sat down. "Maybe if *you* women listened better and did what you were told, then maybe *we* men wouldn't have to do things in such a way that you dislike!"

She clearly wasn't going to lie here and argue with this deranged man, but it wasn't like she could go anywhere. Then it hit her like a bag of bricks, Reece was bleeding! He'd been shot and killed by this man sitting in front of her. Would he kill her too? She wasn't sure. Would he go through all this trouble and kidnap her if he was going to kill her? No, she didn't think so. He would have finished her off at the hospital like he did Reece.

Tears rolled down her face as she thought about what Tate had done. She needed to figure out how she was going to get out of this mess. Lily needed her and she wasn't going to stop until she was with her again. Ashley made that promise to her daughter, and she'd die keeping it.

"In the whole time I've been watching you, I honestly can't remember ever seeing you cry. This man Reece must mean everything to you," he said.

"I'm crying for him and for my daughter," Ashley stated.

He clapped. "Well, *la de da* for them, Miss Ashley. They should be so honored. Maybe, I'll just take away the one thing they cherish most—you."

"You won't kill me," Ashley spat. "You need me, otherwise you wouldn't have gone through all this trouble taking me."

"You think so, do you?"

"What good would come out of it if you did kill me? What would be the point?"

"True, true. But everyone can be replaced," Tate said as he leaned forward, resting his elbows on his knees.

"I agree, but you've gone through too much to stop now. You've had your face changed to look like Rob. It wouldn't make sense to give it all up."

"Ah, now I know why I love you so much and must have you to myself. You are a brilliant woman with a strong will. It makes my dick hard just thinking about it," he laughed.

Ashley turned her head in disgust. There was no way in hell she was going to do anything with him. He could eat dog shit before she would touch him or ever love him.

"Ashley Teodora. You are a fighter; I'll give you that much. But you'll see in time that I'm the right man for you. I can make you happy and please you in many ways. When your mother's guard is down, I will take Lily and bring her here, and then we can be a family. Won't that be wonderful?" Tate asked.

Ashley laughed out loud at his statement when she should be agreeing with him. Especially, if it was her one and only chance to freedom. She could make him believe that she would do whatever he wanted if it would get her out of these restraints.

Acidic bile rose from her stomach, up her esophagus, and entered her mouth. The thought of doing what he wanted her to do made her want to vomit, and in that second, she did. It projected away from the cot and made a splashing sound as it hit the floor. The smell hit her nose and she threw up again and again, until there was nothing left inside her.

Tate jumped to his feet, "Now look what you've gone and done. If you think for one minute I'm going to clean that up, you are so mistaken." He opened the door and stomped out of the room.

Light hit her face. She blinked several times until she could see without spots. Another door stood maybe fifty or more feet away, and she prayed it was the front door. Now all she needed to do was to figure out a way to get out of these ropes and away from this lunatic who called himself a man.

59

Catherine stood beside the bed, peering down at Reece who'd just gotten out of surgery. He was in and out of consciousness as she held his hand, praying to God that he would pull through. That he'd be given another chance at life. Her daughter deserved a good man like him. Someone that would love her the way she needed to be loved.

Reece was found when a volunteer went outside to have a cigarette. She found him on the bench with a blood-soaked shirt, unresponsive, and immediately ran inside for help.

Catherine had asked the woman who'd found him about Ashley being there, but she replied that he was alone on the bench. No one else was around.

When Chief Clarkson showed up at the hospital, he told Catherine in private that Tate had escaped and most likely had shot Reece and taken Ashley hostage. At this time, there were no leads to the whereabouts of Ashley, but she was most likely still alive.

Lily kept asking where her mom was, but Catherine couldn't find it in her heart to tell Lily that the bad man they had just rescued her from had taken her mother. Although she knew the excuses would only work so long before she'd have to tell Lily the truth.

~ ~

The following morning, Catherine's body ached from sleeping on the foldout bed that the nurse had brought in for her. She'd slept in Lily's room that night, afraid to leave her side after everything that had happened.

Catherine was there when Reece woke up. Even though he had been shot and gone through surgery, he was eager to get out of bed and help find Ashley, but the doctor objected and said it would be a bad idea if he tried to do any kind of activity too soon and would not release him.

Chief Clarkson came back to the hospital to check on Reece and to see how Lily was holding up. He talked to Catherine and reassured her that everything was being done to find her daughter and bring her back safely.

There were no new leads, but they were checking his fingerprints in the database to see if they could find anything with his name on it. Loans, mortgages, prior felonies, they would find it. Whatever he'd done in the past would come up, and they would do everything in their power to track him down.

After hearing what the Chief had to say, Catherine needed some time to herself. She took the elevator down to the first floor, stopped at the directory, and walked down the hall until she stood in the doorway of the hospital chapel.

She needed time with God. She needed to pray in His home and feel Him beside her. She needed guidance and positive thinking to get her through this. She needed her higher power to answer all her questions and to relieve her worries. She needed her faith to believe that Ashley was still alive and that she would be brought back to her family.

Catherine jumped when her cell phone rang. She'd forgotten that she had it on her and felt ashamed that it was not on vibrate when she was in the presence of Jesus Christ.

She hit the side to mute the sound and looked at the caller ID. It was her son Paul. She'd forgotten all about Daniel's funeral arrangements.

She stood and left the Chapel, making her way to the exit. The sliding doors sprung open as she walked forward and cleared the entranceway, standing off to the side.

By the time she'd gotten outside the hospital, her phone stopped vibrating. She pressed the callback button and placed the phone to her ear. She needed to tell Paul the truth about what was happening and that Ashley had been kidnapped. He would know what to do, and he could call his brothers and tell them for her. She wasn't sure how much longer her old heart could handle all this pressure and stress that she'd endured this past week.

When she finished talking to Paul, she had the notion to call Ashley's phone. It rang several times until she heard Ashley's voice come on the line. She gasped, but soon realized that it was a recorded message and not her daughter.

Tears formed around her eyes. She couldn't hold it together much longer, but she had to for Lily's sake. She had to be strong if not for herself, but for all her children. They needed her and counted on her to be there for them.

She looked up to the heavens and closed her eyes. "Please bring her back to us, to me. Don't take another child of mine. I couldn't bare it if You did," she whispered as the tears ran down her face.

60

Tate paced the kitchen of the old abandoned cabin, stirring up dust. He hadn't slept much the night before, as he needed to think about how he was going to get Lily out of the hospital. He knew there'd be police surrounding the building, which would make it harder for him to get inside.

He stopped in his tracks and snapped his fingers at the same time. An idea was forming inside his mind.

A brilliant idea.

He'd have to go back to the hospital, looking like someone who worked there, but there was only one problem—he was sure they, meaning the police, would be checking everyone that went in and out of the building. He'd need a pair of scrubs and someone's ID that looked almost like him.

This was going to be harder than he thought. Sure, the idea was great until you factored in the reality of the problem. He'd have to get around the security at the hospital. Then it hit him; he'd use his ID from the psychiatric hospital.

Tate walked over to the room that Ashley was in and opened the door. He stepped back as the smell of puke plunged into his nose. He'd have to open the window a crack to air the room out.

After opening the window, he knelt down next to Ashley. "Hey, I need to go out for a little bit. I'm going to make sure your restraints are good and tight so you don't get any ideas about running away." She didn't respond. "I'm going to go get *our* Lily," he said with a smile.

Tate leaned over her and tugged on the rope tied around her wrists and then checked the one around her feet. They were secure and should hold her until he returned with Lily.

He kissed her lips and left the room, locking it as he went. He was hoping he wouldn't be gone long, but also knew not to trust Ashley. She'd find a way out if she had the chance, and that was something he wouldn't give her.

Once in the van, Tate crawled into the back searching for an extra pair of clothes. Some places made you wear the exact same uniforms as everyone else, but some hospitals or medical facilities weren't as strict. He kept an extra pair of scrubs in the van, in case something happened and he needed a change of clothes.

After changing, he started the engine and drove in the direction of the hospital. He wasn't more than forty-five minutes from the building. The joke was on them because he knew that the cops wouldn't know to look so close to where Ashley had been taken. Nope, they weren't that smart.

As he made his way down the hills of Virginia, he passed an old abandoned building. He had thought about using that spot to hide out in, but when he found the cabin a little further down the road, he changed his mind.

Tate pulled into the parking lot and drove to the rear of the building. He parked in the far corner, keeping the hospital in his view. He wanted to scope out the scenery before making his way inside. He needed to know what the police were doing so he wouldn't get caught.

Most of the cops weren't looking at the people entering or exiting the hospital. He needed to find an exit near his vehicle so he and Lily could escape without being seen.

A door opened and a man in a white coat walked out, got in a red corvette, and drove away. Tate started the van and drove over to the empty spot. There was a sign posted with the name Dr. Elwood Scotsdalle on it. Tate backed into the spot and turned off the ignition.

Once at the backdoor, he hesitated for a second then turned the knob; it was locked. "Shit," he mumbled.

With his hand still on the knob, the door flew open. He took a couple of steps back, but quickly regained his composure before a tall tanned brunette came from behind the door.

"Oh, I'm so sorry. I didn't know you were there. Are you okay?" she asked.

Tate stood tall, grabbing the door before she let go of it. "I'm fine," he growled.

The brunette stepped back as if she had been punched in the gut, and then quickly jogged to her car as she looked over her shoulder.

Tate opened the door and stepped inside. He was standing in a long hallway with florescent lights mounted to the ceiling. The door clicked shut behind him as he moved forward. He'd have to remember his surroundings so he didn't get lost after getting Lily.

He came to the first door that said Janitor's Closet on it. He kept walking. The next door said Electrical Room. When he arrived at the end of the hallway, there were two more doors. The one to his right said Exit, and the one to his left said Pump Room, he opened the door to the right.

It was as if he'd entered a busy highway except with people instead of cars. Nurses and doctors walked through the hall, carrying charts with their heads down. Names were being paged over the intercom. As he looked around the room, he realized he'd entered the emergency area.

The *whoosh* of automatic doors between hospital wings made him turn his head. Several officers stood outside the doors, checking everyone who walked in.

He turned, walked along the wall, and waited for a nurse behind the counter to leave the computer so he could search for Lily's room number. He had to pretend to be busy until she finally strolled away.

He tapped a few keys and plugged in the information needed to find Lily. She had been admitted into the children's ward. There would be too many people up there, and he would have a hard time sneaking her out, more or less getting into the ward without being noticed.

He clicked out of the screen and stood, spotting a white doctor's coat on a chair beside him. He causally gripped the coat in his hand, walked away, and into the first men's restroom he saw.

Once in the stall, he slipped his arms through the sleeves, flushed the toilet, and opened the door. He was relieved when he saw no one in the restroom. Tate quickly opened the door and made his way to the elevator.

He hadn't thought about it until he was in the elevator that he should've grabbed someone's chart so he didn't look exposed.

The moment he stepped inside, he could smell the astringent scent of hand sanitizer with a mixture of body odor. His stomach muscles clenched, then relaxed. The last thing he needed to do was cause a scene in the elevator.

The metallic hum of machinery creaked and groaned before coming to a stop on the fifth floor. The elevator *chimed* and the metal doors slowly opened.

Tate quickly stepped off the elevator, breathing fresh air into his lungs. He stopped at the nurse's station and scanned the room. He grabbed a chart from the counter and walked towards Lily's room.

He stood at the closed door, one hand on the cold metal knob. He turned it to the right, pushed the door open, and went inside.

61

Ashley sat on the edge of the bed, rubbing her wrists. She had waited a few minutes after Tate left before sitting up. She removed the switchblade from her pocket to cut the rope that bound her hands.

She had found the knife in the pocket of her brother's jeans at the hospital. His clothes were inside a bag sitting on the table in his room. After the staff told her Dan had died, she took the bag and went through his things before throwing them away in the garbage. She had hoped to find something that would help her find Lily, but had only found the switchblade, which ultimately came in handy.

She bent over, sliced the rope between her feet and stood. She had heard Tate lock the door behind him before leaving, but she also heard him open the window.

She stood at the window, opened it all the way, and looked over the windowsill. There was at least a four-to-five-foot drop to the ground.

The ground was flat near the house, but if you looked beyond, there was a drop-off. Not a drop-off like a cliff, but a hill with a slight slant to it and many trees. As she searched beyond the trees, she could see the bottom where jagged rocks stuck out of the ground.

Her body shivered as she stood there thinking of what could go wrong. Although the distance from the window to the ground wasn't far, she'd have to be careful not to get hurt by twisting her ankle or worse, falling down the hill.

She boosted herself up, ducked her head under the window, and sat on the edge looking down at the ground. After positioning her hands, she twisted her legs around and dropped to the ground. Her foot slipped on the wet leaves, causing her to slide. It happened so fast as she grabbed at branches to stop herself, but they weren't rooted into the ground.

Her arms flailed around until she was able to grab ahold of a sapling and jolted to a stop, yanking her shoulder out of its socket. The pain was excruciating as Ashley took in a deep breath and exhaled. Tears wanted to surface, but she fought them back, refusing to let fear, defeat, and possibly dying and never seeing everyone she loved ever again, get to her.

Once her feet were supported, she slowly climbed up the hill. With the use of one arm, she rested against the outer shell of the house, taking in slow and easy breaths. She unzipped the pocket of her jacket and took out her phone. The screen was cracked, but she still had power to the phone. She had felt the vibration earlier and prayed that Tate hadn't heard it, but then again, he would have taken it if he had.

She noticed a message and listened to it. It was from her mother. As hard as she tried to fight them back, tears instantly surfaced and slid down her face, but she couldn't waste any more time standing there crying. She hit the call button and started through the woods until she came across a dirt road.

In that time, she hadn't heard the phone ringing and looked at it. No bars, which meant she had no reception. "Shit," she mumbled.

She glanced left and then right, not sure which way to go. She decided to go right, praying that she was going the correct way. She continued to check the phone for reception, but there was no change.

Fifteen minutes later, she saw another road up ahead. She quickened her pace, almost jogging, until her feet met the pavement. She glanced up and down the road, but saw no one.

Ashley looked up at the sky. Now that she was through the woods, she could see the sun and it was at high noon. She had no idea where she was or even if she was still in the state of Virginia.

She pulled her phone from her jacket and checked the time. It was 12:05 p.m. and she saw one bar appear at the top of her screen.

It was the first time she'd felt hope since she had awakened in the cabin after Tate had taken her.

She quickly hit speed dial, which was set to her mom's phone. She placed it to her ear and waited.

"Hello," Catherine answered.

"Mom? Mom is it really you?" Ashley said into the receiver, as more tears escaped, leaving a wet trail down her dirt-covered face.

"Ashley, oh, my God. Thank you, sweet Jesus," Catherine sang into the phone. "I called your phone wanting to hear your voice, and here I am listening to your sweet, sweet voice. I know that sounds silly, but I just needed to hear it."

"Mom, you need to calm down and stop rambling," Ashley said. "I'm somewhere in the woods. Tate shot and killed Reece and took me, but I don't know where I am."

"Reece isn't dead," Catherine replied. "He was found outside. It must have been shortly after you were taken. He was rushed into surgery, but he's doing good. He's alive and well."

Ashley's heart swelled with relief and she smiled. Reece was alive and doing well. "Mom, can you have Chief Clarkson track my phone and find out where I am?"

"Oh, that's a great idea. Hold on a minute," Catherine said.

Ashley could hear voices, but wasn't sure whom they belonged to. She looked towards her left when she heard what sounded like a car coming. She stepped forward, waving her good arm in the air as she held the phone to her ear with the other.

The car swerved around her as the person honked the horn. "Hey, asshole," she screamed at the taillights as she flicked the driver off.

"Ashley, watch your mouth," Catherine hissed.

"Sorry, Mom, but this car came down the road and I tried to get their attention, but they flew right by me as if I wasn't even here," Ashley replied. She could hear a shuffling on the other end of the phone and then a man's voice.

"Do you see any signs around you that might tell you where you're at?" Chief Clarkson asked.

Ashley looked around her, going in circles. She saw something up ahead and started jogging towards it. When she was close enough to see it clearly, she felt defeated once again. The sign was white with the number and words spelling Speed Limit 55.

Ashley kept on walking until she went around a curve in the road and saw a sign with an arrow pointing to her right. The sign had a letter H on it, which meant there was a hospital up ahead in five miles. She wasn't sure which hospital it was, but it was some place she could get help and that's all that mattered.

"Chief, there's something else I need to tell you," she said before walking in the direction of the hospital.

62

Reece slowly raised the bed to an upright position. If he moved too quickly, the pain in his chest would tell him to take it easy. He looked over at the door as it opened and Catherine walked in, closing the door behind her.

"Oh, good you're up," Catherine chimed.

"Yeah, just trying to get comfortable. I never cared much for these beds," Reece said, wincing as he lay back against the pillow.

Catherine filled him in on the conversation she'd just had with Ashley and Chief Clarkson. "I wanted to let you know before I bring Lily in here. The Chief thinks it's a great idea to hide her in your room, and of course, I'll stay with her," Catherine said.

"Oh, thank God she's alright," Reece said, feeling relieved. "I hated myself for not protecting her out there from him, again"

"That's not your fault. You didn't know he was going to shoot you and take Ashley," she said.

"No, not exactly, but I did know that he had escaped and was out there somewhere. I knew he'd come after her."

"How did you know he'd escaped? When did you find out?" Catherine questioned.

"Right after we brought Lily to the hospital. Chief Clarkson told me out in the hall when Ashley was in the room with Lily. He said that Tate knocked out the officer at the scene and grabbed his gun. Told the officer to take the handcuffs off his wrists or he'd shoot him and take them off himself. Tate then ran off into the woods after handcuffing the cop to his patrol car."

"Why didn't you tell us?"

"And what, make Ashley panic? No, I swore to protect her and Lily. And I'll do whatever I can to make sure no one hurts you either," Reece said.

Catherine smiled. "Well, I do appreciate your bravery, but right now, you're not in any shape to save anyone. Lily doesn't know her mom was taken, that's why I needed to speak to you first," Catherine concluded and walked back to the door.

Reece watched from the bed as Catherine opened the door and brought Chief Clarkson into the room.

"Hey, Chief," Reece said.

"How you feeling there, Reece?" the Chief asked.

"Could be better, but otherwise, I'm doing good," Reece replied. "So, tell me what's happening?"

Chief Clarkson spoke as he sat down in the chair next to the bed. "Ashley was able to escape after Tate left her at some cabin in the woods and is on her way to a hospital. My guys are tracking her phone as we speak," Chief stated. "We're not sure what hospital she's headed to. And we don't know where this Tate guy stashed her. She could be hundreds of miles away from here, but what we do know is that he's headed to this hospital to kidnap Lily and take her to her mom."

Reece swallowed, and then his jaw went tight. His blood started to boil under his skin. He was stuck in a bed with a bullet hole in his chest. There was nothing he could do to save either of the two girls he loved with all his heart. He wanted to get out of the bed and help find her, but he knew he wouldn't get far.

"Lily and Catherine are going to stay in here with you, while we go catch this son of a bitch and put him away for life," Chief Clarkson said. "There will also be two Officers outside your door until we get him. No one in and no one out unless it's a doctor or a nurse."

"Thanks Chief," Reece said.

"It's my job to protect. He brought trouble to my town, and now I'm going to bring trouble to him," Chief Clarkson said with a smirk on his face. He stood and walked out the door.

A second later, Lily and Catherine came into the room. Catherine closed the door behind her, locking it.

Lily looked up at Reece. "What happened to you?" she asked. "Did you get a boo-boo too?"

Reece chuckled before answering her question. "I guess you could say that."

Lily walked over to the bed, climbed up on the chair, and sat next to him on the bed. She smiled her toothless grin at him. "Mommy isn't here right now. Do you know where she went?" she asked.

His eyes left Lily's face and looked at Catherine. He had no idea how to answer that. "Well, I wish I knew the answer to that, but I don't know where she went either."

"Are you going to be my new daddy?" she asked without missing a beat. "I saw you hugging Mommy."

Reece's face turned crimson. He already knew the answer to that question, but wasn't sure that he should tell her. Besides, it wasn't the question of *"Was he's going to be her new daddy?"* but that *"He was her daddy!"*

"Well, are you?" she persisted.

"I guess that would be up to your mom, but…" he paused, thinking about what he should say. Ashley had told Lily that he had died. What would Ashley say if he told Lily the truth? Would Ashley be mad, even angry with him? Would she tell him to leave and never come back again? He hoped not because he didn't want to leave either of them.

"You have eyes like mine," Lily whispered. "And we have the same color hair. My mommy has blonde hair so I must've gotten my hair color from my daddy. Did you know my daddy?" she asked.

"Yes, I know him very well," he replied before catching his mistake.

Lily squinted her eyes, looking confused by his words, and then they grew wide with excitement.

"You mean *knew* him very well," Catherine chimed in.

"You knew my daddy?" Lily squealed.

Reece threw his head back and looked up at the ceiling. *He wanted her to know who he was, but Catherine changed everything. Deep down in his heart he wanted her to know. He wanted to hold her like a father should and teach her things like a father does,* he thought to himself.

Catherine spoke. "Kids are resilient, you know. They bounce back faster than most older people. Their minds are still learning, but they know things we don't bother to take the time to see," she said with a smile, nodding as if it was a secret code.

Reece looked from Catherine to Lily and said the words he'd wanted to say since he first saw her. He swallowed. "Lily your dad's not dead," he whispered softly. "I'm your real dad, and I'm not going anywhere."

Lily, who was looking down at the blanket, raised her head. He didn't know how she would react, but in that split second, he found out. Lily threw herself onto his chest and hugged him.

Although, he was struck with pain from her hitting his chest, he didn't care and wrapped his arms around her. She was his little girl, and he loved her more than she knew.

"I knew you weren't really dead. I just knew it," Lily mumbled into the pillow beside Reece's head, then sat up and looked from him to Grandma Cat. "My mommy's going to owe me a dollar for this little fib she told," Lily said in a stern voice. "We're not supposed to tell fibs. Right, Grandma Cat?"

"Right, Lily Bug. God doesn't like it when people lie," Catherine replied.

"Maybe she wanted to surprise you?" Reece suggested.

Lily turned her head to the side as if thinking about what he'd just said, and then smiled. "I love surprises. Do you like surprises, Daddy?" Lily asked.

Reece felt his heart flutter inside when he heard the words come out of her mouth. He hadn't remembered feeling this way in his whole life, except when he first met Ashley six years ago. "I love surprises, especially if they're as good as this one."

Lily smiled and clapped her hands together as she bounced up and down on the bed. "I can't wait for Mommy to get here so we can surprise her."

"Me either," Reece smiled as he pulled Lily into a hug again. He looked at Catherine through Lily's hair. She stood near the window with a smile on her face, but, at the same time, she looked worried and if he had to guess why, he knew she was thinking about Ashley. He was worried about her too.

63

Tate stood in complete darkness. He reached for the wall to his right and felt for the switch. When he found it, he flicked it on and saw nine officers with loaded guns aimed at him.

"Tate, it's a pleasure to see you again," said the officer Tate had handcuffed to his patrol car yesterday.

"Shit," Tate mumbled, knowing he wouldn't get out of this place alive. It was either do or die. He reached back with his right hand and found the knob. He had to be fast if he wanted to get out of here. He also didn't think the cops would start shooting him in a hospital with other people around. He turned the knob, pulled the door open, and turned to bolt out the door. He ran right into the face of Chief Clarkson.

"Well, looky who we have here," said Chief Clarkson, wearing a shit-eating grin on his face.

Before Tate could even think about doing anything, his arms were twisted behind his back and he heard the clicking of the cuffs being put around his wrists.

"This time you're not getting away from me," Chief Clarkson said.

Tate held his head high even though he'd been defeated. He couldn't think for the life of him how they'd known he was even here.

"I know what you're thinking. You're thinking, how'd I know you'd be coming to the hospital? Well, let's just say you're not as smart as you think you are," Clarkson said, smiling.

This time Tate went willingly with Chief Clarkson and the team of officers. They escorted Tate out of the hospital and into an armored police van, where several of the officers accompanying him, climbed into back.

~ ~

Several hours passed as Tate sat in a holding cell. No one had come to see him, which was fine with him. He didn't care one way or another.

His arms folded behind his head. He lay on his back, looking up at the cement ceiling above. He was in deep thought, still amazed how the Chief knew he'd be at the hospital. There was only one way, and that would mean Reece was alive, but still, they wouldn't have known he'd come back to the hospital at that time and try to kidnap Lily again.

Even if Ashley had escaped, she had no means of contacting them. Besides, he knew the restraints were good and tight. So how did they know?

Tate was jolted out of his thoughts with a *clanking* sound on the bars of his cell.

"Get up," the officer said. "Chief Clarkson wants you in the interrogation room."

Tate sat up on the cot and looked at the officer whose hair was freshly buzzed to his scalp. He didn't look much older than Tate himself.

"Come on, let's go," the officer demanded.

Tate swung his legs over the bed, placed his feet on the floor and stood. He walked up to the iron bars, looking the officer in the eyes. Tate stood several inches taller than the man in front of him, and he was much more muscular.

"Turn around, face the wall, and place your hands behind your back."

Tate complied as the officer placed restraints around his wrists and ankles before unlocking the cell door. The officer grabbed Tate's arm and led him down the hall and through two sets of doors.

Once in the interrogation room, the officer chained Tate to a steel ring in the table, making sure that he wouldn't get away.

Tate watched as the officer walked to the door, opened it, and left. Minutes ticked by, then the door opened and the same officer walked in followed by Chief Clarkson.

His eyes followed the Chief as he sat down in front of him. His fellow officer stood tall by the door with his arms crossed on his chest.

"How's your cell?" Chief Clarkson asked. "Hope you don't get too cozy in there. You won't be staying long. Nope, I got a nice place for you to stay for the rest of your life, if I get my way," Clarkson grinned.

Tate sat staring the Chief in the face. He didn't have anything to say to him. He didn't care what the Chief said or what he wanted to do to him. He'd find a way to escape again. They weren't that smart the first time so why did they think they would be this time around?

"No comment?" asked the Chief.

Tate said nothing.

"Well, if you want to play the game that way, then suit yourself. But you're not getting any special treatment from me. What I want to know is, where is Ashley? What did you do with her?" Chief Clarkson asked as he tapped the table with his forefinger.

So, she hadn't escaped after all, Tate thought.

64

Ashley hiked for what seemed like hours in the heat of the day. She wasn't sure what time it was because shortly after calling her mom and talking to Chief Clarkson, she'd lost the connection again, which meant there was no way they could track her phone and find her.

She came upon the next sign that said she had one mile left before she reached the hospital. Her feet and legs were beginning to hurt as she hiked down another hill. She was dehydrated and felt as if she would collapse. There had been no other cars coming up or down the mountain, which seemed unusual to her.

She stopped at the side of the road and stretched her legs. She stayed bent over for a few minutes before standing back up. She pulled one leg back against her butt, and did the same to the other leg. Once she finished stretching, she started walking again.

When she came around the next bend in the road, she saw a large building up ahead. "Thank God," she mumbled. She started jogging, and then her legs took off into a frantic run.

When she reached the driveway of the building, she realized it was no longer a functioning facility. Bricks were faded and falling from the walls. Weeds grew through the cracks of the parking lot and the grass stood a foot tall, which meant it hadn't been mowed in some time. She was lost somewhere in the middle of only *God knows where.*

No water.

No people.

No cars.

No nothing.

She was defeated. There was no way she'd be able to continue walking. She needed to rest. She was beyond exhausted.

She walked towards the entrance of the decrepit building, which had once been a hospital. Most of the windows were shattered into millions of pieces. Her shoes crunched on the broken glass as she pulled open the door and walked inside.

Chairs were overturned, dry-rotted, and faded. Moldy and mildewed magazines and newspapers were scattered around the lobby.

She walked to the counter, which she assumed was once the receptionist desk and looked for a phone. When she found one, part of her filled with joy, but she knew not to get her hopes up. There probably hadn't been any power in this place for years.

She lifted the receiver, no dial tone. Her heart sank, but she had to search the rest of this place. She spotted a sign on the wall, showing stairs. She dropped the phone and limped with her aching feet in the direction of the stairs.

From the corner of her eye, she saw a water fountain and hurried over to it. She pressed the button, and brown dirty water came spurting out. She kept the button pressed in until the water seemed to get clearer, and after a minute or two, she bent over and started drinking.

Ashley couldn't ever remember drinking anything this fast before. No matter how bad it tasted, she kept slurping and swallowing gulps of water down her parched throat.

When she couldn't drink any more, she rested against the wall and slid down to the floor. It felt good to rest. To sit and not have to use any of her body parts that ached so much. She let her sluggish body fall to the floor and closed her eyes.

65

"What do you mean he won't tell you where she's being held?" Reece shouted. "We have to find her and soon. She's been gone for two days now, and she may not have any water or food to survive on."

"I understand your concern, but we're doing everything we can. He won't tell us anything," Chief Clarkson replied. "What do you want me to do, hold him down and torture him?"

"If you won't, I will," Reece shouted again.

"You know I can't let you do that. We'll find her."

"Don't make promises you can't keep," Reece said through gritted teeth.

Reece watched as Chief Clarkson stood not making any effort to calm him down; besides there was nothing the Chief could do or say to make Reece see things his way.

Reece, at times, couldn't control his temper, but only when it came to situations like this. He was never abusive towards people who didn't deserve it. Like the guy he brutally punched and ended up in prison over. But that had been a very different circumstance. The asshole had been beating his girlfriend up in the parking lot of a bar, and Reece wasn't going to stand by and let him.

In the end, the man deserved everything he'd gotten, except for death, considering that the woman was so badly beaten she'd died before the ambulance arrived at the scene.

"Reece, if you're feeling up to it, I'd like for you to come down to the station and talk to Tate, but only talk," Chief Clarkson said in a stern voice. "You can't lay one finger on him. Do you understand?" Chief pointed a finger in Reece's direction.

Reece complied, although inside he really did want to kill Tate.

"Once the doctor releases you, I'll drive you down to the station."

Just as Reece agreed, the door to the room opened and in walked Dr. Richard Durk.

"How are you feeling today?"

"Better. When do you think I'll be able to get out of here?" Reece asked.

"Well, I understand you're eager to leave, but let me take a look at your wound first to make sure it looks good, and there's no infection around the area," Dr. Durk replied.

After examining the gunshot wound, Dr. Durk considered releasing Reece from the hospital, but only under instructions not to overdo it or he could rip the stitches out and end up back in the emergency room.

Reece nodded in agreement and signed his name on the form.

Chief Clarkson and Reece rode to the station with sirens blaring, neither speaking a word. Reece had enough going on in his head to keep him occupied.

Once they parked and exited the car, Reece was on the Chief's heels the moment they entered the police station. They walked straight to the interrogation room where Tate was waiting for them. Chief Clarkson had made a call on their way to the station, requesting that Tate be there when they arrived.

Chief Clarkson nodded at the officers standing outside the room. He opened the door and walked to a set of chairs opposite of Tate. Reece followed behind, but stood by the table looking down at Tate, just as he looked up.

"Well, holyyy shit," Tate said as he stretched out the word. "Look what the cat dragged in. I guess my aim was a little off," Tate snorted. "Coulda' sworn I killed ya'. Too bad though, 'cause Ashley thinks you're dead," he smirked. "Speaking of Ashley, I bet you want to know where she's being held. Is that why the Chief here had to bring you along?" Tate nodded in the direction of Chief Clarkson. "Guess he didn't think he was doing a good enough job and had to go get some backup."

"Shut your pie hole, you worthless piece of shit," Chief Clarkson shouted.

Tate chuckled. "I'm not afraid of you; you donut-eating fat fuck. You'll never find her."

"Yes, we will, and you're going to tell us where she's at," Reece demanded.

Tate chuckled again, but this time it was much louder and deeper. People down the hall could probably hear his evil laugh.

Reece slammed his fist on the table, which jarred his chest causing sharp pain to jolt through his body. He gritted his teeth together, hoping that Tate didn't see his pain. That would just give him one more thing to honor himself and laugh about. "I'm going to ask you one more time, **where is Ashley**?"

"Oh, wouldn't you like to know? You want to be her savior, her knight in shining armor. Well, don't hold your breath because you'll probably be dead before I tell you where she's at."

Reece's anger was rising, but he was in no shape to fight this asshole, but he wouldn't have to because Tate was chained to the table. If Chief Clarkson would let him, he'd pound Tate's head in until he couldn't see out of both his eyes. "I bet you've been wondering how we knew you'd be at the hospital?"

Tate stopped laughing.

"That got your attention, didn't it?" Reece had to make sure Tate was listening and that he'd take Reece seriously. "You never checked the pockets of Ashley's jacket, did you?"

Tate sat still, his gaze settled on the table in front of him as if he was picturing what Reece was saying.

Reece knew he was thinking now. Tate hadn't known, of course, that Ashley had her phone in her pocket and that she'd escaped and called for help. When they tried to track her phone, they'd found nothing, which to him meant her phone had either died or she was out there somewhere in the hills of Virginia where there wasn't any reception. God, he prayed she was okay, and that nothing bad had happened to her.

"Cat got your tongue?" Reece asked.

"She had a cell phone in her pocket," Tate mumbled.

"Yes, she did," Reece replied.

Tate smiled, "You can't track the phone."

"Why would you say that?"

"You wouldn't be in here if you could. She's so deep in the woods you'll never locate her."

"You think she's still in the cabin you left her in?" Reece asked.

The expression on Tate's face changed to horror. "There's no way she escaped," Tate replied.

"Why's that?" Chief Clarkson interrupted.

"Her feet and hands are tied together. I locked her in the room and even if she did get out, she wouldn't know where to go," Tate said in a panicked tone. "You're making this up, just so I tell you where she's being held. Well, I'm not talking!" Tate yelled.

Reece was so close to finding her, but wasn't sure how much more he could get out of the guy. He had to at least get the vicinity of where she was located. The rest they'd figure out once they were out there looking for her. They just needed a direction to start looking.

Reece pulled the chair out from the table and sat down. He placed his hands on the tops of his legs, just to keep them from wanting to choke the shit out of the asshole sitting across from him.

He decided to tell Tate what they knew and see what his face would tell them. If he could get something, anything from him; that's all that mattered.

"I'm going to start with what we know and you tell me if I'm hot or cold. If we find her, I'll make sure that Chief Clarkson here doesn't recommend you get life-in-prison with the whacked-out killers already behind bars waiting for a new piece of ass," Reece lied. He could tell Tate was thinking it over.

Tate nodded.

"Great, now we're getting somewhere. So we know she was in a cabin all tied up. We know for a fact that she got out of the cabin and found a road, but after our brief talk on the phone, the last thing she said was that there was a sign for a hospital up ahead in five miles," Chief Clarkson said. "My question is, where is this hospital?"

"It's not a hospital anymore," Tate replied. "I honestly don't give a shit what you promise me. I'm not telling you anymore." Tate leaned forward, looking Reece in the eye. "If I can't have her, no one will," he said, smiling.

66

She heard the faint sound of a voice calling her name. "Ashley, you have to get up. They can't find you if you don't help them," the voice whispered.

Ashley opened her eyes, blinking until the light didn't hurt her eyes any longer. She wasn't sure how long she'd been out on the cold tile floor of this abandoned building.

She lifted herself to a sitting position, her arm shooting lightning bolts of pain as she rested her back flat against the wall. She looked around the room for the person talking to her, but saw no one. She had been dreaming the whole thing. Hearing voices was the first sign that you were going crazy.

She coughed into her hand, her lung piercing with pain. Her body was getting weak, and she would eventually get sick from not eating and die. She didn't want to die in this place. She didn't want to think of never seeing her Lily Bug again.

She pulled herself to her feet, using the water fountain, and bent over for a drink. She pressed the button and brown rusty water gushed out again. Last time she waited a few minutes for the water to clear, but there was no change in the water. The sight repulsed her, but she had to drink something.

She swallowed the last gulp of water in her mouth and stood. She wasn't sure if it were night or day, but since there was still light outside so she assumed it was the same day, just later.

She walked to the door that led to the stairwell and opened it. She climbed down the two sets of stairs before she was at the bottom. A single door stood to the right of her; she opened it and looked down the hall.

To her left she saw a sign on the wall: **Cafeteria.** She walked into the room, peering into the expansive glass cases that lined the wall. She saw something that was once a sandwich, but was now a moldy greenish gray color.

It wasn't until she slid the glass window open to the case that she smelled the cured meats and sour bread. She was no longer hungry and even if she were, she knew she wouldn't be able to keep it down if she ate the sandwich.

She walked around the counter and in through the swinging metal doors to the kitchen. Cooking bowls and utensils were spewed everywhere. Dirty dishes were piled high in the sink with years of baked food on them. Were the people who worked here in a hurry to leave? She wasn't sure, but it did seem strange to leave the kitchen the way it was. Usually when a place closes, they take everything with them.

Ashley walked around the kitchen, and then went back through the double doors that led to the cafeteria. She wasn't sure how long this place hadn't been in use, but by what she saw, it must have been at least a year or two.

She strolled back to the hall, walked back towards the stairs, climbed the two flights, but decided to check out the floor above it. Once in the hallway, she spotted a nurse's station and walked over to see if there was something she could use. Although the phone downstairs didn't work, she still felt the need to check all three phones she had just stumbled upon. There were no dial tones.

She sat down on one of the old swivel chairs, feeling more defeated than she was when she arrived here earlier. She needed to think of a way to find help and get out of this place. She needed to get back to Lily and her mother, but she also wanted to be with Reece.

In the past week since he'd been back in her life, she'd felt more for him than she had for Rob who she was about to marry. Sure, she had loved Rob, but she couldn't swear on a bible that she was in love with him. And if she weren't in love with him, then why was she about to marry him? The only answer that came to her was *stability*.

She had Lily to raise and dating other men hadn't turned out the way she'd hoped. In fact, they were horrible dates who seemed to only want to get her into bed. The couple of guys whom she had met while in college may have been keepers, but ran the other way when she told them about having a daughter. She guessed that they didn't want to deal with having a girlfriend who had a child by another man. She shook her head, "Their loss, not mine," she mumbled into the empty area.

She took in a deep weighted breath and then exhaled. "It's time to go," said the voice she swore she'd heard earlier. She glanced around the room, feeling crazier by the second.

She stood and climbed back down to the lobby floor and went outside. There was no use staying in a place where she wasn't going to get any help.

She walked out of the parking lot and onto the road, heading in the direction she hoped would be her savior.

The good thing was, she had no more hills to climb up or go down. She turned and looked back the way she'd come, smiled, and then turned back around and continued to walk.

She heard a noise coming over the mountain top, then spotted a helicopter in the distance, flying towards her. She stopped, looked up, and then started waving her arms in the air.

67

Chief Clarkson had jumped on the phone and called in a helicopter to help search the area for Ashley. The computer had shown six abandoned buildings in a hundred-mile radius from where they were.

The chopper circled around the first building, but saw no movement. Officers on the ground went on searching, but found nothing and moved to the next location. By the fifth building, Reece was feeling defeated that he'd never find the love of his life again.

The helicopter flew over the mountain, searching through the trees. The pilot guided the chopper towards the road; close enough to see it wind itself around the mountain like the game of mousetrap.

Up ahead, the last building on their list appeared. Reece spotted something moving. "Can you get closer to that part of the building?"

The pilot dipped down and flew towards the deserted lot. "Over there," Reece shouted as he pointed towards the road. "Do you see it?" he asked Chief Clarkson.

"Ya'," Clarkson replied.

As they flew towards the road, Reece saw someone waving their hands in the air. No, not just someone. It was Ashley. He smiled, his heart beating fast in his chest. He'd found her, and she was alive and well.

The chopper landed in the vacant lot. Reece couldn't wait to get out of the small-enclosed aircraft and hold her. The second he was okayed to exit, he flew out of the chopper, tripping over his own two feet, and nearly falling on his face. He regained his footing and ran to her as she ran to him, his chest aching.

His arms circled around her and picked her up in the air. "Oh, my God, it's so good to see your beautiful face again," Reece whispered into her ear. He pulled back, holding her face in his hands. He looked at her and kissed her lips ever so gently. His stomach felt as if butterflies were fluttering around inside.

"I'm sorry it took so long to find you," Reece said.

"How did you find me? How did you know where to look?"

"Tate," he replied. "When you called your mom, we planted several police officers in Lily's room. You should've seen the look on his face. Hell, I wish I'd seen it. Chief Clarkson said he thought Tate crapped his pants when he opened the door to escape and ran right into the Chief."

They walked back to the helicopter and climbed in. Reece nodded at the pilot. They lifted into the air and flew back in the direction of town.

Reece couldn't take his eyes off her since they'd rescued her. He made her a promise right then and there that he'd never let her out of his sight. Well, actually he wouldn't let anything happen to her again. He would risk his life for her all over again if he had to. She was worth that and so much more, and he'd spend the rest of his life showing her what she meant to him.

Once they landed at the station, Ashley was taken to the hospital for a quick observation and to have her arm reset. Then Reece would take her to go see her daughter who was waiting with Catherine at the hotel in town.

Reece watched as Ashley lay in the hospital bed, waiting for the doctor to come in and check her over. "I love you," he said.

She turned to him, smiling and laughing at the same time. "I love you too. I would like for us to sit down and talk about things once we get back to Ohio," she said.

"I would like that," he replied as he reached out and squeezed her hand in his. He brought her hand to his lips, kissing it as he looked into her eyes. He couldn't ever remember looking into eyes as beautiful as hers.

68

Lily sat on her knees in the chair as she looked out the window of the hotel room, which faced the parking lot. Grandma Cat had told her to watch for her mommy and daddy. Lily didn't want to tell Grandma Cat that she was scared she wouldn't ever see her mommy again because it had been a long time since she'd seen her last.

She hadn't been told that something might have happened to her mommy, but she knew grown-ups didn't always tell their kids the truth. One time, she caught her mommy telling a little white lie about not having Lily's favorite snack in the pantry, but when her mom left the room, she went and checked. Maybe her mommy didn't see it or maybe she just didn't want Lily having the snack before dinner, but still her mommy should have told her instead of lying to her.

One lonely tear escaped and rolled down her face. She quickly wiped it away before Grandma Cat saw it. She tried to be a strong little girl for Grandma Cat, but she really missed her mommy. She prayed nothing bad had happened to her and made a promise never to disobey her again.

No, of course, she didn't want to have something happen to her mommy. Mostly, because she was the only mommy Lily would ever have. Don't get Lily wrong, she loved Grandma Cat, but every little girl needed their mommy to be around and help them with things and to love them, no matter what. Sure, little boys needed their mommies too, but she didn't think it was as much as girls did.

Lily couldn't wait to see Sierra when she got back to Grandma Cat's house. She had so much to tell her. Lily twisted her lips to each side and thought real hard about what she would tell her friend. She didn't want to tell her anything that would scare her and possibly give her nightmares.

Lily jumped from her thoughts when she heard a car door shut and sat up on her knees to see out the window. She could only see part of the car because of a tree planted in her view of the other half of the car. Reece stood at the front of the car looking to his right. He reached his arm out and walked towards the stairs with her mommy, holding her hand.

Lily squealed in excitement as she climbed down off the chair and ran to the door. She tried to open it, but there was a chain latched to the door from the wall. "Grandma Cat, help me, please," she hollered. "Mommy's coming. Mommy's coming."

Lily was jumping up and down waiting for the door to open so she could run out and hug her mommy.

"Hold your horses, Lily," Catherine demanded. "I'm not as fast on my feet these days."

Once the chain was unhooked, Lily walked out the door, looked up and down both sides of the hall until she saw her mommy. In the distance, Lily could see her mommy holding daddy's hand. That made Lily happy.

Lily screamed, "Mommy, Mommy," as she ran down the hall. Ashley slowly knelt down when Lily came running. Lily collapsed into Ashley's open arms that wrapped around her and squeezed her tight.

"Oh, Lily Bug, it's so good to see you," Ashley whispered. "I'm so sorry I was away from you for so long. I promise to never leave you again."

Lily smiled at the words, but also knew that her mommy couldn't be around every second of the day, although, the thought was nice.

Grandma Cat was waiting in the doorway when they walked back down the hall to the room. She looked sad to Lily, but then she smiled the moment they got closer.

"Ash," Grandma Cat whimpered.

"Hi, Mama," Ashley replied as they hugged each other.

Lily watched them both as if they could communicate without speaking to one another. This made her think of Sierra again because sometimes when they played together they didn't always have to say what was on their minds. It was like each of them knew what the other was thinking.

Lily sat on her mommy's lap looking from one person to the next, while Grandma Cat and Daddy talked about the bad man named Tate who had kidnapped Lily. Reece said that they could go back to Ohio as soon as tomorrow, and that Chief Clarkson would keep in contact with them about the ongoing case. Her mom looked relieved by what Reece had said. Grandma Cat, on the other hand, just looked exhausted.

Lily glanced at the clock by the bed; it was after 2:00 p.m., way passed Grandma Cat's naptime. Thinking of naps, Lily yawned and snuggled into the crevice of her mom's arm and closed her eyes.

69

The following evening when they all arrived at Catherine's house, there was a note attached to her door.

> *Catherine,*
> *Please call me when you get in. I would like to speak with Lily about Sierra.*
> *Karen Miller*

Catherine swallowed; she'd forgotten all about Sierra Miller being found in the river. After everything that had happened, she didn't know if she could bear to tell Lily about her friend being killed. Lily would be devastated by the news of her friend.

Catherine quickly slipped the note in her sweater pocket, but not fast enough for Ashley not to see what she did.

"Mom, is everything okay?" Ashley asked.

"What? Yes, everything is fine."

"Then what was on the note you placed in your pocket?"

Catherine closed her eyes and then opened them as she pulled the piece of paper from her pocket and handed it over to her daughter.

Ashley read the note and then handed it back. "What would she have to talk to Lily about?"

"Well, they were close friends. They played together every day she was here. Sometimes Sierra would even sleepover," Catherine replied. "Lily needs to know what happened to her."

Ashley sighed, "I know, but she's just been through so much lately. Can't this wait until tomorrow?"

Catherine nodded, "Of course." She turned and with shaky hands, she unlocked the front door. The sweet smell of her home entered her nostrils and made her smile. She relaxed her shoulders and walked inside, placing her purse on the bench by the door. She was exhausted from the drive and couldn't wait to sleep in her own bed tonight. There was just something about the comfort and feel of your own bed and pillow that nothing could replace.

She walked into the kitchen and grabbed a glass from the strainer in the sink, filling it with water from the tap. She opened the cabinet to her right and took out a bottle of Tylenol as her hand began to shake again. She popped three in her mouth and swallowed.

She hadn't heard Ashley come into the room when she turned around, leaned against the counter, and saw Ashley staring at her.

"Mom, are you okay? You seem, I don't know, not yourself."

Catherine took another sip of water, using both hands to hold the glass steady. "I'm just tired, that's all."

"Are you sure that's it? You look a little paler than usual."

"I'm fine, really I am," Catherine said. She felt relieved that Ashley hadn't seen the way her hands shook. She hadn't told Ashley or anyone about what the doctor had told her. She needed to take better care of herself. She didn't need to develop diabetes, although it was common at her age to have low or even high blood sugar levels.

"Do you want us to stay here with you tonight?" Ashley asked.

Catherine hadn't thought about being alone in her own house when they arrived back. *Did she want to be alone? Did she feel safe here without anyone? She'd been on her own for years now; why would she suddenly feel insecure about being by herself?* The sad part was, she knew the answer to those questions.

With everything that had happened in the past week, she was emotionally, mentally, and physically exhausted. Period!

Catherine stepped away from the counter and her legs went weak. She reached for the island counter in front of her to keep herself from falling.

"Mom," Ashley shrieked as she reached out to hold her mom up. "Reece, can you come in the kitchen, please," Ashley hollered.

Reece flew into the room as if the place was on fire. "What's wrong?" he asked.

"My mom isn't feeling well and I need help getting her to the sofa in the living room."

"Sure," he replied as he slipped his arm around Catherine and helped her to the couch in the next room.

"Thank you," Catherine said. "I just need to rest is all." She fluffed up the pillow on the sofa before placing her head on it. She instantly fell into a deep sleep.

~ ~

Hours later when she woke, she found the house dark and an afghan over her. She lifted herself to a sitting position, waiting for the dizziness to dissipate. She couldn't remember the last time she'd eaten something and was scared to walk to the kitchen by herself. *What if she fell and no one found her for days? Was Ashley even here with her? Did they stay the night upstairs?* There was no way she'd be able to make it up the stairs on her own.

She stood, using the arm of the sofa to help her up. When she felt like she could stand on her own, she let go and walked to the window in the foyer. Catherine peeked out into the driveway and saw her daughter's SUV sitting there, along with her own car.

Relief ran over her as she dropped the curtain in her hand and walked into the kitchen for a glass of water. She sat down at the table, her eyes catching sight of the container filled with cookies that her and Lily had made earlier that week.

With so much trauma going on, it was the first time she'd thought of Daniel since they arrived home. A vision of him came to her. Daniel was sitting across from her eating his favorite cookies and drinking milk.

He seemed cheerful, more like himself than the old Daniel she'd once known. She wished she'd told him that she was proud that he was doing so well in the Army and that he'd made time to come see her. Even if she came second after seeing his boyfriend.

She shook her head in disgust. Not because he was gay, but because it had been with Ashley's fiancé. She had always known he was different. When she cleaned his room when he was young, she had found magazines of naked men under his bed. She hadn't mentioned anything to him, of course. She wanted him to have his privacy; besides, he would have been furious even though her intentions hadn't been to snoop through his things while he was at school.

She took another sip of her water and placed the glass back down on the table. Her heart sped up when she heard the floorboards creak. Her eyes swept over the dark and empty kitchen around her. She heard another creak, but this time it was in the next room. The same room she'd just been sleeping in.

"Mom, are you in here?" Ashley asked as she flipped the switch on the wall. Light illuminated the room.

Catherine blinked several times until her eyes adjusted to the light.

"Why are you sitting here in the dark?" Ashley asked.

"Didn't feel like turning the light on; besides, sometimes it's nice to sit in the dark. It helps you to relax and clear your mind of the day's troubles," Catherine replied.

"Do you want me to make you some tea or coffee?" Ashley asked.

"Tea sounds nice," she replied.

Catherine watched as Ashley walked to the sink, filled the teakettle, placed it on the stove, and ignited the burner. She then gathered two teacups and placed them on the counter by the stove. She removed the lid on a red ceramic container in front of her and took out two herbal tea bags.

Ten minutes later, the kettle began to whistle and she turned the dial off. She poured the hot water in the cups and carried them to the table. Once she placed the sugar on the table, she sat down across from her mother.

"I'm so proud of you," Catherine said as she looked over her teacup.

Ashley smiled. "Thanks mom that means a lot to hear you say that."

"I didn't get a chance to say it to Daniel before he died," Catherine said, choking back her tears. "I don't want to wait anymore to say how I feel. Life is too short. We don't know when it's our time, you know?"

Ashley nodded.

"So, if you love Reece, tell him, be with him because I can tell he feels nothing but love and respect for you. A man that loves that deep and true, should be held onto with both hands," Catherine stated with a smile. "Don't let him get away. Lily needs her father around her. They need each other."

Ashley nodded, "I know she does, but I have to make sure it's what he wants too."

"Oh, I can tell you he does want that."

"And how do you know? Did he mention something to you?" Ashley questioned.

"More than once. He loves both of you so much. He was shot and nearly died, but that didn't stop him from getting out of bed to go searching for you," Catherine replied. She could tell that Ashley was listening and starting to question herself. "You've made some really great choices in life, but with men maybe not so much. I can tell this one is a keeper, and he'll love you until the day you die."

Catherine knew her daughter well and that she would consider all the angles. She'd think things through before responding right away. "Think about what Lily needs too. That little girl is very fond of him and she has a right to get to know her dad."

"I know I need to tell her the truth about him," Ashley said.

Catherine smiled behind her teacup. "Maybe she already knows."

70

The next day, Ashley helped her mother call everyone in the family about the upcoming funeral for her brother. She also helped write the obituary for the newspaper. Catherine had been notified that Daniel's body was being brought to Craven Falls Funeral Home later today and would be readied for the funeral being held in two days.

Ashley ran errands and helped her mom prepare meals for the Memorial Repast after the funeral, while Reece worked in the yard setting up several large tents and chairs. It was almost like they were having a huge party instead of a gathering with friends to pay their respects to the family.

The Teodora family wasn't enormous, not by any means. Catherine was an only child and both parents had been dead for many years now. Her husband Charley was also an only child, but the friends they had, could fill up three average-size churches. Carven Falls's population was at times no more than 2,800 people, and they were friends with almost all of them.

Catherine mixed and stirred, while Ashley placed finished foods to be cooled on an extra table that Reece had brought in the house. Lily helped Reece outside with the chairs and taping down the table cloths.

At 4:00 p.m. that afternoon, Catherine's oldest son Paul and his family arrived along with Kevin, Catherine's third son. Matthew and his family would be picking up Saul who was landing at the Youngstown airport at 4:45

p.m. from California. This would be the first time in two years that the whole family would be together.

~ ~

Ashley had been feeling nervous all morning as she worked alongside her mother. She replayed their conversation over and over in her head from last night. *What had she meant by, "Lily may already know?" Had something happened when she was in that place in the woods? Did Reece go behind her back and tell Lily the truth?*

She wasn't sure how she felt about him doing that. They were supposed to talk about it together, but what if he thought they'd never find her, and then the courts would take Lily away from him. He wasn't on her birth certificate. She was sure that her mom would step in and make sure that didn't happen.

"Earth to Ashley," Saul said.

Ashley blinked several times before realizing that someone was talking to her. She'd been in her own little world. "Hey, Saul. How have you been?" she asked, smiling.

He hugged her before answering. "I'm good, staying busy with work."

Ashley looked around the room. "Where are Julia and the boys? Didn't they come with you?"

Saul pointed to the front door that led outside. Once they stepped onto the porch, they sat down on the swing at the end of the deck.

"What's going on?" Ashley asked.

"Julia's divorcing me and taking the kids. She said I work too much and don't spend any time with them," he whispered. "I told her about the funeral, about Daniel dying, but she's been a little bitchy lately and, well, she told me to go alone; that they didn't really know him anyway. That the boys wouldn't be missing anything," he concluded.

Ashley was at a loss for words. She'd met Julia a couple of times, but never had she thought the woman was capable of doing such a thing. Saul loved her. He loved his kids too. That much Ashley knew. "Does mom know?"

He shook his head.

"You think she'll be upset?"

"Don't you?" he asked.

Ashley thought for a second and then answered, "Nope."

Saul looked at her in surprise. "Really? As religious as she can be, you don't think she'd be mad at me and my choices?"

Ashley filled him in on Reece being Lily's real father, and everything that had happened in the past week.

"Do you love him, Ash?" Saul asked.

"Yes, I've loved him since we first met all those years ago, but how do I tell Lily about him? I told her he was dead."

"Why don't you let her make that decision? I know she's only, what five years old now? Kids can adapt quicker and easier than us grownups can. First, you should sit down, talk to Reece, and find out where you both stand. If he feels the same as you do, then go for it. Don't let him get away for the second time," Saul said.

"You sound like Mom," she laughed. "He is a great guy, and I do really love him."

"Then what are you waiting for? You almost lost your life this week, and from what you've just told me, so did Reece. If I were you, I'd be on him like peanut butter on jelly."

Ashley laughed even harder, making her bend over holding her stomach. "Peanut butter on jelly, really?"

"Well, they are my favorite foods these days," he laughed along with her.

The screen door opened and Reece came walking out. "Oh, there you are. I was wondering where you went off to," Reece said.

"I was just talking with my brother about you," Ashley replied, still laughing.

"Really, am I that funny?" Reece said with a smile. "Well, I hope it was all good."

Saul stood and stretched. "I'm going to head out back and see how everyone else is doing," Saul said, pointing his thumb towards the back of the house. He turned and winked at Ashley before leaving them alone on the porch.

Reece came and sat down next to Ashley, throwing an arm behind her as they swung back and forth.

Ashley swallowed. "Reece how do you feel about me?" she asked, knowing they'd already discussed this at the hospital days ago.

He turned and looked at her. She could see a sparkle in his eyes as she waited for him to answer.

"I told you that I love you with all my heart. I have loved you since the first day I met you, and I've never stopped loving you," he replied.

She smiled, her heart growing warmer with each word.

"And how do you feel about me?" he asked.

She leaned over and kissed him deeper than she'd ever kissed any man. When she pulled away, they were both breathing heavy. "I love you with everything I have and everything that I am," she said before kissing him again.

The screen door banged shut, making Reece and Ashley jump. Lily stood fifteen feet away with a gigantic smile on her face. "Did you tell her our surprise without me?"

Reece shook his head. "Nope, I was waiting for you, pumpkin."

Lily bounced over to where they were sitting and squeezed in between them.

Ashley felt the warm wetness form behind her eyes. Seeing them all together like this was more than a blessing, it was beautiful. "Lily Bug, I have something I need to tell you," Ashley whispered.

"We have something to tell you too," Lily said, covering her mouth as she giggled.

Ashley looked puzzled by her daughter's statement and decided to let Lily talk first. "Okay, you first," Ashley said.

Lily looked up at her dad and then over at her mom. "Reece is my daddy," Lily announced. "We wanted to surprise you first before you told me he was my real dad who really wasn't dead, which by the way, you owe me a dollar in the fib jar," Lily said in a stern almost adult voice.

Ashley's jaw fell open. She was speechless again within the past half hour. "You knew?" she asked.

"Well," Lily looked at her dad before continuing. "When you were gone and Daddy was in the hospital with his boo-boo, we were talking and I told him that he and I looked like each other. He said that you were going to surprise me and tell me he was my real daddy, but he kinda' told me first," Lily said, looking up at her mom.

Ashley looked from Reece to Lily. "Oh, well that's definitely a surprise," she said with hurt in her voice. "Are you happy about him being your dad?"

Lily nodded. "He's the best dad ever and he told me to tell you that he loves you very much."

"He does, does he?" Ashley replied with a smile.

"Yes, I do," Reece said.

A child screamed inside the house and both Ashley and Reece jumped up off the swing and ran to the door. Once inside, Ashley saw her mom lying on the living room floor with blood coming from her forehead.

71

Catherine woke with a headache the size of Detroit. Once the blurriness in her vision dissipated, she realized she was in the hospital.

She touched a hand to her head and felt a bandage and a huge lump underneath. She remembered feeling dizzy and falling in the living room, but nothing else.

"Mom, you're awake," Ashley said, taking her mom's hand in hers.

Catherine turned towards her daughter's voice and swallowed to moisten her throat before speaking. "What happened?"

"You had a nasty fall. The doctor said your blood sugar got to low and you passed out. He said you were going into a diabetic coma, but that we got you to the hospital in time. The doctor said you should be fine now. You have Type 2 Diabetes, but with the pills he prescribed, it should help regulate your sugar levels, and this shouldn't happen again," Ashley stated. "As long as you start eating a healthy diet and checking your sugar a couple of times a day."

Catherine nodded.

"I'll go let the doctor know you're awake and let everyone else know that they can come in and see you, if you're up to it?"

Catherine nodded again.

~ ~

The following morning, Catherine was released from the hospital and was sent home with a list of healthy dietary foods and a pamphlet on how to maintain her diabetes.

It wasn't until she arrived home that she recalled the events leading up to her dizzy spell. She'd come in from the backyard where everyone was gathered to retrieve several of the photo albums she'd kept since the kids were all born. That was until a few years ago when no more paper photos were being developed by her family, only digital photos.

She'd walked into the living room, bent over to grab the albums off the lower shelf and her head began to feel fuzzy. She fell, hitting her head on the coffee table beside her.

The photo albums were now sitting on the kitchen table open to pictures of Daniel when he was a baby. Tears spilled from her eyes. She had held them in for too long. Although with everything that had happened up to and after Daniel dying, no one could blame her.

Catherine turned around and clasped into Ashley's arms, releasing everything inside her. Once Catherine felt better, her daughter led her to the sofa in the family room. Ashley grabbed several tissues and sat down next to her.

Catherine wasn't sure how she'd be able to handle what tomorrow will bring, but as she looked around the room and saw her three sons, their wives, her only daughter, and her five out of the eight grandchildren, she knew she'd make it through the funeral and the gathering they would have afterwards. Her loving family would help her through it, along with themselves.

Daniel wasn't just her son, but a brother and an uncle too. No matter how troubled he'd been growing up, he was still loved by her and by his siblings.

Some families struggle and fight to stay together, while others stand by and let their families split up and never forgive each other for wrongdoings.

Catherine's family, the same family she'd taught to stand up for one another and never walk away without solving the issue at-hand, that's the family that was in this room right now and would hold each other through the sadness of what tomorrow will bring to each and every one of them.

No matter what, they would cry and they would laugh at all the funny things Daniel did as a kid. They will remember him as he was and not what happened in the end. Catherine could and would forgive him for his wrongdoings. Surely, God would too. It's who she was, and Daniel was her baby who had his faults, but also loved with all his heart.

She squeezed Ashley's hand and smiled at all of them. They'd help her through this and see that she lived a long and healthy life because she still needed to see her great-grandchildren one day.

There were still many things to do and see in this life. Catherine didn't care to see the world; all she wanted was everything sitting in front of her. Her family meant more to her than anything.

72

L ily stood between her daddy and mommy, holding their hands in hers as they all stood during the Minister's words at the church. Although she was afraid of this man lying in the casket in front of her, she knew he wouldn't and couldn't hurt her anymore. Actually, he had never really hurt her, just scared her.

Uncle Dan had saved her from the man named Tate and told her he was taking her some place safe, even though he should've just brought her back to her mommy. Then maybe he wouldn't be dead now.

Lily didn't think her mommy and daddy knew that she could hear them talking about Uncle Dan and the bad things he did. She heard them say something about Uncle Dan being in a mental hospital with her ex-daddy Rob, who her mommy had said disappeared into thin air since they last saw him.

Lily didn't care if she saw him or that Tate guy ever again. She had a daddy now and not just *a* daddy, but her real daddy, the one her mommy kept smiling at and kissing.

Lily looked up at her daddy and smiled as he looked down and smiled at her. She let go of his hand and wrapped her arm around his leg, hugging it tight. She didn't want anything to happen to him. She didn't want to lose him like she had lost Rob.

When the speech was over, everyone in the church sat down and bowed their heads in prayer. Minutes later and one-by-one, each person in a row walked up to the casket and paid their respects before going outside and getting into their cars while they waited for the casket to be carried out and placed in the back of the Hearst that would be driven to Dan's final resting place.

Lily hid behind her daddy, not wanting to see Uncle Dan's face again; it was bad enough that he was in her dreams. Dreams she tried hard not to have, but sometimes she couldn't keep her eyes open any longer and would fall asleep.

Lily prayed that one day the bad thoughts would go away now that he had gone to heaven. On the other hand, would he go to the bad place Grandma Cat said bad people go to when they do bad things? Lily couldn't say the word because her mommy said it was a bad word, even though she heard Mommy say it when she was mad. Lily smiled at this before finally realizing that her mommy and daddy were walking away from the casket. Lily was looking straight ahead, but couldn't see inside the casket, which was a good thing. She turned and bolted to catch up to her mommy.

After placing the casket in the Hearst, they all climbed into the limo that was waiting outside for them. She had never been in a limo before, and according to Grandma Cat, she hadn't ever been in one either. Grandma Cat said they were too expensive to rent, but Lily's Uncle Kevin, insisted that he'd take care of getting a limo for the family.

Lily liked to watch the lights on the ceiling of the car flash on and off. It looked like stars twinkling. There were different colored lights that changed from blue to orange to red and then to yellow as they drove down the road.

After they all left the cemetery and her Uncle Dan was now resting peacefully, as Grandma Cat had said, the limo dropped them all off at Grandma Cat's house where they would all eat, play, and talk about all the things they remembered about her Uncle Dan. Well, that was what Grandma Cat and Mommy had told her, but Lily didn't want to remember him and the things he did. Lily wanted to forget the things that happened and just be happy and play with her friend Sierra.

"Mommy," Lily said as she tugged on Ashley's shirtsleeve. "Can I go over and invite Sierra to our party? I haven't seen her in a long, long time." She watched as Mommy, Daddy, and Grandma Cat looked at each other as if she'd said something wrong. "Well can I?" Lily asked again. "Daddy can go with me. He hasn't met my friend Sierra before. I can show him the way," Lily pleaded.

"Let me call and make sure it's a good idea," Grandma Cat replied as she quickly walked towards the back door of her house.

"Okay," Lily sang as she watched Grandma Cat slip into the house.

Lily looked up as she heard Mommy and Daddy whispering and then stopped when they saw her looking at them. "What?" Lily questioned. "Why are you whispering? You said it wasn't nice to talk in whispers around other people, and no secrets either," Lily stomped her foot on the ground.

"You're right, Lily Bug, but sometimes it's okay to talk in a hushed voice," Ashley replied.

"Are the secrets about me and my friend Sierra?" Lily asked. "Did we do something wrong?"

Ashley tried to stifle a cry, but failed terribly. She bit her lower lip as she knelt down to look Lily in the eye. "No, sweetie. Neither of you did anything wrong. Come with me and we'll go talk somewhere quieter," Ashley suggested as they walked to the front of the house and sat on the swing.

Lily watched her mommy's every move, waiting for her to tell Lily what was going on. The way her mommy was acting, Lily knew it couldn't be good, but she couldn't think for the life of her what it could be about. She hadn't seen Sierra in forever.

"Lily Bug," Ashley said as she smoothed her hand down Lily's arm. "With everything that has happened I forgot to talk to you about your friend Sierra," Ashley swallowed. "Before we found you, there was a girl found in the river."

"Sierra loved playing near the water," Lily stated, smiling.

"Did she?" Ashley wasn't really asking a question, but just confirming what Sierra liked to do.

Lily nodded. "But Grandma Cat said to be careful down there. Sometimes when it rains, the water can get really deep and you can slip in and dro…" Lily stopped before she spoke the last word. She wanted to say *drown*, but as it entered her little mind, it was as if she could actually see it happening. She shook her head back and forth, as if she knew what her mommy was trying to tell her.

Lily looked up at her mommy as if the answer would be written in her eyes. It wasn't, of course, but she could tell by the wetness forming in her eyes that something bad had happened to her friend; otherwise, why would her mommy start crying?

"I'm sorry, sweetie, but Sierra had an accident and…" Ashley paused. "Well, she's with God now, just like Uncle Dan."

"No!" shouted Lily. "Not like Uncle Dan. Sierra was not a bad person. She didn't do mean things to people," Lily said as she started to cry.

Ashley went to hold Lily, but Lily shrugged away and ran off the porch and around the back of the house. She had to get away from her mommy, from everyone.

Lily ran into the woods as fast as she could, trying not to trip over any branches. She ran past a tree with a yellow X on it and then a second and third tree. She ran until she got to the end of the trail where it dropped off a couple of feet. Sierra and Lily would always grab the saplings growing out of the ground to make their way down.

When she got to the bottom, she walked over to a big rock that her and her friend Sierra would always sit on. She climbed up on the rock and sat, placing her head in the crock of her arm and cried for the loss of her friend.

73

Reece spotted Lily on the rock and made his way down the small incline. He sat down beside her and placed his arm around her, pulling her into him. Lily didn't give him a fight; instead, she turned towards him and wrapped her arms around his waist, crying harder. Reece didn't know what to say to his daughter, who was hurting for her friend who had died too young.

Before finding out that Lily had ran away, Reece had talked to Sheriff White, who was at the gathering for Dan. The Sheriff had told Reece that although they'd thought the Miller girl was murdered, they did some investigating and searched the surrounding area, thoroughly checking everything. The results came back from the autopsy showing that there had been no foul play. Sheriff White concluded that the most likely scenario was that the little girl had been at the river alone, slipped, hitting her head, and landing face down into the river. Cause of death indicated that she drowned and was then carried down the river to the outskirts of town.

Reece had then gone in search of Ashley and Lily, and he was told that Lily had run off, but Ashley thought she'd gone somewhere around the house. When they couldn't find her, Reece remembered an area down by the river that looked as if some kids hung out there. He'd mentioned it to Ashley and Catherine before heading into the woods to search for her.

As he held his daughter close, he looked around the perimeter still taped off with yellow caution tape. He replayed the scene in his head about what the Sheriff said had happened, and by the look of the area, he could see the little girl falling and hitting her head on the rock by the water's edge.

"Daddy," he heard Lily say. "Why did God have to take my friend? Why couldn't he take only the bad people?"

Reece smiled inside at this. *Wouldn't it be so simple to just take the people that didn't care? Who steal things, kill, and hurt other people? It would sure clean up this world if that could actually happen,* he thought. "I'm sorry, sweetie; I wish I had the answer to that question, but I'm just as confused as you are," he replied, thinking of his mother.

"Grandma Cat says that God has a plan for everyone, but if that's true, then what was Sierra's plan? I don't think five years old is much time to live your life."

"I have to agree with you on that," Reece replied. He had never told anyone what he was about to tell Lily. "My mom died when I was about your age."

Lily looked up at him, her face smeared with tears and dirt. "Your mommy died?"

He looked up, over the water, and then up at the sky. "Yeah, she got sick and went to heaven."

"Oh, Daddy, I'm so sorry. I don't know if I could be without my mommy. I would be really, really sad. Were you really sad when your mommy died?"

Reece nodded, "Yes, I was, but I still had my dad to help raise me."

They both sat quietly for several long minutes, staring out over the water. It wasn't as if they were waiting for something to happen. They were sitting on a large rock holding one another and sharing a father-daughter moment together.

"Hey, what do you say about going back to the house? I bet your mom is worried sick about you," Reece said.

"Okay, but I want to do one more thing," Lily said.

"Sure, what do you have in mind?"

Reece watched as Lily slid off the rock and walked to the spot where her and Sierra always stood, right near the water's edge. She pulled the flower from her hair and knelt down by the water. She kissed the flower and whispered to it as if it was a person. She placed the flower on top of the water and watched it float away. It went under the bridge and out of sight.

Reece touched his hand to her shoulder, letting her know that he was beside her. They walked the longer trail around and made their way up the hill to the path leading to Catherine's house. He then bent down and scooped Lily up into his arms.

He could see Ashley waiting at the edge of the woods for them to return. She looked like an angel standing there with the light beaming around her. She was the most beautiful thing he'd ever seen in his life; besides his mother, of course.

Before he could even think about the question he was about to ask her, as they stood face-to-face, he just opened his mouth and said, "Ashley, marry me. Be my wife and mother to our future children," he said. "I don't want to spend another second without you sand Lily. What do you say?"

74

"Yes," Ashley squealed in excitement. "Yes, yes, yes, I'll marry you!" She knew she didn't have to think about her answer. She loved him and wanted a life with him, more than Rob, more than any man she'd been with before. She didn't want to wait any longer. She was happy and in love with Reece. With everything that had happened in the past week, losing him would destroy her.

Ashley kissed him and he held her in his arms along with Lily. They would be a family. The family she had always wanted with this man.

When they let go and turned around, everyone at the gathering cheered and said congratulations. Although it was a get-together to celebrate her brother Daniel's life, she would make sure that it stayed that way. No matter what he'd done, he still deserved to be remembered by the people who loved him and would miss him.

~ ~

Later that evening after everyone had left, Catherine and Lily went into the family room to relax and watch some TV. Ashley and Reece cleaned up the yard and had started on the kitchen when the phone rang. Since Ashley was washing the dishes, Reece answered the phone.

"Hello."

"Good evening, my name is Claudia Hills. I'm the Adult Unit Director at Clearwood Psychiatric Hospital in

Pennsylvania. Is there a Miss Ashley Teodora at this residence who I can speak with?"

Reece seemed to hesitate a moment before confirming. "Yes, there's an Ashley Teodora that resides here," he said.

"May I please speak with her?" Claudia asked.

"May I ask what this is about?" Reece questioned.

"I'm sorry, but I can only speak with Miss Ashley Teodora about the reason for my call. It pertains to our Patient-Doctor confidentiality," Claudia concluded.

"Sure, yeah, I understand," Reece said as he rolled his eyes. "Hold on for just a minute and I'll get her." He placed a hand over the receiver. "Ash, it's some lady named Claudia Hills from some hospital in Pennsylvania."

"Hospital in Pennsylvania? What does she want?" Ashley asked as she wiped her hands on the dishtowel hanging from the oven handle.

"She wouldn't tell me. Said she could only speak to you."

Ashley straightened the towel back on the stove before walking to the phone that Reece held in his hand. "Hello, this is Ashley Teodora."

"Hello, Miss Teodora, I'm sorry to bother you this late in the evening."

Ashley looked at the clock on the microwave, which read 8:05 p.m. "It's no problem. What's this about?"

"Well, I'm afraid I can't discuss the matter over the phone. Would you be able to come to my office tomorrow, say around 1:00 p.m.?"

"Can you at least tell me the patient's name who is at your hospital?" Ashley asked, getting annoyed. Claudia had called her, not the other way around. Yet, the lady wouldn't release any information over the phone?

"We're not just a hospital; we're one of the top five Psychiatric Hospitals in the state of Pennsylvania," Claudia protested.

"Psychiatric Hospital?" Ashley repeated.

"Yes," Claudia replied. "Will you be able to make the appointment tomorrow at 1:00 p.m.?"

"Umm, yes, we'll be there," Ashley replied.

"*We'll* be there?" Claudia questioned. "I'm afraid I can only talk to you."

"Well, then, if I can't bring my fiancé with me, I guess we won't be speaking tomorrow," Ashley concluded.

"This is a matter we need to discuss. I can't make any future decisions without speaking to you first. If you must, bring him along tomorrow, 1:00 p.m. sharp," Claudia said, and then gave Ashley the address to the Psychiatric Hospital.

Ashley hung up the phone, tearing the paper from its holder. "I guess we have somewhere to be tomorrow," Ashley said.

"She didn't tell you what it's about?"

"Nope, said we have to talk in-person."

"Didn't Tate say he met Rob in a facility like that?"

Ashley thought for a moment. She hadn't heard or seen Rob since their last encounter here at her mom's house. Part of her thought it was strange that he hadn't been calling her cell phone or continuing to beg her to come back to him. Maybe their last visit knocked some sense into him. She still couldn't believe that Rob had hid the secret of him being in a mental institution all these years.

Thoughts came rolling in, but she had no answers to them. Maybe she'd find out all the answers tomorrow at this meeting.

75

The next morning buzzed by quickly as Ashley kept herself busy by cleaning her mom's living room and the rest of the kitchen. All three of them had spent the night at her mother's house because Ashley was still very worried about her mom and the fall that she'd had.

After the phone call the night before, Ashley's mind had gone into overdrive. She couldn't think of anything else so she and Reece had given Lily a bath and put their daughter to bed before crawling under the blankets. As much as they wanted to make passionate love to one another, Ashley couldn't do it under her mother's roof. So, they snuggled in close before finally falling asleep in each other's arms.

~ ~

Ashley continued to look at her watch as Reece drove them to the Psychiatric Hospital in Pennsylvania. She was nervous about leaving Lily after she'd gotten her back and with her mother's health, Ashley was on edge. What if something happened to her mom while they were gone and poor Lily, what would she do? She eased her mind, knowing that her brothers were still in town and that they would call her if anything happened.

Ashley looked out the window and then down at her watch. Out the window, down at her watch. She wanted to fast-forward time so they could get there, find out what this was all about, and get back home to her mom and Lily.

Although part of her knew it must be about Rob because if it had been about Daniel, wouldn't they have wanted to talk to her mother instead of her? This she knew to be true. They weren't close, maybe in age, but definitely not as brother and sister. She wanted to stop her mind from spinning out of control, but it was useless. Soon they would arrive and find out what and whom this was about.

Reece squeezed her hand; she looked over at him and smiled; he nudged his head to the left. Up ahead was a huge sign indicating that they were finally there. She hadn't expected the drive to take as long as it had, even though Reece had Googled the directions. MapQuest had noted that it would take at least two hours; still it seemed much longer then she had anticipated.

Reece turned left onto the access road, which seemed to go on forever with twists and turns. Once over the last hill, Ashley could see the weatherworn stone pillars and rock walls, which made the building look like ancient ruins instead of a Psychiatric Hospital for crazy people.

Crazy people. Is that what she thought her brother Dan was and her ex? Rob had never seemed crazy or unstable around her or Lily. But Dan, on the other hand; well, he was surely different then her other brothers, that was for sure, but she had always been told by her mother and father not to make fun of him just because he was different. To her mother, Daniel was a unique boy, a gifted boy that just needed special attention *sometimes*. Although, Ashley knew her mother meant to say *all the time*.

Ashley thought back to a time when her so-called *special* brother ran after a rabbit and twisted its neck until it lay limp in his hand. No, there was nothing *special* about her brother. Maybe a killer or a kidnapper, but definitely not *special*.

They entered the parking lot and parked in the first spot Reece saw before shutting off the engine. She looked up the moment the vehicle went still, looking at Reece. Neither said a word—what was there to say?—she knew he was just as anxious as she was to find out the truth.

Ashley unbuckled her seatbelt, opened the door, and stood. The wind blew her blonde hair into her face and her body back against the car. She hadn't remembered feeling the wind thrust against the car as they drove.

She regained her footing, stepped away from the car, and closed the door. By the time she went around the vehicle, Reece was waiting for her.

Ashley lifted her face, closed her eyes, and inhaled the fresh scent of cut grass and blooming flowers. She looked around the parking lot and noticed the black pavement was riddled with cracks that were long overdue to be filled.

Her gaze then went to the hospital in front of them. There was a ten-foot iron fence around the building and an iron gate when you walked up the walkway towards the front door. Apparently, they wanted to keep everyone inside, which to her made sense if the people were too unstable to be out in the world. The scenery looked frightening and like something you'd see on a horror show.

A keypad stood to the left, which she assumed was used to call the receptionist on the other side of the doors.

"Ready?" Reece asked.

Ashley snapped out of her zone, nodded, and pushed the call button.

"Hello, how can I help you?" a man asked.

"Hi, my name is Ashley Teodora and I have an appointment to see Director Claudia Hills at 1:00 p.m." The man must have had his finger on the button still because she could hear papers being flipped through.

"Ah, yes, I see your name here. Please come in. We're at the top of the stairs to your right," the man said before the box went silent.

A buzzer sounded, which indicated that they could open the gate and go in. They climbed the stairs, opened the massive large doors, and walked to the counter on the right.

"Miss Teodora?" the man questioned.

She nodded.

"Please sign your name here and…" the man looked Reece up and down before finishing his sentence. "And his as well. All visitors must be signed in whether they are going beyond these doors or not. We like to keep track of who comes and goes."

"I understand," Ashley said as she wrote both her and Reece's names down.

"You can wait over there," the man pointed to a set of sofa chairs against the wall. "Someone will come get you shortly."

They walked over and sat down on the dark green velvet love seat. Reece smoothed his hand over it like a little kid would do. "Nice," he smiled.

Ashley couldn't help but giggle at him, which echoed off the walls.

The man at the counter cleared his throat.

She looked over at the man behind the desk who gave her a dirty look. She turned back around and raised her eyes at Reece. *The people who work here soon become the people locked up here,* she thought.

She looked down at her watch. It read 12:59 p.m. Soon, someone would fill them in on what this whole meeting was about and her mind would be free of stress or at least she hoped so.

The clatter of heels against the tiled floor ricocheted off the walls. If the male receptionist thought her laugh was loud, he was so wrong.

The woman stopped in front of Ashley and Reece. They both looked up at the same time. The woman had long slender skeletal legs that connected to her bony hips. The blouse she wore hung from her shoulders, giving her an even thinner look. Her face, also thin, showed her cheekbones that had way too much blush on them. The aroma, not too pleasing, of cigarette smoke lingered in the air.

There are some people that by the way they look you know how their voice will sound, but Ashley couldn't have been more wrong. "Miss Ashley Teodora," the lady said in a deep manly voice.

Ashley blinked before clearing her throat to speak. "Yes, I'm Ashley Teodora." She wanted to laugh because she wondered if the lady was once a man.

"Please, follow me. Come on, we don't have all day. In fifteen minutes, you don't want to be caught in these halls beyond those doors without supervision," she said.

Ashley and Reece quickly stood and followed her down the hallway to a set of double doors with a keypad.

She entered a pin and the doors slowly opened. Once through, the doors shut and beeped to indicate that they were locked.

Ashley gripped Reece's hand as they walked past an open door. She saw a hospital bed with a plastic mattress cover. White sheets and a white blanket lay folded on top. On the side of the bed, she saw padded restraints, which she assumed were used to strap the patient to the bed.

Their footsteps echoed down the corridor and fists pounded on the locked doors as they passed by. The further they walked, the more Ashley smelled disinfectant which they probably used to sanitize the walls and floors around them.

They came to another set of double doors. The lady punched in her code and they walked through. They turned the corner and stopped outside a gray metal door. The lady pressed her thumb on a pad on the wall. A bright light scanned her thumbprint and then the door *clicked*. She opened the door and they all went inside.

There was a set of chairs along the wall with a small table covered with magazines. In front of them, sat a dark cherry desk assorted with your typical office supplies: pencils, pens, notebooks, stapler, etc. Beyond the desk was another door with the name "Director Claudia Hills" inscribed upon it.

They followed the slim-looking woman towards the door. She knocked, waited for Claudia to tell them to come in, and then opened the door.

The room was twice the size of the one they'd just come from. Frames of diplomas and degrees hung on the wall to Ashley's right, and a window that overlooked the outdoor quarters was to her left.

From where she stood, she saw no one outside in the secured yard. Ashley turned back towards the desk when Reece pulled gently on her arm to indicate they were to sit.

"Ashley Teodora and Reece Garran, is that correct?" Claudia asked.

"Yes," Reece replied for the both of them as if Ashley was mute.

"I know you're both wondering why I asked you to come here so I'll just get right to it. The quicker we discuss his medical needs; the faster I can get him treated."

Ashley and Reece looked at each other.

"He has been a client here on-and-off for the past seventeen years. For the first ten years he was admitted, he wasn't allowed any guests or even to leave the facility, but then after years of treatment which showed stability and improvement, patients can come and go as they please," Claudia said with a smile. "As long as they come every three-to-six months for an evaluation, we feel that they should *blend in* with society. This means that when they start to feel like they're going to lose themselves, they can come to the hospital and we can admit them for however long we see fit, although..." Claudia paused. "They can still check themselves out even if we don't agree. But this can only happen when they have checked themselves in, not when they're admitted through a hospital or by a Psychiatrist," Claudia concluded before placing the sheet of paper in her hand down on the desk.

Ashley looked stone cold as if she were somewhere in a freezer full of dead, skinned animals hanging from the rafters. She had no idea that Rob had or was ever committed in a place like this. He had never told her. She was about to marry this man and would've had children with him.

Her stomach flipped. She swallowed down the sour bile rising up through her esophagus and into the back of her throat. If she let herself think about this, she'd have to run from the office or grab the trashcan next to the enormous oak desk, which seemed too far away from her grasp because there was no way she would be able to hold down the breakfast she'd eaten earlier this morning.

"Ash, are you feeling okay?" Reece asked.

Ashley looked over at him, her skin white as snow. She swallowed again before saying. "I don't know. I don't feel too good at all, but I want to hear more. I want to know more," Ashley said, but she wasn't sure if she really meant it.

Claudia Hills continued, "So the reason I called you is because your name is listed for any medical procedures needed only if the patient is incoherent."

"Incoherent?" Ashley asked almost in a whisper.

"Yes, it seems that since Tate Lanier's arrival back at our facility, we recommend that he gets treatment. At this point, he isn't able to make these decisions on his own."

76

"Tate?" Ashley questioned, sounding confused. "What does this have to do with Tate? And why would I be on his call list?" She felt angry, all of a sudden.

Claudia sat back in her chair, flabbergasted.

"I thought you were talking about Rob Mahan," Ashley said.

"Rob Mahan? Why would this be about him? He isn't a patient here," Claudia Hills stated.

"But you know him?"

"Yes, of course, I know Rob Mahan. Everyone knows who he is. He's worked here for over fifteen years. Came here right after high school. He did some college courses to get a degree in nursing."

"Nursing?"

"Yes, he's one of the male nurses in the ward. Very good at his job too. Sometimes he gets too close to some of the patients, like Tate, and a man named Daniel Teodora…" Claudia stopped. "Wait? Daniel Teodora. Any relation to you?"

"Yes," Ashley whispered. "He was my brother."

"Was?"

"Yes, I'm afraid he died from an automobile accident a few days ago." *She hadn't known for sure that Dan had been in a mental hospital; her mother had never mentioned it to her. Had her mother even known? It was possible that he'd kept this from the whole family.*

"Oh, dear. I'm so sorry to hear that. He was such a good kid; really, he was. We tried real hard to help him, but no matter what treatment we did, he still heard those awful voices in his head," Claudia said, shaking her head back and forth.

"He heard voices in his head?"

"Yes, sometimes they tried to control him and get him to do things he wasn't comfortable doing. Most of the time we had to have him sedated and chained to his bed, afraid that he would hurt himself or the people around him. We did some shock treatments on him, and we thought it had finally worked. He wasn't talking to himself anymore," Claudia said. "So, after the past few years we let him socialize with the other patients. He became close with Rob. He seemed so much happier. When he felt that he could go back into the world and for the first time visit his mother, whom he talked about daily, we were all for it. He had only been gone a couple of weeks," Claudia added.

"So, you said that Rob and Tate were close. Have you even seen Tate lately since he's come back?'

"Yes," Claudia said in a hushed voice. "He was gone for almost six months. I see that he has changed his appearance to look exactly like ..." Claudia paused and swallowed. "Oh, dear God. He looks exactly like Rob."

"How did Tate get here?" Reece asked.

Claudia looked down at her notes. "A Chief Clarkson from Virginia."

"Did Chief Clarkson fill you in on what Tate had done with his time on the outside?"

"No, it's not his job to evaluate the patient. He was just told to have him transported back to our facilities requested by the judge."

Ashley and Reece went into telling Director Claudia Hills about everything that had happened in the past week. "He said that he had been watching me for a long time," Ashley said.

Claudia's hand flew to her mouth. "I'm so sorry you had to go through all of that. I do hope your daughter is fine and that she isn't traumatized by what happened."

"So, why would Tate have Ashley's name down when they're not even a couple or related for that matter?" Reece asked. "Why would he leave her in control of his fate?"

"That's a good question, but an easy one to answer now that I know what's happened in the past week. I believe he thought he could take Rob's place and marry Ashley; then she'd be his wife and she could make any decisions that were needed, but only if it came down to him not being able to make the decisions himself."

Both Ashley and Reece nodded in agreement with what Claudia said. Claudia quickly stood when a light on the wall started to flash.

"What does that mean?" Ashley asked.

"That there's a serious problem with one of our patients in the ward. You both need to stay here while I tend to this matter," Claudia said as she went out the door.

Reece stood and looked at the papers on the desk.

"What are you doing?" Ashley asked.

"I'm looking for the room number that Tate is in. I want to have a talk with him."

"Oh, okay. Well, I'm coming too," Ashley persisted.

"No, you're not!" Reece demanded. "I want you to stay put. If she asks where I went, tell her I had to use the restroom."

A few minutes after Reece had left the room, Ashley went after him. She wasn't going to sit there and wait; besides, what if he needed her help? She'd been through an ordeal and wasn't about to go through another one alone.

She walked out the door and down the hall in the same direction they'd come in. She looked through the glass window of the door before punching in the code she'd seen Claudia's assistant use.

She peeked into the rooms through a small window on each of the doors. She had to use her tippy toes to see, but still wasn't able to get a look inside and see who was in them. When she went around the next corner, she ran straight into Rob.

"Ashley, why are you here?"

"I think I need to ask you the same question. Why didn't you tell me this is where you worked? Why the secret?" Ashley asked.

"Come with me. This isn't the place for you to be." He led her down another hall and into a small janitorial closet. He flicked the light on in the room.

"Well, are you going to answer my questions now?"

"Look, I didn't want you to know that I worked with mentally ill people. I just thought you wouldn't like me if you knew."

"Why would it matter where you worked? And it sure would've explained why you went out of town all the time. Did you know about Tate?" she asked.

By the look on his face, she had her answer to that question.

"I didn't know he was planning on kidnapping Lily to get to you. I didn't know he was watching you all those months."

Ashley felt a chill run through her spine. *How did he know that Tate had watched her, and that he was the one that took Lily?* She hadn't known who had taken Lily the last time she saw Rob so he wouldn't have heard it from her, unless... she looked up and focused on his face.

"I was wondering how long it would take you to figure it out," Tate said.

"Tate?"

"Yep, your one and only," he said with a smirk.

The hairs on her arms stood straight up. Now what was she going to do? How was she going to get away from him?

"I bet you're wondering how to get away from me? It worked like a charm to get you here, putting your name down as the person to call if I couldn't respond to the staff. It was a beautiful and clever idea, don't you think?" he smiled at her. His grin, long and wide, all he needed was burly teeth and he'd look like an animal that was hunting for his prey. He had been for a long time, watching and waiting for her.

"You won't get away with this!" she said.

"And how do you think I won't? I have my own ID and I know all the passcodes to this place. I can come and go as I please. How do you think it was so easy to come and see you?"

"Where's Rob? What did you do to him?"

"He's fine. Don't go worrying you're pretty little head off. He's pretending to be me right now, except he's not able to talk so he won't be able to tell them who he really is," Tate said. "It wasn't hard to switch places; well, except for looking exactly like him."

"What is that supposed to mean?" Ashley asked.

"Oh, you will know in time, my sweet beautiful, Ashley," he replied with a smile, reaching his hand out towards her face.

Ashley backed away before he could touch her.

"Other than me looking like Rob, we are two of the same. As a child, I was quite different than most other kids my age. My father placed me in here so that I'd get the help I needed," Tate looked down at the floor, but it was the look in his eyes when he looked up that frightened Ashley the most.

"No one had to battle the headaches that I endured. The ones that drove me to do bad things as a kid. Rob owed it to me, to give me his life and be happy like he was. I deserved that much. I deserved to have you." Tate laughed so deep and loud, it shot sparks of electricity through Ashley's body.

She honestly had no idea what he was talking about and just wanted to get away from him and back to Reece, but how was she going to escape this maniac?

Tate turned slightly and Ashley saw the syringe in his hand and knew what he was about to do to her. He was willing to alter her mobility just to get her out of here. She'd be in the state Rob was in right now. Stuck in a world where he couldn't speak or move.

She bit back a cry and stood taller. She had to be strong and figure out a way to survive. A way to get out of here and find Reece. *Shit!* Why didn't she just go with him earlier? Then they would've been together.

The sound of shoes running down the hall filled the small room. Tate grabbed her and placed a hand over her mouth.

"Say one word and I won't hesitate to inject you with what's in this syringe," Tate said through gritted teeth.

Ashley relaxed herself before lifting her leg and kicking back with as much force as she could muster into his shin. She turned and kicked him again, but this time in the most delicate part of a man's body, bringing him down to his knees as if he was begging her for forgiveness. She kicked him again, this time in the head until he fell over. It made her feel good, strong, and powerful to finally let out all her frustrations and anger that this man had caused her and her family.

She turned and grabbed the door handle and pushed it open right when one of the orderlies in the hospital came running down the hall. The weight of the blow knocked him down to the ground and her against the door jam. The man looked up to see what it was that knocked him on his ass, but Ashley wasn't going to stay and find out what would happen if Tate got to his feet.

"The man you want is in there," she yelled as she went around the guy on the floor and ran down the hall where she'd come from a few minutes earlier. She could hear commotion ahead and decided that she would be safer in a crowd of people, whether they were crazy mental patients or doctors and nurses, than to be alone.

"Ashley."

She heard her name and turned around. Reece was by the wall, looking right at her and waving his hand in the air. She made her way to him and fell into his arms. "Oh, God, it's so good to see you again," she said.

"Where did you go? I went back to the room and you were gone so I went looking for you," he said in a panicked voice.

"Tate, he took me. He's pretending to be Rob. He said that Rob is the one that's chained up and can't talk."

"Is that so?" Claudia said before turning on her heels and entering a room three doors down.

They followed Claudia and stopped just inside the room to see her talking to Rob who was still chained to the bed. She was asking him questions, but he seemed incoherent and unable to answer them. She shouted orders for the nurse to get her Scopolamine, an adrenaline-like drug that could sometimes be used to help a person become more coherent.

"I want this whole facility locked down. We have a patient on the loose," Claudia spoke into the radio that was clipped to her side.

"He has an ID," Ashley said. "He said that's how he was able to get in and out of this building whenever he wanted to and he knows all the codes."

The radio in Claudia's hand chirped. "Director Hills, I have the known patient. Where do you want me to take him?" said a man.

"Bring him to room 4B right now," Claudia demanded.

A minute later, the same man Ashley had knocked down in the hall came walking in with Tate in his possession. Ashley huddled in close to Reece as she watched Tate stumble as they tried to restrain him in a chair.

A male nurse with bushy dark hair came into the room holding two syringes. He handed one to Claudia and was about to insert the other needle into Tate, when Tate head-butted the bushy-haired man and started stabbing him repeatedly with a screwdriver.

77

Claudia picked up the syringe the instant it fell out of the male nurse's hand while Tate was stabbing him. The moment Tate moved towards Ashley, Reece grabbed Tate so fast and spun him around, locking his arm around his neck so Claudia could inject him with a needle filled with Fluphenazine. Once Tate dropped the screwdriver, Reece released his hold. Tate slinked to the floor like a limp flower.

By the time security arrived at the scene, Tate was lying motionless on the tile floor. His eyes were wide and focused at the wall. The look of him sent tingles down Ashley's spine. He looked dead.

Half an hour later, Ashley and Reece sat in the ambulance outside the Psychiatric Hospital, waiting to be released. Neither one of them was hurt, but the hospital insisted that they both be checked out. When they were cleared to go, Ashley told Reece that she wanted to see how Rob was doing before they left.

Back inside the hospital, but in a different room, Rob was lying in a bed with his eyes closed. Ashley strolled up to the bed and sat in the chair next to him. Rob must have sensed someone was there and opened his eyes.

"Hey," he said, his throat sounding hoarse.

"Hi," she said with a slight smile. After everything that had happened in the past month, starting with finding Rob, or maybe it was Tate, in bed with her brother and then Lily being taken, she still felt something for the guy. Of course, she would. She'd spent two years with him, and then *poof* it was all gone as if their relationship hadn't existed.

"I'm sorry about everything," he said. "I never meant for you to find out about me and your brother. He asked for me not to tell you or your mother that he was in a Psychiatric Hospital," Rob stated. "I was helping him to get back on his feet again after he was discharged from here. He was just supposed to stay with me for a while. It sort of just happened. One thing led to another and... I should have told you and ended it with him."

Her stomach dropped. Had she heard him right? Did he say he was in a relationship with her brother? She had for one second, maybe two, thought she'd been wrong and it had actually been Tate and not Rob in bed with her brother Dan. The feelings she'd thought she felt the moment she sat down and looked at him lying in this bed disappeared. Did she feel angry with him? That would be an understatement. Angry, sad, disgusted, betrayed, used, lied to, what else could she add to the list?

"Ash," Rob whispered.

She raised her hand to indicate he should stop talking. "Don't," she said, shaking her head. "Don't try to justify what you have done to me, to Lily or to us. Rob, if you don't already know, we are over. No wedding, no future, and don't even try to be a part of Lily's life. You've done nothing but lie to me over and over again. Don't contact me or try to contact her." She knew the last part would hurt him the most. "Goodbye," she said as she stood and walked away.

"Can you at least tell Dan that I'm..."

She didn't even turn around. "Dan's dead!"

"What!" he shouted. "Dead? How? When?"

He hadn't known what happened. She turned around to face him one last time. "He died a few days ago from injuries in a car crash. We just buried him yesterday," she said, then turned and walked out the door. She hadn't wiped the tears away because there weren't any to wipe.

78

A couple of hours later, they pulled into her mom's driveway. Reece closed the car door just as Lily ran down the porch steps and jumped into his arms. She started telling him about her day and that Grandma Cat and she had gone to the cemetery to place flowers on Sierra's grave. Then, they went for ice cream and worked in the greenhouse outback.

"Wow! You sound like you had an awesome day with Grandma Cat."

Lily nodded her head. "We were just about ready to take a nap until you and Mommy showed up."

"Ah, a nap sure does sound good right now," Reece said. "How about we all three go upstairs and lie down for a little while? I'm sure Grandma Cat would like to rest too." Reece looked over Lily's shoulder to see Catherine sitting in the swing nodding off.

They helped Catherine to her feet and up the stairs, suggesting as they climbed that they should help bring all her things downstairs later to the guest bedroom.

Catherine didn't argue the fact that she was getting beyond her years to continue to climb up and down the stairs, especially after being in the hospital.

Ashley had also told her that it would be better that she slept downstairs because Ashley, Reece, and Lily would be going back to her place to live, tomorrow, that was *if* her mom felt stable enough to be on her own.

~ ~

An hour later, Ashley woke to find Reece missing beside her. With Lily in the same bed, she tiptoed out of the room and down the stairs. She looked in the living room and then the kitchen. She glanced over the backyard; still, no Reece. As she walked back through to the front of the house, she heard chains creaking against metal.

She opened the screen door and saw him sitting on the swing. He smiled up at her. She walked over and sat down beside him. He placed an arm around her shoulders and she folded into him.

"Hey, beautiful. How did you sleep?" Reece asked.

"Good and you?"

"I got some sleep. I didn't want to wake you so I crept out of the room and came outside to enjoy the weather." He kissed her head.

She melted into his body, feeling almost as light as air from his touch. She couldn't help herself; she was totally in love with this man next to her.

"I want to say I'm sorry about yesterday," Reece said.

Ashley turned her head and looked up at him. "Sorry about what?"

"It was your brother's day, and I shouldn't have made it our day asking you to marry me like that."

She frowned, "You don't want to get married now?"

"What? Yes, I want to marry you, but I want to ask you in a proper way. I want us to have a day to remember, not the day of your brother's funeral."

She nodded, "I understand."

Reece slipped off the swing and bent down on one knee. He pulled a small black velvet box from his jeans pocket and opened the lid.

Her eyes lit up like the night sky on the fourth of July. "When did you get this?"

"It was my mother's ring. I've been carrying it around since my father passed away. He said to give it to the woman who captures my heart," Reece smiled. "He said that I would know who she is the moment I meet her. Although it was six years ago when we met, I don't want to lose you ever again. You are the only one besides Lily who has my heart, and I want to spend the rest of my life loving you, caring for you, and protecting you. I want to come home every day from work, see your beautiful face, and make love to you every chance I can. I want to be a father to Lily and hopefully to many more children," he said with a wink. "What do you say? Will you marry me?"

She reached down and kissed his lips. "Yes, I'll marry you Reece Garran," Ashley said as she whispered the words against his lips. They kissed and he placed the ring on her finger.

"Oh, my sweet Jesus, that was the most romantic thing I ever heard," Catherine said from the doorway. She wiped a tear from her cheek. "I'm sorry for being nosy, but I just couldn't help myself. I can't wait to tell everyone," Catherine bellowed.

"Mom," Ashley said. "They were here yesterday when he asked me the first time. Now, it's just more official."

Catherine laughed, "Yes, I guess you're right, but we do have a lot to do. Wait, don't you still have the cake and flowers ordered and the church is still reserved, right?"

Ashley nodded, "Yes, I guess I haven't gotten around to canceling it yet. That's only if Reece wants to get married in a month."

"Are you kidding me? I'd do it right now if we had someone here to marry us," Reece laughed.

Catherine clapped her hands together. "Then it's settled; in one month, you'll be Mrs. Reece Garran.

~ ~

As the days passed slowly by, Ashley and her mom were busy mailing out the invitations and arranging the food, flowers, and several large tents to be set up outside in the yard. Practically, the whole town was invited to the wedding. She also knew they'd all fit in the yard because of Daniel's funeral.

Catherine, Reece, Ashley, and Lily all went to the fair that was held the following weekend in the park of Craven Falls. Reece played some games and won Lily a stuffed bear and Ashley a lion. They walked around, enjoyed the food, and shared cotton candy.

Ashley introduced Reece to a couple of contractors in town and Reece said he'd contact them on Monday and set up a meeting.

The following Monday, Reece was hired and was working on an addition to the local diner in town. The owner of the diner wanted to extend the roof and have an outdoor sitting area for summertime.

~ ~

On the day of the wedding, Ashley stood in front of the mirror, turning from one side to the other. The sheath, off-white, pearl-beaded gown had a plunging deep Vneckline that hugged her waist and accented her hips. She looked and felt gorgeous.

She stepped into her heels, bringing the dress just above her toes. She smoothed down the fabric against her body and smiled into the mirror. Ashley turned when she heard a soft knock at the door. "Come in," she sang.

The door opened; Catherine and Lily came into the room, along with everyone in the wedding party. Lily was hopping up and down in excitement. "You look so pretty, Mommy," Lily said.

"Thank you, sweetie."

"I'm lost for words," Catherine said. "I don't think there are any words to describe just how stunning you look. You are going to turn a lot of heads today."

"The only head I want to turn is Reece's," Ashley smiled.

Catherine walked over and hugged her daughter. "You are so beautiful, my sweet child. Your father would be so proud of you. I mean, he is very proud of you. I just wish he were here to see you and walk you down the aisle."

"Mom, don't get me started. I don't want to mess up my make-up."

"Oh, you can't mess up beauty," Catherine said, kissing Ashley on the cheek. "The music is about to start and your brother Paul is waiting to walk you down the aisle."

Ashley held her mother's face in her hands and then kissed her cheek. "I'm ready," she smiled back.

"Ashley, you look so beautiful," Carla Michaels said.

"So, do you. I can't thank you enough for coming," Ashley replied. "For being my maid of honor."

"I know I've been going through some rough times, but this is my best friend's wedding. Do you really think I'd miss it?" Carla said. "Besides, I wanted you to meet Samantha."

The first time that Ashley had met Samantha was two days ago when she and Carla arrived for the wedding. Carla had told Ashley everything that had happened after she'd left last month from visiting her in Illinois. All the hidden secrets her late husband had kept from her came exploding out of nowhere. The best part was finding out about Samantha. She too, like Carla, had some twisted secrets that had been kept from everyone.

Paul knocked on the door as he peeked his head in. "It's time, ladies," he said.

They all walked out the door and down the hall. The doors to the main church were closed, allowing the wedding party to lineup.

The doors opened as Ashley stood off to the side with her arm in Paul's, watching the wedding party begin their descent down the aisle. When it was their turn, they both stepped into the doorway as the wedding march began.

Ashley glided down the aisle, smiling with her eyes on Reece the whole time. She hadn't realized just how good-looking he was. The sparkle in his eye and that gorgeous smile on his face took her breath away.

They stopped just short of the alter. Paul turned towards his sister, kissed her cheek, and placed her hand in Reece's before sitting down next to his wife.

The ceremony took less than half an hour and they were pronounced husband and wife. Reece enveloped Ashley in his arms and bowed her down, kissing her deeply on the lips.

It wasn't until that night when they were dancing under the string of lights decorated like the stars in the sky that she knew she was married to the greatest man on earth.

She watched as Reece twirled Lily around and around, her laughter filling the night air. Her daughter was everything to her. In that terrified week that she had lost her daughter, it had felt like the world come crashing down around her.

Lily was more than just her daughter; she was her life, and she'd do anything to protect her and so would her father who Lily already had wrapped around her little finger. But isn't that what little girls were supposed to do?

79

The door creaked open as Rob stepped into the dark room. He walked to the bed, stopped, and stared down at Tate who was strapped to the bed with restraints.

Tate turned and looked up at Rob.

"I can see that you're awake now," Rob said. "I think it's time we start working together and figure out how we will get our revenge."

Tate's lips curved up into a devious grin. "I thought you'd never see things my way."

"Oh, how we are so alike, but yet, so different? There's so much to plan before we each get what we want. There can be no mistakes this time," Rob said. "You can have Ashley, but only if you help me kill Reece."

Tate smiled, "It will be my pleasure, little brother."

Acknowledgements

I want to give many thanks to my wonderful and extraordinary editor, Deborah Bowman Stevens, for turning this novel into something great. I owe you more than I can offer for all your hard work and kindness. Thank you so much. I wouldn't have come this far without your expertise.

About the Author

Donna M. Zadunajsky started out writing children's books before she accomplished and published her first novel, *Broken Promises*, in June 2012. She since has written several more novels and her first novella, *HELP ME!* Book 1 in the series, which is about teen suicide and bullying.

HELP ME!, won Awards in:
The Great Northwest Book Festival-**Winner**
Global EBook Awards- **Gold Medal Winner**
The Great Southeast Book Festival-**Winner**
IPA Award- **Winner in Grief Category**
Reader Views Awards- In 3 different categories:
*Children-Teen 12-16 year olds
*Children-Young Adult 16-18 years old
*Best Teen/YA Book of the Year
eLit Awards- **Silver Winner**

Talk To Me, Book 2 was a **Finalist in the Author U unpublished contest**, 2016.
IPA Award- **Winner in Death and Dying**

The author is available for speaking on the matters of teen suicide, bullying and for author events. To find out more about the author and her books go to:
http://www.donnazadunajsky.com

63830210R00213

Made in the USA
Lexington, KY
19 May 2017